WALKING SHADOW

THE DARKWORLD SERIES: BOOK TWO

EMMA L. ADAMS

"The mind is its own place, and in itself
Can make a Heaven of Hell, a Hell of Heaven."
John Milton, 'Paradise Lost'

1

THE VAMPIRE

The moon glared down at us from between the black spires of the cathedral, its cold light giving the gravestones an unearthly glow. I couldn't help but imagine what Cara, my superstitious best friend, would say if she could see us, sitting by the entrance to the cemetery on a night like this.

"It's a full moon! You're just asking for it!"

But despite everything that had happened over the past few months, I still didn't believe the dead could rise under the light of the full moon and walk amongst the living. Nor was I concerned that any of us were going to transform into hideous monsters at any moment.

Besides, we waited for a vampire, not a werewolf.

I hadn't believed Leo when he'd first told me that a vampire wanted to meet us in confidence. He'd given me no reason to believe he would lie, but it sounded so outlandish I was convinced he was playing a joke on me.

It was during the first meeting of the new term. Well, we called them "meetings," even though they were more of a casual gathering of magic-users who, for one reason or other, refused to join with the Venantium, the organisation that policed other sorcerers. Only Leo and I had shown up early, and he'd wasted no time in commandeering the sofa in the Games Room. He lay back with his head over the arm, waiting for the Xbox to load, looking at me upside-down with his wavy dark hair practically vertical. Today his t-shirt proclaimed Armageddon was nigh.

"A vampire wants to meet with us tomorrow night," he said.

"Uh, what?" I said, looking up from the book on demons I'd just picked up, one of the ones Claudia left lying around. "Is that a joke?"

"Nope, really. There's a vampire asking for our help."

"And I have a werewolf on speed-dial."

He flipped the right way up. "Honestly, Ash, vampires do exist," he said with all sincerity, though given that he was about to start shooting down a battalion of zombies on an Xbox game, I wasn't entirely convinced.

"Pull the other one," I said. "I thought we dealt with demons, not Dracula."

"Not that kind of vampire," said Leo. "They don't drink blood, they drain the life energy out of people."

"What, just like demons?" I said, sceptically. Demons were, as Claudia put it when she'd first told me, magical parasites that could possess anyone and drain his or her life energy in the blink of an eye. They were spirits, creatures that resembled formless black smoke, apart from their violet eyes. "Or… or human-demons?"

I fought to keep my voice even, to suppress the shiver of hope that began to stir inside me, like a bird awakening from slumber.

"No, nothing like that," said Leo, killing that metaphorical bird stone dead. "It's a magical condition, it affects about one in ten magic-users. Basically, they can't function without magic energy, so they have to take it from others. So a bit like demons, yes. Except they're fully human. It's like a genetic thing."

Told you so, a voice in my head chided the part of me that dared hope, for a second, there were other people like me out there. Human-demons. Freaks of nature.

"Okay," I said. "So what does the vampire want to speak to us about?"

"He's asked us for help," said Leo, "because seven vampires have been killed in the area in the last month. He wants our protection."

"*Our* protection?" This didn't quite add up with the image I had of vampires in my head. "I thought vampires were crazy-strong and super-fast. Why would he need our help?"

"Vampires aren't any different from other magic-users," said Leo. "Except they can't function without draining someone else's magical energy. The Venantium have them labelled as monsters, even though most never intentionally harm people. So they generally lead a solitary existence."

"I can imagine," I said. "So how are they being killed? I take it they aren't allergic to sunlight or anything?"

"Nope. You'd think staking them through the heart would be more ironic, but the way they were killed… well, it's bizarre. All seven of them had their throats cut, but the actual cause of death was from their life energy being drained out of them. Which, as far as I know, can only be done by another vampire. And two of the victims were students."

"So you think there's an evil vampire on the loose?" I shivered at the mention of the recent student deaths, which had been all over the news. The Venantium worked hard to cover up any demon-related incident, by any means possible, but I guessed even they wouldn't be able to hide those gruesome deaths. For smaller incidents, they used Influence—meddling with people's memories, even removing them entirely. As the organisation responsible for protecting the public from demons, they strived to ensure no non-magic-users ever became aware of it. This was supposedly out of fear demons would take advantage and, I guessed, find a way to manipulate non-sorcerers through the Darkworld. Anyone with a slight awareness of the Darkworld was vulnerable to demon interference—and magic-users, or sorcerers, were most vulnerable of all.

"That's what the Venantium seem to think. But whatever they might say, vampires aren't usually a threat to us. I mean, they can be dangerous when in a frenzy, but they can't help what they are, any more than we can help having a connection to the Darkworld."

Or than I can help being part demon, I thought. But I didn't feel ready to share that yet. Unlike most magic-users, my parents weren't sorcerers themselves. I was one of the few who developed magical powers—and the ability to see demons—independently. Seeing shadowy, purple-eyed demons everywhere I went had led me to conclude I was losing my mind, and it was only when I'd met Claudia and the others that I'd learned the truth about the Darkworld.

I'd originally decided to come study in Blackstone because it was a demon-free zone, not that I'd known *why*. It turned out to be because we were right on the doorstep of the Venantium. The Barrier they maintained kept the demons from escaping from the Darkworld into *our* world. Out of fear of discovery, and my determination to find out why the demons seemed to be interested in me, I'd reluctantly joined up with a small band of magic-users at the university who wanted nothing to do with the Venantium.

But neither I, nor anyone else I knew, could have

guessed the reason for my connection to the Darkworld was because I was descended from a higher demon, and I'd vowed never to tell a soul. Who would believe me if I said that the family's depository of magical energy was currently sitting around my neck in the form of an amethyst pendant, given to me by the woman I'd believed to be my aunt? It had nearly got me killed once already, when one of my flatmates, secretly a magic-user, had tried to claim its power and use it to control a demon. But the demon had turned on its summoner, killing him and acknowledging me as its superior.

I knew I was lucky to be alive, as much as I detested the idea of owing my life to a horrible secret I could never tell anyone about. The descendants of the so-called Seven Princes, the higher demons who could apparently take on human form, had been hunted by the Venantium in the past, and I had no intention of finding out whether things had changed. Even the rest of the group had no idea what really happened that night. Only Aunt Eve—whoever she really was—and I knew the full truth.

And I was positive there was more she wasn't telling me.

IN THE END, curiosity won me over, and so I joined my fellow magic-users Leo, Claudia, Cyrus, Howard, and Berenice, in Blackstone Cemetery, where, for whatever reason, the vampire had requested we meet.

I wasn't fond of the place, and not for the obvious reasons. Last time I'd been here, when we'd sneaked into the Venantium's library, I'd been attacked by a harpy, one of the creatures the Venantium used to carry messages and to intercept intruders. I'd dreamt of the place too often, my morbid imagination conjuring up images of the dead suddenly bursting from the ground with a spray of earth and grass, dragging their decaying limbs through the village of Blackstone, or of me plunging to my death off the cliffs that overhung the ocean, a five minute walk away.

"Why a graveyard?" I asked Claudia.

"I think he might be coming through one of the tunnels," she said.

I blinked, surprised. I knew there were tunnels underneath the village, including the one that led to the Venantium's library, but I'd assumed they were generally out of use.

"No, everything's underground," said Claudia, when I mentioned this. "Where do you think the Venantium have their headquarters? It's not easy to hide a huge building."

I looked down at the grass under my feet in amazement. "What, it's under here?"

"Sure is. Well, not *here*. If you dig up this ground all you'll find is a bunch of coffins. But it's deep under the village, yeah."

"Wow. What would the Venantium do if someone did try to dig it up?" I said, remembering something I'd seen on the news the other day, about grave robberies.

"It's too deeply buried. Even below the catacombs. Did you see that news report about the Ghouls, by any chance?"

"Yeah," I said. "What kind of a name is that for a gang of grave-robbers?"

"Who knows?" said Claudia.

The graves that were dug up had also been spray-painted with obscure graffiti. There were rumours that they were some kind of cult.

"Can we not talk about that here?" said Berenice.

Clearly, I wasn't the only one feeling uneasy. Berenice

hovered near Howard, who seemed more interested in joining Leo in creating fireballs in his hand and shooting at the harpies that circled above the city. When either of them hit one, it exploded in a storm of feathers which swiftly turned to smoke and dissipated.

Cyrus turned to his younger brother and scolded him. "Stop that, Leo. We don't want to draw attention to ourselves."

"Sorry," said Leo, still grinning. "Never gets old, this."

I was with Cyrus. I'd felt the pain of a harpy's talons once before and had no desire to repeat the experience.

Only Cyrus and Claudia showed any signs of disquiet. Claudia paced back and forth between two rows of crumbling tombstones, her dark red hair the only splash of colour in the gloomy night. Cyrus sat on the wall, but looked alert, uneasy. Leo lounged beside him, now making a small flame dance between his hands.

Howard was entirely at ease, his large frame sprawled on top of a grave. Cyrus had said it would serve him right if the grave's occupant came out and attacked him, but Howard responded that if they did, he'd "beat the shit out of the *venator* scumbag." Almost all of the people buried there were Venantium members. Howard reserved a special hatred for them, apparently even the dead ones.

Berenice leaned on the grave for support, her elbows resting atop the head of a gargoyle. She was one of those nauseatingly pretty girls who always seem to look flawless, the type who woke up in the morning with salon-perfect hair. She was also a complete bitch. I'd have pitied her attempts to gain Howard's affections if she hadn't hated me without reason from the moment we first met. Whilst at the end of a night out, the two of them inevitably ended up at Howard's place. He was completely oblivious to the fact that Berenice might want more than casual sex.

That was us. The "Circle of Sinners," as Leo had named us, based on the rumoured belief of some of the Venantium: that all magic-users were Hell-bound devil-worshippers.. The original idea of Hell had apparently come from the Darkworld, and I could see why. It was a black pit, devoid of life, warmth or light, the realm of spirits in which demons dominated. Apparently it was possible, through the use of a certain spell, to separate from one's body and to travel to the Darkworld, but there was no guarantee of returning to the physical world at all. Some sorcerers had tried it to gain power, but it never ended well. The Darkworld was place of pure magical energy, the reason we could use magic. And that made magic-users irresistible to demons.

Knowing I couldn't be possessed like everyone else could didn't make me any less scared of them. Even though I'd killed one myself—well, sent it back to the Darkworld, since demons couldn't really die.

It was kind of funny that I didn't expect to see demons in a place like this. The creatures tended to gather wherever a lot of people were, but the Venantium's barriers kept them away from Blackstone. The only shadow-creatures here were the harpies, which constantly swooped overhead, looking misleadingly like large black birds. In fact, up close they resembled old crones crossed with eagles, and were as hideous as they were vicious.

Berenice said, through chattering teeth, "How long is this guy gonna keep us waiting? I'm freezing my ass off here."

It figured she'd be the first to complain.

"You didn't have to come," said Leo, shooting down two harpies at once. "Beat that," he added, to Howard.

Berenice shrugged. "What if he attacks us?" she said.

Howard shot a couple of harpies out of the air, too.

"He won't. Vampires aren't savages," said Leo. "They're people, like us."

"They bite people." Berenice shuddered theatrically.

"They can't help it. It's an instinct they can't control." Leo threw another fireball, igniting three harpies at once.

"Whatever. I'm not getting too close to it, anyway. I hear they live like animals."

"That's bullshit," said Leo, with so much venom that Berenice looked at him in surprise.

"Don't tell me you're a vampire's advocate now, Leo?" she said.

Leo glared at her. "I just don't believe in prejudice." I was surprised too. He'd never reacted to Berenice's barbed comments like that before.

An uneasy silence fell all the same; whatever he said, maybe there *was* the possibility of an attack. Almost unconsciously, the way we were arranged covered all directions, in case anyone sneaked up on us. I found myself seeing shadowy figures behind every grave. Why *had* the vampire insisted we meet here?

As this thought crossed my mind, I saw movement out of the corner of my eye, and a figure came out from behind one of the large tombstones. He walked towards us at a slight crouch, as if unwilling to draw attention to himself, his head bent. The air seemed to tighten as he approached, and my own breathing sounded unnaturally loud. I tried to make out his features, but beneath the towering graves, I could only discern his white-blond hair.

When he stood a few feet away from us, he hesitated. At that moment the moonlight fell on his face, and with a sinking heart, I recognised him.

Oh, God, I thought. *Not him.*

2

CONRAD

T he week before, I'd gone out with my flatmates, Alex and Sarah, and a few other people from the Literature Society. There was a book-themed pub crawl in Blackstone, and Alex, Sarah, and I had dressed as the nineteenth-century poets, Byron, Shelley, and Keats (although Alex kept forgetting which of us was which). We sat around a table at the Coach and Horses, Blackstone's most popular pub, reciting terrible attempts at poetry, when I noticed a guy staring at me from the other side of the bar.

He was short and slightly chubby, with white-blond hair almost the colour of snow. He had a nervous look about him that reminded me of a rodent. His eyes kept darting around, as if looking out for someone, but they'd always come back to me. It was a bit unnerving, to say the least. When we got up to leave, and move on to the next pub, he appeared behind me.

"Hey, you're Ashlyn, right?" he said.

"Yeah," I said warily.

His face broke into a smile of relief. "I've wanted to talk to you for ages. I'm Conrad, by the way."

"Um… nice to meet you," I said. "Um, why did you want to talk to me?"

"Can we talk alone?" He shifted from one foot to the other.

I glanced at my friends, who were looking at me curiously. "Sure."

We moved away from the group. I saw Alex give him a suspicious glance as he beckoned me down an alleyway.

"You're not planning to murder me, are you?" I said.

I'd meant it as a joke, but he flinched. "No! No, of course not, why would I kill you? You're beautiful. Sorry, that came out wrong. I'm making a mess of this."

Dear God. "You're wasted," I said. And it was true. I should have guessed from the way he'd been putting away pint after pint in the pub. He could barely walk in a straight line.

"Sorry, I was just nervous. I wanted—I wanted to ask you… will you come to the Valentine's Day ball with me?"

I stared at him. "Um… what?"

"Want to come? To the ball, I mean?"

Was this some kind of joke? Quite apart from the fact that I didn't generally have guys falling at my feet anyway, the ball was nearly a month away. Besides, I hadn't been planning to go at all. Fancy events were definitely not my thing, the winter dance being the exception.

"Um. I kinda already have plans…" His eager look made me want to back away, which was probably the opposite of what he intended. I was pretty certain my face was on fire. Plus I still wore that ridiculous Percy Shelley wig and a costume like one of the admirals from *Pirates of the Caribbean*.

This couldn't possibly get any more embarrassing.

"Oh, it's okay. Just thought I'd ask. I'm doing English too, by the way. I've seen you around. I've never had the courage to speak to you before," he babbled, and I actually did back away as he made to put a hand on my arm.

Jesus. He didn't seem particularly threatening—not that I judged by appearances, considering everything that had happened in the last few months—but all the same, I automatically reached out to the Darkworld and felt my fingertips begin to freeze. I could defend myself, in theory, but I'd rather not cause a scene.

He saw me move away and gave me a wounded look, all puppy-dog eyes. "Sorry if I'm freaking you out. I'm not good at this. Um, I'll see you around? I'll be at the editorial meeting on Monday? I signed up for the student paper, when I saw your name on the list."

"Oh…kay." Definitely borderline-stalker behaviour. "And you knew my name… how?"

"From our course's Facebook group, of course! I sent you a friend request." He beamed at me.

I didn't have the heart to wipe the hopeful expression from his face. "Um, maybe, yeah. See you around."

You handled that well, said a sarcastic voice in my head. I ignored it. There *was* no way to handle that situation without plunging it deeper into awkwardness.

Alex gave him an evil look when we emerged from the alleyway. I could tell she'd been prepared to intervene.

"What did he want with you?" she asked, as soon as he was out of earshot.

"He wanted to ask me out. Even though we've never spoken before. It was the most embarrassing thing ever."

"Seriously? Man, you're popular lately."

"Because one guy asked me out?" I said, steering them in the direction of the rest of the group. William Shakespeare led the bar crawl, accompanied by Charles Dickens,

Sir Walter Raleigh, and T.S. Eliot. As I'd expected, Rex Golding, Alex's not-so-secret admirer, showed up dressed as Aragorn from the Lord of the Rings. At least, unlike the Role-Playing Society members, he hadn't challenged anyone to a duel. Even I thought that was a bit much.

"What about your little friend from GameSoc?"

"He's not little, and he's just a *friend.*" In fairness, the only time Alex had seen Leo was when he'd been standing near Howard, who would make any person of average height look short. But there wasn't anything between us, anyway. He'd said I looked *pretty* at the winter dance before Christmas, but he'd been drunk at the time, and I didn't exactly put much faith in things people said when inebriated. Another reason to avoid Conrad like the plague.

And now here he was, in Blackstone Cemetery at midnight. It was absurd.

He looked at me now, eyes widening. "Ash?"

"Um," I said. "Hi, Conrad." There was no point in pretending. I was a terrible liar.

"You two know each other?" said Berenice, looking from him to me with a calculating expression I didn't like at all.

"Um, I know Ash, from our course. I'm Conrad, by the way. The vampire."

I felt a bizarre urge to laugh. I couldn't imagine anyone *less* vampire-like. How many vampires were short, chubby, and blond? More to the point, he looked so timid that the idea of him attacking anyone was incongruous. He trembled all over, and he moved closer to us, giving the nearest row of graves a wide berth as though expecting their inhabitants to rise from the ground and attack him.

Berenice sniggered openly. "The *vampire,*" she said, tossing her hair imperiously. "And you have something to say to us?"

Conrad gaped at her, as if he'd momentarily lost the ability to speak. I'd have felt sorry for him under normal circumstances. Berenice wasn't known for her kindness to strangers. Or to anyone, really, apart from Howard.

"Well?" she said.

Conrad stuttered, "Um... I... er... well, I don't want to be annoying, but could you help me? Other vampires are being killed, and I... I think I might be next." His voice rose an octave.

"How do you know?" said Howard, sitting up and swinging his legs over the tomb he sat on. Like the others, he now gave the vampire his full attention.

"Well. Um, the last vampire to die was a student, right?"

"Yeah," said Cyrus. "Will Reynolds. He was a third year, on my course. Do you know who might have killed him?"

Conrad hesitated. "Um. I'm not sure. I just thought, since students were dying, that I might be next and I panicked. I saw Ash with you guys and I figured you might be able to help me..." He trailed off.

"Well, you thought wrong," said Berenice. "We won't be your bodyguards. Whatever's happening to your sort isn't our problem."

"Berenice!" said Cyrus. He turned to Conrad. "Sorry."

"It's fine," said Conrad. "I wouldn't ask, only I'm desperate. Do any of you have an idea about who's killing people?"

"We thought *you* might," said Leo. "Even the Venantium are clueless."

"Look, we're disturbed by this, too," said Cyrus, "but there's no proof yet that it's only vampires who are the targets. Any of us is a potential victim."

"Thanks for the reassurance!" said Berenice. "I'd

rather not risk my chances by associating with a walking target, thanks."

"Then don't," said Leo. "Take your selfish ass elsewhere."

No one could pull off the wounded expression quite like Berenice. Everyone either rolled their eyes or shook their head at her, except Howard, who looked Conrad up and down suspiciously.

"Prove it," he said. "Prove you're a vampire. How do we know this isn't a joke?"

"Do I look like I'm joking?" said Conrad. He looked white-faced and desperate.

"We've met some pretty good actors," said Howard, eyes narrowed.

"Are you wearing a shield?" said Claudia, squinting at him. "Damn shadows make it hard to see."

"Um, yeah. My dad taught me how to do it, I…"

"He's telling the truth," said Claudia. "He's not a threat, or a spy."

"It's true," said Leo, nodding. *Are they seeing something I'm not?* I stared at him, too. He stood half in shadow, white hair gleaming in the moonlight. *They must mean a shield like the one they put on me*, I thought, and made a mental note to ask how they could see one on other people. The whole point of a shield was to make a magic-user inconspicuous.

"Okay," Howard relented. "But we can't act as his bodyguards."

"I… I'm not asking you to. I just… would you let me know if you find anything out about the killer? I don't… I don't wanna die."

"Oh, *Jesus*," said Berenice, rolling her eyes.

"Okay, we'll let you know," said Claudia. Even she sounded as though she wanted to get as far away from Conrad as possible.

"Thanks," said Conrad, gratefully.

The silence hinted at an end to the meeting, but he continued to hover nearby. It didn't escape my attention that he kept furtively glancing at me.

"Well," said Berenice, "I for one don't want to spend any more time in this damned graveyard. You coming, Howard?"

Howard pushed himself off the tomb. "Sure," he said.

As the two of them left, hopping over the low stone wall, Cyrus said, "I have to get back to mine. Might get some work on my dissertation done."

"What, at this time?" said Claudia.

"I only have a week left to get five thousand words done," he said.

"How'd you manage that?" said Claudia, raising her eyebrows.

"Changed my topic at the last minute. I know, I know."

"Serves you right for being a psychology major."

"Yeah, whatever. See you later, bro." He high-fived Leo, leapt over the cemetery wall, and disappeared into the alleyway.

"Suppose we ought to go, too," said Claudia.

"How about a quick stop at the Coach and Horses?" said Leo.

Claudia sighed. "I would, but I actually have to go to my seminar tomorrow, or my tutor will skin me alive. Missed too many already."

To my relief, Conrad didn't follow us back to campus. I felt him watching me as we left, though. *A vampire stalker. Just when I thought life couldn't get any weirder.*

The wind was freezing cold, so we walked back to campus swiftly. Our breath fogged the air in front of us, and the frost-hardened ground cracked beneath our feet. We conjured lights to see our way through the forest, and it crossed my mind that we probably should have taken the bus, even though it was a ten-minute journey which never seemed worth paying full bus fare for.

Now the forest seemed an impenetrable wall of darkness, the thick bare-branched trees forming a stern line on the edge of the road.

"Lights," said Leo, and conjured one in the palm of his hand. It gleamed, a round white orb that lit up a circular area around him. Claudia and I did the same, and, lights in hand, we attempted to find the path. The stream had frozen mid-flow, its water spectre-white against the gloom of the surroundings. Every shadow looked uncomfortably like a dark space.

This was definitely a bad idea. Especially given that there was apparently a murderer somewhere nearby.

Well, neither of the actual murders had taken place anywhere near the university, but two student deaths had caused a campus-wide rumour-fest that lurked beneath the usual gossip and talk between lectures. One had been a girl who'd lived in Preston, the other a guy in York. Two places that had no connection, two people who didn't know each other, and the only thing they had in common was they went to this university, and they'd both died from blood loss after having their throats cut with a sharp weapon.

I rarely paid attention to the news, but this gave me the chills before I'd even found out they'd been magic-users. And vampires. Thinking about it, it proved the Venantium couldn't hush *everything* up, though they'd be hard-pressed to make the world forget a story that had been on the national news for the past month. From what I knew of memory adjusting—and, to be honest, I wished I didn't—you had to be near the person whose memory you wanted to erase.

"What did you do to Conrad earlier?" I said to Claudia. "How could you tell he wasn't lying?"

"My parents used to work for the Venantium," she said. "Part of their job was identifying whether people were potential threats. They taught me how to read whether someone's a user of hostile magic. He's safe."

"Okay," I said. "I was confused. You seemed to know it just by looking at him. I thought you couldn't see shields, isn't that the point of them?"

"It's because we knew he was a magic-user already," said Leo. "My guardian taught me how to see shields, but even most *venators* don't know how until they enter formal training."

"You have to be trained to work for them?"

"Well, yeah. Which section you work in dictates how much, but they run some pretty thorough tests on you."

"Sounds fun," I said.

"You know, I did consider working for them, for a bit," said Claudia. "My parents taught me a few things, like how to see and make shields, but I think they expected me to join."

"Really?" I said.

"The way my parents described them made it sound like what they do makes a real difference. I'm not saying I believed that—well, not wanting to be like my parents was one of the reasons I refused to join—but if you don't know what *we* know about them, then they sound... like protectors, I guess. Protecting the world from demonic threats."

"That's what you told me," I said. "But you also said they threaten people themselves."

"Like Howard, yeah," said Leo. "He did kind of provoke them, but blocking his magic like that was totally out of order. As for what they did to *his* parents..." He shook his head.

I remembered Claudia telling me Howard's parents had been arrested when he was a child for breaking the Venantium's rule against experimenting with magic. He hadn't seen them since, and had his own magic temporarily blocked for trying to break into their Headquarters to find them. In some ways they sounded like crazy dictators determined to keep all magic-users in line.

But I could sort of see why a lot of people, upon learning about their connection to the Darkworld, would want to use it for a good purpose. The Venantium maintained the Barrier, who kept the demons at bay. Their name meant *hunters* in Latin, because that was what they used to do: hunt demons. Now, however, they were apparently paranoid about unregistered magic-users.

"Yeah," said Claudia. "I mean, most of the *venators* are just ordinary like us, but I swear the higher-ups are on some kind of crazy power trip. Constantly looking out for unregistereds causing trouble. They've got harpies flying around in broad daylight when they know sometimes non-magic-users can see them. And they keep tailing people. It's driving Berenice nuts. They followed her back from Satan's Pit the other night. Unfortunately for them, the only dirt they got was the lovely sight of her giving Howard a hand job in an alleyway."

"I really didn't need to know that!" I said.

"Neither did I," said Claudia. "I know, it's a scarring image. Anyway, she's really pissed off. Her dad's a lecturer here—Dr Payne, how appropriate—she doesn't want him to think she's experimenting with evil magic."

"Or that she's giving people hand jobs in public places, I imagine," I said. "So her dad's a lecturer, even though he's a magic-user?"

I'd never really thought about whether magic-users could have normal careers. As much as I didn't know what I wanted to do after university, I'd realised when I was at home for the holidays that I should probably start to look at my options.

"Course," said Leo. "You could even be a stripper if you wanted to."

"No thanks," I said. "I was thinking of going into research, actually... I'll probably do a Masters. Maybe a PhD. Not sure I want to be a lecturer though."

"You want to be known as Dr Temple?"

"Yeah, I realise that sounds more like an Egyptologist than an English lecturer," I said. "So do you have any ideas? About what to do with your life?"

"Oh, the usual. World domination. Make a deal with the devil and get into trouble for boxing the Pope's ears and making people sprout antlers."

"Right," I said. "Like Doctor Faustus. I don't think you want to end up dismembered, though."

"If you want to use your powers for good, you could set up as a freelancer like Madame Persephone," said Claudia. "I haven't ruled that out."

"Hm," I said, biting my lip.

I hadn't seen the fortune-teller since that night in the Lakes, the night when I'd nearly died. Knowing she was really my Aunt Eve, and not really my aunt at that, made me clueless about how I was supposed to act around her. And besides, she'd lied to me. I still didn't know her real identity. She guarded herself well.

"I was wondering," I said, voicing something that had been on my mind a lot recently. "Is it possible to use magic to change your appearance? You know, disguise yourself?"

Claudia frowned. "Not that I know of. I guess you

could use a mind-trick, make people think you're someone else. But that would take a hell of a lot of skill."

"More than breaking into someone's mind?" I referred to what we'd done to my former flatmate, David. It still didn't sit well with me that we'd erased twenty-four hours' worth of memories from his mind so he wouldn't report us to the Venantium, his bosses. Worse was how easy it had been.

"Well, yeah, it'd have to be done on a massive scale. Low-level Influence, like making yourself effectively invisible to people, that's fairly easy. But maintaining an illusion like that… well, you'd have to be tuned into the Darkworld all the time. Most people would burn out."

Using any magic required this connection, but I didn't feel it like other people did. From carefully questioning the others, I concluded that to most people, it was a tenuous connection at best, and quickly drained energy from the body. For me, the penetrating cold made me feel alive in a way that was one part scary and one part strangely thrilling. *Perks of being part-demon.* Yet sometimes, I'd sell my soul to be like other magic-users, not caught in a web of secrets that might constrict around me at any moment.

"I'm not the best with mind-tricks," said Leo. "Pity, since they're useful. But unless you have specialist training, there's only so much you can do."

"It's because the Venantium like to guard all the secrets of magic," said Claudia. "Like in their library. There's still no sign of the *Sorcerers' Almanac*."

"I know," said Leo. "Well, I vote that if our little friend bothers us again, we point him in their direction. There'll be someone sympathetic enough to take an interest in protecting him. Or just getting him out of our way."

"That's not very nice, Leo," said Claudia.

"Hey, I have every sympathy for his condition. I just think he's a whiny moron."

I laughed at that. "A bit whiny, yeah." I hadn't told the others about him asking me out, and I didn't intend to bring it up if I could help it. I hoped he'd leave me alone.

Famous last words, I thought, as we emerged from the trees to see Conrad waiting up ahead, on the path that led directly to the student village. My heart sank.

"Can't he take a hint?" I muttered.

"Maybe he's seen something?" said Claudia.

Conrad stood stock still, visibly trembling.

"What's up?" Leo called.

He said something I didn't hear. Then three voices cried, "Ash! Look out!" just as a large shape barrelled into me, knocking me off my feet, and sharp teeth sank into my arm.

3

MR MELMOTH

The world flipped over. I was suddenly overwhelmed by the stench of earth and leather. And, lurking beneath, a more subtle scent, metallic and salty. Blood. My arm throbbed. I rolled out of the way of my attacker—a big man, broad and wild-looking. He wore the tattered remains of what must once have been a pristine suit, which was now torn and stained with mud. His steel-grey hair was matted and his teeth were bared in an inhuman snarl.

"I found you," he hissed.

I couldn't move. Even though he wasn't touching me, I felt as though I was frozen to the spot. It was like one of my nightmares which ended in sleep paralysis, with me unable to even move a limb, or scream for help. But before anything else could happen, there was an explosion of fiery light and the man leapt aside, roaring in pain. Claudia faced him, and she looked incredibly pissed off.

"What," she said, "is your problem?"

"This is none of your concern," he growled.

"I'd say it is," said Leo, and threw himself at the man.

This was an incredibly foolish thing to do, given that his opponent was twice his size, but the guy clearly hadn't expected such a direct assault. They both fell away down the hill, and judging by the flashes and yells of pain, both were using magic. I hesitated to follow, not wanting to get in the way. I'd never seen Leo display the slightest bit of aggression before, but now he looked livid. I was ashamed at myself for holding back, but it didn't seem a bright idea to get in the way of the flames. Being part-demon meant I'd never be able to summon fire myself, although I could still overwhelm a demon using ice that burned like flames. But I couldn't make myself immune to burning, like Leo and Claudia could. In a fight like that I'd burn alive.

"Get away from her!" yelled a voice.

I'd forgotten about Conrad. He ran towards us, but his feet slipped on the wet grass and he went head over heels. I would have laughed at him if I didn't have more pressing matters to deal with.

Ignoring my throbbing arm, I contacted the Darkworld and felt the familiar surge of coldness, of pure energy, rush through me. Without thinking, I threw myself after the other two. Claudia hung back, perhaps hesitant to shoot a fireball in case she hit Leo by accident. But I didn't really have a plan. I just wanted to get him away from Leo.

Ice spread out from my palms rapidly as I latched onto the man from behind.

"Leo, let go of him!" I shouted, not wanting him to get caught in the spell, too. He backed away, gaping as ice flowed over the man before him.

Drained, I dropped to my knees.

"How the hell did you do that?" said Leo. "I've never seen magic like it."

"I have no idea." Light-headedness swept over me. I pressed my forehead to the cold ground, my body trembling. *This big guy attacked me for no reason.* "Tell me I didn't imagine that. Who was he? A werewolf?"

"No, he's another vampire," said Leo, and he wasn't laughing. "His name's Bill Melmoth, and he's my guardian."

My heart missed a beat. "You what? Your guardian?" I looked up at him, even though I felt dizzy.

"Yeah. Shit." He knelt down to examine the perfect vampire ice-statue. "Holy hell. He's totally iced over."

"I don't understand," I said. "He's… a vampire?" I held up my arm. "He bit me. Am I going to turn into one of them?"

"No, of course not," said Leo. He'd pulled out his mobile phone. "Vampires often bite people to make it easier to take their magical energy from them."

"Ouch," I said, examining the ring of teeth marks. He'd barely drawn blood, but it stung from where the bite had overlapped on the scars from where harpies had attacked me last year.

"Cy! Cyrus! Oh, for God's sake. He's not picking up."

He turned back to me. "Hell. We're in a mess. Do you need something to put on that arm? I have antiseptic cream somewhere in my flat. Let me look at it."

That seemed beside the point, but I let him check it anyway.

"I think you're fine. I'm so sorry about this. I never thought…" He shook his head.

"I don't get it," I said. "He's really your guardian?"

"Yeah. After Mum died, Dad didn't want anything to do with his kids any more. He left us for the Venantium. Melmoth here took Cy and me in when he retired. And he's…" Leo shook his head again. "It's been getting worse. Vampirism worsens over time, and he's had it his whole life. But he's *never* attacked anyone deliberately. He seemed to recognise you. It's weird."

"I've honestly never see him before," I said. "I don't understand."

"Nor me," said Leo, punching numbers into his phone. "Maybe he's cracked. I'll look after him, since Cy's decided to turn his phone off."

"So… what do we do?"

"I'll figure it out," said Leo. "You'd better get back to your flat—Claudia, too. I don't want us to get caught out here. I don't know what he was thinking, coming so close to the Venantium. They're not exactly best friends. He only stayed in Crowley because his family's buried there…"

"You can't stay out here with him alone!"

"Trust me," said Leo, "he won't attack me. I can handle him. Go."

The spell began to wear off. I could see the ice melting, water dripping from Mr Melmoth's hands.

"Jesus," said Claudia. "I've never seen anything like that ice-spell. Are you a direct descendant?"

"A what?" I said, blankly.

"They say the descendants of the original Inner Circle had extraordinary magic."

"I've no idea," I said. "I never found my entry in that book, remember?"

"The *Almanac*? That's a point. I wonder if it's back in the library? Worth a look, I suppose——"

"Leo!" said Claudia, gesturing at Mr Melmoth's prone form. "Bigger problems?"

"Oh, right. You two should go."

"Okay," said Claudia. "Come on, Ash."

She half-dragged me back to the flat, ignoring my

protests. She was surprisingly strong for someone barely taller than I was.

"Did you want him to attack you again?" she said, as she used her fob to get into the building.

"I didn't want him to hurt Leo. He—he never told me his guardian was a vampire."

"It's not something he or Cyrus really talk about. Cy's pretty private, but he did tell me about his family one time. Apparently that Melmoth guy used to be really high up in the Venantium, until it came out that he had the Vampire's Curse, and he had to step down. They're so prejudiced there."

"I can imagine," I said. "He kept it a secret, then?"

"Must have done."

"It's weird." I sighed. "I just don't get why he attacked me."

"I don't get it either. And how did you freeze him like that? It's the same thing you did to David, right?"

"I don't know. It must have been instinct, I just... did it."

Claudia sighed. "We need to look into this. And I think we should talk to... you know, *her.*"

"Ash?" said a voice from behind me. Once again, I'd forgotten about Conrad. He stood awkwardly outside the block, swaying slightly as though he might faint.

"You'd better go, too," said Claudia. "Why'd you follow us here?"

"I live here," said Conrad. "Well, in the block over there." He pointed.

"Then what the hell was up with making us go all the way into Blackstone?" she demanded.

"Um, I didn't want to be overheard. No one knows what I am here. They don't even know I'm a magic-user."

"Join the club," said Claudia. "Doesn't mean you had

to drag us right up to the Venantium's doorstep. We've been attacked there before. Well, Ash has."

Conrad looked alarmed. "I'm sorry, Ash. I didn't realise! I'm really, really sorry."

"It's fine." I wasn't used to guys falling over themselves to apologise to me; it made me feel uncomfortable. "I should be getting to my flat now, anyway. My friends'll be wondering where I am."

To my annoyance, Conrad followed me into the building, and right up to the door to my flat. *Great. Now he knows exactly where I live.* At least I was in the habit of checking the shield I'd placed on my room to stop intruders getting in, after what had happened last term.

"Goodbye, Conrad," I said firmly, as I let myself in, making sure to shut the door behind me.

Maybe I'd been a bit mean to him, but I genuinely didn't know how to deal with this situation. I'd wasted far too much of last term wondering if a guy liked me or not, and now I had the opposite problem. This had *never* happened before I'd come to Blackstone. I wasn't the type to turn heads, and it had never particularly bothered me. Guys at home were usually only after one thing, so I didn't take it as an insult.

I have to tell him I'm not interested.

I groaned. Like that mattered. A vampire had attacked me, for crying out loud.

I took a long shower, since sleep was impossible. Adrenaline still fizzed through my veins from the fight, and my body temperature felt out of control, going from boiling to freezing more rapidly than the shower did. Ordinarily I could only feel temperature in the extremes; even the coldest night didn't bother me. But the Darkworld brought a chill of its own, the kind that penetrated to the bone, and always awoke when I used magic.

My magic was different to any of the others'. I couldn't summon fire, which was easy for most sorcerers, but I could freeze things. And, in defence against demons, I could fight them with ice that burned like fire. None of the others had a clue why I was different, and I feigned ignorance, too. I knew my magic wasn't the same as the others' because I was part demon, and demons were creatures that thrived in the dark and cold.

The demons had tried to get me to join them once before, and I'd resisted. Every time I left Blackstone, they were waiting for me, whispering promises in my ears, bowing their heads to accept my authority over them. Like I'd join them after seeing what dealing with demons had done to Terrence, my former flatmate.

I still revisited that night in the Lakes in my dreams. Terrence had been a covert sorcerer tempted by demonic magic, and he'd finally summoned one in an attempt to coerce me into surrendering my demon heart to him. But he hadn't known—and neither had I—that I couldn't be possessed. I couldn't even imagine what that must feel like. That was the demons' ultimate weapon, the ability to pierce your mind from within and take over. The demon could choose whether to take control of their victim's magic, leaving the sorcerer conscious whilst it wreaked havoc using his or her body, or simply to kill them. Either way, no one survived very long after letting a demon in. Terrence hadn't.

I might have killed the demon, but I knew it wasn't over. The demons were cunning, cruel and merciless, and it chilled me to the very soul that I had any kind of connection to them.

I stepped out of my en-suite bathroom and changed into my warmest pyjamas. I might not be able to feel the frigid air seeping in through the gap beside the window the way normal people could, but I could still catch a cold. I examined the ring of teeth marks on my arm. They weren't bleeding, but still stung. I made a mental note to wear long sleeves for a while. At least the other scars—from a harpy's talons—were invisible to most people's eyes.

I shook the tangles out of my dark hair whilst flicking absently through my required seminar reading. Work had piled up now term had started properly. I'd come back to Blackstone a week early, since Cara had gone back to Edinburgh that week. I'd missed campus, and most of all I'd missed going out without running into demons everywhere. Every time I saw one, I thought of Terrence's face contorting, and his body dropping to the ground like a stone. Nothing should be allowed to have that kind of power.

At home, my parents didn't take much notice of me either; both were working most days—Dad was an electrician, Mum worked part-time in a shop—and our Christmas had been a quiet one. I'd pretty much had free reign to do whatever I wanted, which, ironically, made it less likely that I'd do anything adventurous. At university, there was always something happening, and it had been weird suddenly having nothing to do but play video games and read. Of course, I didn't miss people trying to kill me, but home didn't feel the same anymore, and not just because I was away from the shields which kept me from seeing demons in Blackstone. Cara and I had enjoyed shopping in the January sales, but other than that, I'd looked forwards to coming back to campus.

Outside, the sky began to lighten. Once again, I was already awake to see the dawn. I always seemed to get into the habit of sleeping at odd hours during term, especially when Claudia and the others dragged me on night-time excursions. Not that I'd been back to the library since the harpies attacked us last time. Howard had taken enough books to occupy us for a good while, and the Venantium didn't seem to have noticed their absence.

This included the one on my desk, *The Seven Princes of the Darkworld*. That book had been my saving grace when I'd been paranoid that my part-demon state meant I had other demonic traits, such as immortality. Unlike Sarah, who was a *Twilight* fanatic, I imagined it would get boring after a few centuries or so. Thankfully, though, immortality was reserved for spirits alone.

The higher demons, one of whom was supposedly my ancestor, were the only demons able to take on human form completely, mainly for the purpose of seducing humans and leaving their traits in the genetic line. I couldn't completely work my way around the old-fashioned language of the book, but I gathered that their aim in doing this was to create a generation of super-humans in order to overthrow the Barrier. They'd almost succeeded once, apparently, back in the fifteenth century, but the human-demons had not proven immune to ordinary causes of death and were particularly vulnerable to burns. In the ensuing battle it had been the pure demons who'd put up the strongest front, which may have been one of the reasons why human-demons were all but forgotten these days. Except for me.

The sun crept over the treetops as I watched, sitting in the windowsill with my feet tucked in. Frost covered the tree branches, glittering in the rising sun. The moon still floated in the sky, though it looked faded and washed-out. A robin sang outside my window. Its feathers were fluffed up against the cold.

"Dan-ielle," sang a mournful voice. I jumped. That definitely wasn't a robin. "Dan-ielle!"

There came the long, drawn-out twang of someone

inexpertly plucking a guitar string, and my flatmate Pete staggered into view. Dishevelled and totally mortal-drunk, he fell to his knees in the middle of the field and howled to the sky.

"Shut the hell up, you loser!" someone yelled from an upstairs window.

Pete didn't move. Totally besotted with a second-year student, Danielle, even after four months of continuous rejection, he constantly did everything he could to get her attention. Penniless as a result of splurging on alcohol in the first few weeks of last term, it was left to Alex, Sarah, and me to make sure he didn't starve for the rest of the year by letting him "borrow" cash to buy food.

My phone buzzed. I picked it up, hoping fervently that Conrad hadn't somehow got hold of my number. But it was from an unknown sender.

The message said, "A shadow has your face."

I stared at the words. *A shadow has your face?* What could that possibly mean? I scanned over my recent messages, but couldn't find any from the same number. Was it a prank?

I sighed. Yeah. Weird shit had started happening again.

SARAH AND ALEX were in the kitchen when I went in to get breakfast, both looking sleepy. I felt surprisingly alert considering I'd been awake all night. I wondered if Leo would come to the lecture. I hoped to see him, for reassurance that he was okay and that nothing else had happened.

His guardian was a vampire. It sounded even more absurd now. If I hadn't seen it with my own eyes, I'd have dismissed last night's events as lunacy.

"Looking forwards to another joyous lecture on Wordsworth?" said Alex.

"Can't wait," I said, putting bread in the toaster.

"Late night, was it? I didn't hear you come in." Alex skimmed through her anthology, trying for a last-minute bit of preparation.

"Um." What had I said I was doing? At a GameSoc social, probably. "Yeah, pretty late."

Maybe I should have gone to bed. I was used to concocting alibis, but this just got confusing.

"I haven't read the *Prelude*," said Sarah. "Have you, Ash?"

"Some of it," I said.

"That's not like you," said Alex, scrutinising me. "Whatever happened to Ash the workaholic?"

"Wordsworth's not depressing enough," I said, munching toast. "Too many daffodils, not enough fire and brimstone."

"Well, we're done with *Paradise Lost* now, you crazy person. Ugh, I give up with this." She shut the anthology with a snap. "Also, we're going to be late if we don't get a move on."

"Fair point," I said, grabbing my last piece of toast and putting my plate in the sink.

I snatched up my bag and followed Alex and Sarah out of the flat, trying to pull my mind away from vampires and murders and graveyards.

Unfortunately, I didn't bargain on Conrad waiting for me outside the building.

Great.

"Hi, Ash!" He smiled at me. I caught a whiff of after-shave and almost gagged. It smelt like manure. Had he doused his whole head in it?

"Hi," I said, whilst Alex and Sarah sniggered behind

me. Ignoring them, I began to walk through the student village. Conrad hurried to keep up.

"How're you doing?"

"I'm going to a lecture," I said. I wasn't exactly in a conversational mood.

"Me too. I'm on your course, remember?"

My lack of enthusiasm didn't deter him from trailing me all the way to the lecture theatre, and by the time I took my seat, trying to ignore my friends' incessant giggling, I was in a thoroughly bad mood. Leo wasn't there, either, but since he had a habit of skiving early morning lectures, this wasn't unusual.

One snore-fest later, I joined Alex and Sarah for some studying in the library. Our workloads had begun to pile up again, and our first-year exams seemed much closer from this side of Christmas. To my relief, Conrad had another seminar now, so he couldn't tail me to the library. Since we had another essay due in a couple of weeks, I wanted to stay ahead of the game.

"Ash, you're like an essay-writing machine," said Alex, reaching to pull my hand away from the page so she could read what I'd written. "You do know first year doesn't actually count towards our final grade, right?"

"Yeah, but I don't want to fail," I said.

Alex rolled her eyes. "You, fail? Didn't you get that scholarship for being a genius?"

"For my A-Level grades," I muttered, flushing. That was true. I'd almost forgotten about it. The extra money had been a welcome addition to my meagre student loan.

"Maybe that's why all these guys are after you. They think you'll do their references for them."

I snorted. "Yeah, that's totally what's on most guys' minds."

"Well, either that or they're enraptured by your femi-nine charm," said Alex.

"You've been reading too much love poetry," I said. "In case you've forgotten, when Conrad and I met, I was dressed as Percy Shelley."

"He wrote love poetry, didn't he?"

"Er... no. Have you done *any* of this term's reading?"

"Who are you, the new professor?" said Alex, but her tone was light. "To be honest, I'd come to one of your lectures. Be a lot more helpful than that waste of an hour."

"Me? Public speaking?" I mock-shuddered. "No way in hell."

Alex laughed, nudging Sarah. "Come on, Ash should totally take over our English lectures, right?"

Sarah gave a faint smile.

"What's up?" said Alex.

"Nothing." Sarah stowed her phone in her bag. I'd seen her texting someone.

"Nothing's nothing," said Alex, with her typical Alex logic.

"Does that even make sense?" said Sarah.

"Who cares? Who were you texting?"

"Liam. Does it matter?"

Sarah was usually soft-spoken, so this outburst took me by surprise. Liam was her boyfriend—he studied at university in London, hours away. Sarah and he had been in a long-distance relationship since summer, but if I was honest, I'd forgotten she even *had* a boyfriend.

"Okay, that's definitely not nothing," said Alex. "Spill it. Do I need to drop-kick anyone?"

Alex had the same philosophy as my oldest friend Cara when it came to guy trouble—she'd once remarked that a kick to the bollocks worked better than talking things over. No wonder Rex hadn't made a move on her yet.

"No!" said Sarah. "It's really nothing. He's just being... I mean, I don't think he's coming to visit next weekend."

It had slipped my mind, but I remembered her being really excited. They hadn't seen much of each other over the holidays due to his visiting family in the south.

"That's not cool," said Alex. "Did he say why?"

"Some football game."

"He plays?"

"Sometimes. Like I said, it's cool."

"Uh, no, it isn't. Tell the dickweasel that you have to come first. How long have you guys been together anyway?"

Funny, neither of us had asked that before, even though we'd lived together for the best part of the past four months. I guessed it was because of the way university worked—several random people were thrown together, and in the rush to adjust to spending every day with each other, basic questions were often got forgotten.

A good thing for me, considering how many things I'd kept from them.

"A year," said Sarah.

"Okay. Definitely tell him it's not cool." Alex perched on the edge of her seat, as though tempted to take Sarah's phone and text him herself.

"Alex," said Sarah. "It's really fine. Besides, if I get this job, I won't be free Sunday anyway."

"Oh yeah, forgot about that," said Alex. Yet another new development that had slipped my mind. "When's the interview again?"

"Tomorrow at three."

"You'll be fine," said Alex. "You'll nail it."

"Ugh." Sarah shuddered. "I hate interviews. They'll think I'm the least eloquent English student ever."

"You should've seen me at my Oxford interview!" I

said. "I talked about a book I hadn't even read. Beat that for embarrassing."

"Wait, there's a book you *haven't* read?" said Alex, raising an eyebrow.

"Ha ha," I said.

I was well-practiced in feigning levity when I was around my friends, but the mention of that interview stirred other, equally unwelcome memories. Like what had happened after the interview, when I'd run through a dark space and everyone had thought I was crazy. The memory raised goose bumps on my arms and gave me the creeping feeling of being watched by unseen eyes. Habitually, I looked around, even though I knew it was in my own head.

Most students in the library were final-years, like Cyrus, finishing dissertations and projects, so the noise was at a low level. But I also detected the undercurrent of gossip that had pervaded campus since we'd returned a couple of weeks ago, concerning the two murders. Everyone who didn't know the people in question whispered about whether it was a coincidence that they'd died within days of each other. No one, however, seemed to find it odd that only the local news had reported it. Copies of the paper were everywhere, even though within a week, speculation had slipped off the radar again, at least as far as the papers were concerned. The latest headline concerned another grave robbery in a nearby town called Filburn. Three bodies removed, graffiti left everywhere. A copy lay open on the table, and I couldn't stop my gaze drifting onto it. An image of several graves dominated the cover, with words sprayed in neon across each stone, *The Ghouls were here!*

Ghouls. I remembered a certain night in Redthorne in which Claudia and I had dragged a giant, shaggy shadow-beast out of Satan's Pit, the student night club, and were then ambushed by a group of shadow-foxes and a couple of ghouls. Hideous as harpies, their heads looked like sunken human skulls and their bodies like deformed apes. I pushed the thought away. It was unlikely that these grave robberies had anything to do with the Darkworld. *Probably.*

I returned to my Wordsworth notes, but before I could write a word, someone called my name. I looked up to see Claudia making frantic motions towards me from across the room. I went over to her, heedless of Alex and Sarah's curious glances.

Claudia looked like she hadn't slept either, and her usually glossy dark red hair was in disarray and her face bare of makeup.

"What's up?" I asked. "What's happened?"

"It's…" She shook her head. "It's awful. Have you seen a newspaper today?"

"I saw one on the table back there. There was something about grave robberies on the cover."

"That was yesterday's. Check this out," she said grimly, and held up a crumpled copy of the *Blackstone Herald*. I glimpsed the headline, *Businessman Murdered in Blackstone*. Then my eyes focused on the photograph beneath it.

It was Mr Melmoth.

4

MURDER

"How——?" As I spoke, I scanned the text, horror rising in my chest.

"This one's more accurate. When I saw that headline I panicked and swiped this one from a couple of *venators.*" Claudia handed me another paper, a smaller one, printed on thick, stiff paper. I took it. This one was headlined, *FORMER INNER CIRCLE HEAD FOUND WITH THROAT TORN OUT.*

My stomach turned over. It was a horrible enough image without associating it with someone I'd met only yesterday.

I read on: *"William Edward Melmoth, former leader of the Venantium's Inner Circle, has been found murdered in Blackstone.*

Mr Melmoth was discovered in the early hours of the morning of the 28th January, in a field just outside the village. A known recluse, he has lived in the area for most of his life, and even after his retirement has been a trusted helper to the Venators' cause despite his suffering from a debilitating condition. His brutal murder, almost a parody of the method of killing favoured by the creatures from which his condition takes its name, has shocked locals and Venators alike.

Having retired early, Mr Melmoth raised siblings Cyrus and Leo Blake, children of the current Inner Circle member——"

I stopped reading. "Leo," I gasped. "Is he okay? I mean, he was *with*——"

Claudia shushed me. I'd forgotten we were in the library, and people were beginning to stare at us.

"Let's get out of here," she said, and grabbed me by the arm, dragging me after her.

Once we were on the front steps, she said, "Leo's fine. Shaken up, of course, but he's okay. Apparently he couldn't reason with Melmoth, and once your spell wore off, he legged it. Leo went after him, but he'd disappeared into the village by then. He walked around all night looking for him, but he ran into a couple of *venators* and they told him… they told him they'd found the body. Then they took him in for questioning."

"They what?" I said, my heart somersaulting. "They can't think Leo killed him!"

"I don't know what they think. But it's bad for us, too."

"Why?"

Claudia took a deep breath. "Don't ask me how, but they know we were there last night, too. You and me. They want to question us."

My chest tightened, as though a vice squeezed the air from my lungs. *It's finally happening.*

Ever since I'd learnt that I was one of the few people to have developed a connection to the Darkworld even though I had no relations within the Venantium, I'd come to regard them as an enemy, based mostly on my impressions from the others in the group. I'd even let Leo and Claudia put a shield over me so that if any *venator* cast a spell to find out whether I was a magic-user or not, it'd come up blank. Apart from that one trip into the library, in which I'd been attacked by the Venantium's own harpies, I'd done everything I could to stay out of their way.

Now I was implicated in a murder case.

"Relax, Ash," said Claudia, seeing the fear in my eyes. "We can get out of this. Honestly. We'll bring in Madame Persephone. She'll help us."

"Fine." My voice came out in a croak.

"But we'll have to go now. They want to see us *today.* Five o'clock this evening."

"You're *joking*," I said.

"I got a message from them this morning. Check your phone, you might have one, too."

"They don't have my number, do they?"

"Did David have it? They will if he did. *Venators* can't hide anything from their superiors."

"Shit." There was indeed a message waiting for me. "Miss Temple. We request that you present yourself to us at 5 p.m. this evening for questioning. Your friend Miss Delaney will help you find our Headquarters. Good day."

"Oh God." I slid down the wall to the ground. "Oh God." I was going to kill David. I'd known he was thinking of selling me out as a rogue magic-user, but I'd never have thought he'd give my number to his bosses. *Bastard.*

"Panicking will only make it worse. If anything, Leo's in deeper shit than either of us."

"True." I said, willing my heart to stop beating like it was trying to leap out of my chest. *Don't panic.*

But returning to my friends and getting on with my work was impossible, not now. I went to retrieve my books, muttered an excuse, and fled with Alex's curious stare behind me.

I needed to speak to the fortune-teller. Maybe she could get me out of this.

I kept questioning Claudia all the way into town, more

to stop my imagination from taking over than anything. Knowing what the Venantium thought of independent magic-users, I couldn't help but envision interrogation chambers full of harpies and worse. The Venantium didn't like to let magic-users out of their sight. Claudia's parents had stopped working for them, but their daughter's name had automatically been put on the register. The only reason mine hadn't was because no one else in my family had ever had anything to do with them. In theory, a magic-user could go their whole life without ever coming into contact with the Venantium. If I hadn't come to Blackstone, they wouldn't have known about me unless I'd done something stupid like using magic in public.

Making a secret society of magic-users at university, even an ironic one, was a step against them in their book. The Venantium liked to think they ran the universe. In a way, I was more afraid of them than I was of demons, because I had no idea what they could do to me. That message was so impersonal, I could get no meaning out of it. The sender didn't even leave a name.

I thought of the other message I'd got yesterday. Had that been from someone else David had given my number to? *A shadow has your face* read more like a prank sent to freak me out, but this…

We found the fortune-teller's tent in its usual corner in the town square, hidden from anyone but us. "Madame Persephone," as she called herself, opened her services to the public during the weekly market, but she wasn't a real fortune-teller, merely one of the most perceptive people I'd ever met. It was a cover-up for her true identity as a freelance magic-user, dedicated to helping magic-users who were in trouble and didn't necessarily want to have anything to do with the Venantium.

I just didn't appreciate the way she'd pretended to be

my aunt for years. Whenever I'd been in town, I'd stayed well away from the fortune-teller's tent in case she ambushed me with some other unwelcome revelation. I couldn't evade the problem forever, but right now life was complicated enough. It was typical that she was the only person who could help us now.

On the inside, the tent was set out like a standard fortune-teller's, complete with charms, crystals, and incense candles. The woman behind the black-draped table was beautiful enough to spark envy in most women. Her silver-fair hair glowed faintly in the gloom, and her eyes were a startling blue-grey, somehow older-looking than the rest of her. There was something unearthly about her, like she wasn't totally of this world. I had no idea how old she really was, but as she could change her own appearance, it was understandable she'd opt for a face that would make any other female hate her by default.

"Well, it's been a while, Miss Temple."

I shrugged, happy to let Claudia do the talking. My heart still beat erratically, and my hands shook.

"We need your help," said Claudia.

"I thought as much. I saw Master Blake earlier, too."

"Is he okay?" I said, forgetting that I wasn't speaking to her. "Do the Venantium have him?"

"He's been to identify the body, but they've scanned him and he came up clean. They know he's innocent."

"So is he free?"

"Yes. You, however, might not be so lucky." And the knowing expression in her eyes said it all. Would they know I was part demon if they ran tests on me to see if I was guilty? The thought made my blood turn to ice. It wasn't as though I could run away. They no doubt had ways of tracking people. They seemed all-knowing, like they had eyes everywhere.

"What do we do?" said Claudia, who wore a puzzled expression; clearly she hadn't missed our silent exchange.

"For a start, you'll have to remove your shield. They'll see right through it anyway. It'll only get you into more trouble. Ash, you'll have to tell them that you don't know who your ancestors are. Tell them you discovered your connection to the Darkworld independently, and that Miss Delaney and Master Blake helped you."

"Isn't that the truth anyway?" said Claudia.

"Of course," I said—well, it was *part* of the truth. "So you think I should be honest?"

"As honest as you can be. Tell them what happened the night you encountered Mr Melmoth, as accurately as you remember. Leave nothing out."

"They've got no evidence against us, right?" said Claudia.

"No, but you'll come under suspicion as an unregistered magic-user all the same. Just relax, tell them what happened, and hope that the truth's enough."

"Very encouraging," I muttered. "And if they lock me up?"

"They won't. The worst is that they'll do a full magic scan on you, which is less scary than it sounds, and won't hurt you."

"So what's the fuss about?" said Claudia.

"Nothing. I don't want to be arrested," I said. "Criminal records count against you for life."

"It's not quite like that with the Venantium," said the fortune-teller.

"Please don't tell me it's worse," I said, swallowing.

Her expression softened. The effect was surprising, like an ice mask had cracked.

"You'll be fine," she said. "Is there anything else you wanted to say?"

"Just that I got a weird text message last night," I said. "It said, 'A shadow has your face.' It was from a private number."

"Indeed." The fortune-teller looked troubled. "I would guess that it was a practical joke. The important thing is to focus on the present."

And that was the end of our discussion. There were a fair few more things I wanted to say, but with Claudia there, I couldn't.

So we left.

There were still two hours before our appointment, so for lack of anything better to do, we went and sat in the Coach and Horses. I kept glancing at my watch every few minutes. The seconds seemed to drag by, yet at the same time a jolt of fear went through my veins every time another five minutes of freedom passed.

Leo arrived with half an hour to go. He looked pale and tired.

Stupidly, the first words that came out of my mouth were, "Are you okay?"

He shrugged. "I've been worse."

His apparent nonchalance surprised me. I mean, his guardian had been killed, he'd been interrogated about it, and now we were facing the same. He had none of his usual bravado, but didn't look to be in the depths of grief either.

"Melmoth was going to die anyway," he said, as if feeling the need to explain himself. "The Vampire's Curse was killing him. It kills most of them in the end. It burns up your life energy, makes you age way faster than normal people do. It was a matter of time."

"But... someone *murdered* him," said Claudia. "If he was dying anyway, why would they do that? Did he have something to hide?"

"You could say that," said Leo. "I found out today he was still working for the Venantium after all, for their medical division. People are saying he was developing a cure for the Vampire's Curse."

"Seriously?" said Claudia. "Is that even possible? I thought it was incurable."

"Melmoth always insisted it wasn't," said Leo. "After he left the Venantium, he went into research. He was adamant that there was a way of controlling the killer instinct, and he's been helping loads of people who had it really bad. I didn't know he'd actually found a cure, but there are rumours. They've pretty much torn our house to pieces."

"Oh, Leo," I said. "I'm sorry."

"Don't be. It could have been worse for me, but now it looks like they've got a bunch of new clues to help them catch the killer. They're looking into whether any of the other victims had anything to do with Melmoth."

"And do you... do you have any idea who it could have been?"

"No. There was a hell of a lot of shit Melmoth didn't tell me, evidently. I'll find out somehow." He glanced at his watch. "I think we ought to leave now. I'll come with, but I don't think they'll let me back in."

"Is the entrance still in that old crypt?" said Claudia.

"Where else would it be?"

"I dunno. They're paranoid these days. I thought they might have switched back to using the tunnels."

"Yeah, I guess the higher-ups didn't fancy getting their feet dirty."

"It's underground, isn't it?" I said.

"Yeah, but you wouldn't think it if you saw it from the inside," said Claudia. "We'd better get going, anyway."

I trembled all over as we made our way to the graveyard. Dusk brought with it a low, heavy fog that hung over the buildings like a wreath of cobwebs. The streetlamps spilled butter-yellow light across the cobblestones. Above, the towering spires of the cathedral loomed ever closer. We climbed over the wall to the cemetery. *Second time in two days. People are going to think I'm a graveyard junkie.*

This time, Claudia and Leo led me to a large dome-shaped tomb, with a pair of doors made of dark wood set into it. Beside it was the Blackstone memorial, appropriately a large slab of black stone.

Without warning, the edges of the tomb's doors blazed with a fiery light. I stared at the word carved above the doors: *Blackstone*. It seemed to come alive with the same light, like fire was contained within the wood itself.

Then the words faded, and the doors swung open.

I'd expected to see a gloomy, narrow staircase twisting down into the darkness, but instead a dark hole in the ground greeted us, like an open grave.

"You have to jump in," said Leo. "Don't worry, it doesn't hurt or anything. It's only a mind trick."

That didn't make me any more prepared to jump into a freaking *grave*. It reinforced my private fear that I wasn't going to come back.

Shit. I'm not ready for this.

Leo gave me a hug, a move that startled both Claudia and me. An unexpected rush of warmth ran through me, a brief respite from the choking fear that tightened around me.

Then he let go. "Hope you come back," he said.

"Me too," I said, not quite managing a smile.

Then, her face set, though her eyes told a different story, Claudia grabbed me by the arm and pulled me after her. A scream escaped my mouth as we dropped into the grave.

5

THE ANGEL BOX

My own yell echoed in my ears, cut off in a squeak of surprise as we landed. The fall only lasted a second, but it was enough to completely shake me up. I lay with my face on the ground, and it took a moment to process that there wasn't cold stone beneath me, but thick carpet.

"You okay, Ash?" said Claudia from somewhere nearby.

I got to my feet, looking around me in growing bafflement. This might have been the entrance hall to a posh hotel, not an underground organisation. The carpets were a deep blood red, and ran the length of the hall, up to a pair of heavy iron doors. Marble pillars stood at intervals, rising to support the dome-shaped ceiling. The walls were glossy black and embellished by paintings that reminded me of the religious-themed pictures at the Art Gallery above ground, depicting Miltonic scenes of sinners confronted by the monsters of the underworld. These were juxtaposed with paintings of actual demons, shadow-beasts, and harpies.

Blue flames shone from old-fashioned brackets, casting eerie reflections on the glass picture-frames and making the eyes of the demons flicker creepily. This was enough to stopper my awe and strike cold fear into my heart once again. We stood in the place where humans resisted the demons. They showed no mercy to anyone they thought might have a connection to them.

I turned on the spot, looking for a way out. Several other doors were set in the walls, beneath elaborately carved archways. Above each perched a hideous bird-crone creature with black feathers, a harpy. The memory of talons slicing through my arms made me shudder, and I hugged my arms tight to myself, resisting the urge to hold the pendant. I'd tucked it inside my jacket, and a sudden thought gripped me. What if someone recognised it as a demon heart?

Don't think, I told myself, as panic stoppered my throat again. I began to shake uncontrollably.

It was so quiet I'd thought we were alone, so Claudia's sharp intake of breath gave me a start.

"You," she said, in tones of disgust.

I turned to see a sharp-faced youth standing over us, scowling heavily. He had thick dark hair and equally thick eyebrows. The effect was that his features looked as though they had been etched on his face in black marker pen. He couldn't be older than we were, yet he regarded us in a way that suggested we were scum beneath his feet.

"Me," he said. "I'd be a bit more respectful of Mr Priestley when he arrives."

"You slick bastard," said Claudia, through gritted teeth. "Are you their front-boy now?"

"I have duties," said the boy haughtily. "I'm supposed to make sure you don't attempt to escape."

"Like we'd try it." I could almost feel the animosity

coming from Claudia in waves. She and this guy clearly had some kind of history.

"Come on. I'm meant to take you *downstairs.*" He placed a delicate emphasis on the last word, and there was a twisted smile behind it.

Downstairs turned out to be through one of the arched doorways. A passageway sloped downward in a manner similar to the tunnels leading to the library, and the walls and floor were stone and seemed to exude coldness. The light had dimmed to a faint glow from the flickering blue candles in brackets along the walls, and I didn't dare conjure my own light. I was in enough trouble as it was. A sense of suffocating claustrophobia descended on me.

"Nervous?" said the boy.

I didn't say anything. I wasn't sure I *could* speak.

"I wouldn't worry," he said. "You might get lucky and miss out on the Angel Box, since it's your first time."

"The what?" I croaked.

His white teeth shone in the darkness as he grinned. "You'll see."

Asshole, thought the part of me that wasn't paralysed with terror. I stumbled after Claudia, feet catching on the uneven ground. A steady dripping came from somewhere up ahead, and apart from our echoing footsteps, no other sound penetrated the silence until we reached the foot of the slope, where the passageway branched off in several different directions.

A bloodcurdling scream rent the silence. I jumped sideways into Claudia, my heart leaping into my throat.

"What the hell?!" Claudia gasped. In the gloom, her face was deathly pale, a mirror of my own.

"Don't worry. We're not going that way."

"I hope not," she said. "The Venantium solicit torture now, do they?"

"If it's deserved." The boy's smirk grew more pronounced. I wanted to hit him.

The passage we took was even narrower than the one we'd come down through, so we had to walk in single file. My breath fogged the air in front of me as I walked on and on, feeling as though we were travelling down into the depths of the earth. But finally the tunnel widened, and a bright light hit my eyes, making me cringe away into the shadows. Once my eyes adjusted, I saw it came from behind a door that stood ajar at the end of the room we were in.

The room was more like an underground chamber than anything, except the walls and floor were a dark, shiny metal rather than stone. It had an odd, clinical smell, mixed with the scent of earth from the tunnels, and the faint, but unmistakeable aroma of burning.

Someone was waiting for us, in front of the oblong of light. A tall, spindly man whose face was completely expressionless stepped forwards.

"Are you Claudia Delaney and Ashlyn Temple?" His voice was as empty of life as his face. I couldn't tell how old he was—he might have been any age between thirty and sixty.

"Yes," said Claudia. I merely nodded. I felt as though I'd left my voice behind in the tunnels.

"Leave, Jude," he said, and the boy departed. "Miss Delaney, go into that room." He pointed to one of the identical metal doors inset in the walls. She nodded and turned away. She was shaking, too.

"Miss Temple, come with me."

A shiver of dread danced across the back of my neck, as he led me into the room with that alien light. The glow turned out to come from a human-sized glass case that stood in the centre of the room. If it hadn't been for the door which lay ajar, I wouldn't have said a person could stand in there without suffocating.

"Have you ever been here before, Miss Temple?" said the man.

"N-no," I said, my legs weakening.

"Then you will be unfamiliar with the Angel Box. This is a device used as a magic scanner. I'll need you to step inside it. You will not be harmed."

The last thing I wanted to do was step inside that box, but what choice did I have? It muted all sound the instant I entered, and I felt the mad urge to scream in terror. I clenched my fists instead, willing myself to stay calm. The eerie light was all around me, and if I was Leo, I might have made jokes about alien abduction. As it was, I shut my eyes and tried to pretend I was somewhere else. It didn't work.

I must have stood there for at least ten minutes whilst he walked around me, examining me from every angle. A gap above the door meant I could still breathe normally, but panic made my chest tight. I kept my eyes on my feet to avoid looking at my examiner's blank face, stealing the occasional glance at the rest of the room. Apart from the glass case and metal walls, it was furnished like a regular office. A desk sat in the corner, topped with piles of paper and two computers. How on earth did they still work, this deep underground?

Finally he gestured, and the glass door sprang open.

"Please come and sit here." His voice was emotionless. I couldn't tell if it was good news or bad.

The chair looked uncomfortably reminiscent of pictures I'd seen of electric chairs, but I was so relieved to be out of that box, I collapsed into it. The man peered at me. His eyes were a dull shade of dark grey, but with an odd intensity to them.

"You're a magic-user." It wasn't a question.

"Yes," I whispered.

"But unregistered."

"Yes," I said. "My parents aren't magic-users. I didn't know about it before."

"How long have you known?"

"About…" I swallowed. "Four months, I think."

"There is something unusual there, but your reluctance to approach us is understandable." I blinked in surprise. "It's very rare for the connection to develop independently. Do you know of any history of magic-users in your family?"

He doesn't know, I thought.

"No," I said. "I don't have a copy of my family tree, and I'd never heard about anything until it happened."

He nodded. *He believes me,* I thought, the tiniest spark of relief beginning to glow within me.

"But there is something that concerns me. How have you used magic? In what capacity?"

"I—" I stumbled. He had a surprisingly intense stare for someone with such a plain face. "I don't remem-ber—I've made lights appear, you know, to see in the dark…" It was my Oxford interview all over again. My mind blanked itself completely.

"You have never harmed anyone?"

Did turning someone to ice constitute harm? I didn't want to mention that, in case it made him suspect what I really was. The Venantium had to be aware of human-demons, right? Either way, I couldn't risk it.

"No," I said. "Honestly. I've never hurt a single person."

Unless I counted Terrence, but as he was possessed by a demon at the time, I wasn't sure he qualified as a person. I did my best to meet that level stare. I wasn't lying, was I?

He nodded, and I breathed again. "All the same, we feel it is prudent to set a watch on you. If you see any harpies—you know what harpies are?"

"Um, yeah," I said.

"They will report back to us. If we suspect any illicit activity, we will send for you again."

Great. As if one stalker wasn't bad enough. Now the evil crone-birds would be on my tail.

"But there is another important matter which needs to be addressed. Do you know who murdered Mr Melmoth?" The directness of the question disarmed me.

"No," I said.

"You saw him last night?"

"I—yeah. He attacked me and my friends when we were walking back to our flat."

"You defended yourselves?"

"Yes." There was no point lying. "I didn't hurt him. He—Leo—" My thoughts were all jumbled together. "None of us harmed him," I said. "Honestly."

"I have spoken to Mr Blake. He was the last person to see Mr Melmoth alive. I merely wanted to know if you saw anything. I know from the scan that you have not performed any harmful magic of late, nor have you physically harmed anyone in any way. You're clear."

A rush of relief made my legs turn to jelly again. "And Claudia?"

"I'm sure your friend is clear, too. As you may be aware, Mr Melmoth's is only the latest in a series of murders we are currently investigating, and we have to question all witnesses. Had you lied, I would have known."

I nodded, suppressing a shiver at his last words. They implied a hidden threat, not quite masked by his blank, robot-like face.

"However, there is one thing that concerns me about this particular case. Were you acquainted with the man beforehand?"

"No. I'd never met him before. I don't know why he attacked me."

"Well, I have knowledge that his condition was worsening. It could have been random, of course, but we will keep an eye on the case nonetheless."

This sounded ominous to me.

"Tell me, Miss Temple, are you acquainted with the story of the Blackstone family?"

I hesitated. "The whole family died in a fire... that's what I heard."

"That's the common story. The untold part is that around a century and a half ago, a stranger knocked on the door of the Blackstone family's manor. He was a sorcerer, a traveller, and they were happy to let him into their home. He seduced their daughter, Melivia. When her father found out, he unleashed his wrath upon the man. But he was too late. The man had already tricked Melivia into summoning a demon.

"In the Demon Wars that followed, the entire clan was wiped out. As it was such a momentous event people tend to forget the origins. But here in Blackstone we do not forget. The family's grave stands as a monument to those who met their fate at the hands of a demon. For such a contract inevitably leads to death. Although the stories of the events are uncertain, mainly based on eyewitness accounts from the time, the one thing we know is that no one left that house alive. And the demon escaped, leading to a conflict that spanned the entire country, even the world. All the Venantium fought the demon invasion and killed Lucifer, the sorcerer, after years of conflict."

I swallowed. I didn't know what to say. I'd completely forgotten about the Blackstone family and the weird way everything in the village seemed to be connected to them. It made sense that they'd been magic-users—but had one person really caused a war?

"What happened to her?" I asked.

"Melivia? She died in the fire, too. Set herself alight, it's said, in order to exorcise the demon that possessed her. The poor child."

I remembered the paintings at the Art Gallery in Blackstone: David had said they were Melivia's work. Scenes of the dead rising to drag the damned into hell. *She burned alive?*

"I just wanted to stress upon you the consequences of contacting the Darkworld. Here, we have no choice. It is our job to keep the world safe. But the reason we keep an eye on independent sorcerers like yourself is precisely because of incidents like this one. We never forget."

He paused. The intense light flickered in his eyes.

"If you wish to register and join us, our doors are always open to you."

His tone was welcoming now, inviting, but something about it set me on edge. *Like I'm going to say yes.* But he clearly expected an answer.

"Um, okay."

He bowed his head. "That is all, Miss Temple. You may leave."

It seemed too good to be true, but I nodded and left the room as fast as I could. I found Claudia waiting for me outside. She looked pale, but composed.

"Clear?" she said in a tremulous voice.

"Yeah."

"I thought so," she said, not quite masking the relief in

her voice. "Let's get outta here. I don't suppose that prick Jude will be back to show us out."

The tunnel didn't seem as long or threatening this time, but we hurried regardless. The memory of that blood-curdling scream came back, and I couldn't help but imagine what could have happened had we not been so lucky.

Claudia seemed to think the same. She muttered, "It'll wipe that smirk off Jude's face to see us unharmed. He'd love to think we were suffering some awful punishment."

"He and Berenice should get together," I said.

"I think they dated once, actually. Before Howard came into the picture. And before he tried to get my parents arrested for not registering me with the Venantium."

"What?"

"I know. He told the Inner Circle they were traitors. Thankfully they took no notice. He's always trying stuff like that, to get himself into the higher-ups. But they're not interested. He's just their front boy. He's at our uni, too. Studying politics. God help the world if he becomes a politician."

Jude wasn't even there when we came out of the tunnel. The entrance hall was deserted.

"Damn," said Claudia. "I can't remember which door leads to the exit."

As if in response to her words, one of the doors sprang open, although there was no one behind it.

"I'm guessing it's that one," I said.

"They have all the magic of the Darkworld at their fingertips, and all they can do is mess with technology and make underground automatic doors," Claudia said, shaking her head. "Let's go, anyway."

Another passageway awaited us, this one sloping

upwards. We raced up it, feet barely skimming the stone floor, striking out a path for light and freedom.

It was dark when we emerged from the ground, although I instantly recognised where we were. The large black slab of the Blackstone memorial loomed over us; we were now behind it, rather than in front.

Claudia turned to me, and gave a shaky laugh. "No harpies this time, right?"

"Ash!" Leo pushed off from the stone wall.

"Leo? You're still here? You must be freezing!"

"Little bit," he said, holding up his hands, which had gone an interesting shade of blue. "Never mind that. How did it go?"

"Considering we're here and not still down there, it went pretty well," said Claudia. "We're both clear."

"Thank God," said Leo. "I planned to go down there myself if you hadn't come out by midnight."

"Can you even get down there?" I said. "I thought the way only opened for us because they wanted to see us. I mean, that's what it looked like."

"There are other ways," said Leo. "The tunnels."

"Ah." I thought of the winding passageways. Not my favourite place. Even now, it was such a relief to breathe the fresh, cool night air.

"Don't the locals know about all those tunnels?" I said. "I'm surprised they can exist right under our feet without anyone knowing."

"The Venantium protect them. The entrances are concealed, generally near old mine tunnels, and marked as hazardous. Of course, they use Influence, too. Like the fortune-teller's tent."

"Ah."

"And those harpies make sure no one gets near them

who's not supposed to. Specifically, unregistered magic-users."

"Yeah, I got that much," I said. "I'm surprised they didn't go for me again."

"You had permission to be there this time," said Leo. "They're brainless, they can only obey orders. Otherwise, I'd be screwed. They'd know I'm the one who keeps attacking them."

"Aren't you and Howard worried you'll get caught?"

"Daft question," Claudia broke in. "The words 'Leo' and 'worried' rarely work in the same sentence. He has no concept of it."

"Well, it's pretty low-risk," said Leo. "If you hit a harpy, it just disappears back to the Darkworld. It can't tell anyone about it. It's not like I'm leaving evidence."

"It's the overt use of magic that worries me," said Claudia. "But I've given up arguing."

Were the harpies watching us right now? I looked up and saw a flock swoop past, casting dark shadows in the moonlight. Leo was right: they were everywhere these days.

I *really* didn't like the thought of them spying on me. I thought of David, how he'd spied on me last term. He'd clearly told the Venantium about me after all, the lying bastard. That, or they'd got hold of my number some other way—a thought that didn't sit well with me, either.

Claudia and Leo talked about the interrogations all the way back to campus. I told them about mine, too, but I had half my gaze on the sky above, on the dark, wheeling shapes. They'd carried messages to David, I remembered. How many other students led double lives? That Jude was a student, too…

Maybe no one was who they claimed to be. Maybe the

Venantium had a grip on everyone at the university. For the first time, I fully empathised with Howard's attitude towards them. Who were they to think they owned the universe? I had never broken any laws. I hadn't asked for any of this. I'd tried to make the most of a bad situation, associating with Claudia and the others only to learn more about what I was. Was that a crime, in the eyes of the masters?

I didn't know, but I had an inkling that my days of leading a relatively peaceful double life were over.

6

GRAVE-ROBBERS

Sleep came easily after the day I'd had, but it wasn't a restful night. I dreamed I was back in that glass box, on display to the world as a part-demon freak. Cameras flashed, people jostling to get to the front of the crowd. I could see my own reflection in the glass, and for a second, my hazel eyes appeared violet. Demon eyes.

People jumped back, letting out cries I couldn't hear behind the glass. I pressed my hands to it and cold bit at my fingers. It wasn't glass. It was ice.

I hammered at it desperately until the skin on my hands cracked and beads of blood began to pepper my skin. Then heat seared my back, and I smelled burning. Someone behind me brandished a torch, and in the heat, the ice began to melt.

More torches flared, blue flames like those in the Venantium's tunnels. Ice dripped onto my head and trickled down my back. I couldn't get out, but there was nowhere to run. A paralysing sense of hopelessness seized me as the crowd closed in around my shrinking prison. As the first flame touched my skin I cried aloud, and awoke tangled in my bedcovers and drenched in sweat.

Breathing heavily, I examined my burning arm. Pain had flared along the not-quite-faded scar from the harpy's attack and around the faint ring of bite-marks from where Mr Melmoth bit me. I had no idea if this was normal. Shuddering, I made for the shower to wash away all thought of the dream.

At least today was Saturday. I couldn't handle a day of lectures, not after last night. Alex wanted to go book-shopping in Redthorne, so Sarah and I joined her. Nothing could calm me quite like browsing around bookshops, and later, people-watching in Starbucks over hot chocolate.

"Oh my God!" Alex shrieked, causing people across the room to stare at us. "It's Ash's boyfriend."

Not again. She pointed out the window, grinning, as Conrad tripped over the kerb and executed a spectacular face-plant.

"Please don't come in here," I muttered.

"Where else would we get our entertainment?" Alex snickered. "Oh. He's gone. Shame."

I exhaled in relief. Good job they had no idea he was a vampire. I'd never hear the end of *that*. A vampire stalker. What a novelty.

"Come on, Sarah, lighten up." Alex nudged Sarah, who almost dropped her phone. "Hey—did you find out about the job?"

"Yeah, I got it," said Sarah, in a surprisingly less-than-enthusiastic tone. Not that a job at the on-campus restaurant was glamorous, but money was money.

"But that's awesome!" said Alex. "Why didn't you tell us?"

"Um, I only found out now. They were trialling a few people."

"Told you you'd nail it," said Alex. "What'll you be doing, waiting tables?"

"Yeah, I guess so. I didn't think the trial went that well, but they're desperate. I think one of their staff left over the holidays."

"Nice going, anyway. Just make sure you don't miss any LitSoc socials. We're planning something epic this term, seeing as the social organiser screwed up massively at Halloween."

"Was something supposed to be happening at Halloween?" I said, scrambling to remember what crazy thing had dominated my thoughts at that particular time. Oh yeah. Claudia and I had battled a bunch of ghouls.

"Hell, yeah," said Alex. "We were meant to be spending the night in a haunted house."

"No freaking way am I doing that," said Sarah. "I'll pass."

"Come on," said Alex. "It's all in good fun. A sleepover in an old house, telling ghost stories by the fire… Ash?"

"What?" I said.

"You in?"

"Haunted houses?" I said. "Not really my thing."

"Scared of ghosts?" Alex pulled a ghoulish face that startled the couple at the table next to us.

I knew ghosts didn't exist—that was precisely the problem. *Other things* waited in the darkness. An old house, with history, in this area… *Yeah. Count me out.*

"I just don't fancy freezing my ass off all night in an old house at this time of year."

"You're both spoilsports," muttered Alex. "Well, I'm going."

"I don't know how you find the time," said Sarah. "I mean, you're in what, seven societies?"

"Eight," said Alex. "I joined archery last week."

"Remind me not to come near when you're practising," I said. "You almost poked my eye out with a cocktail stick at the winter dance."

"That was an accident!" Alex insisted, spilling coffee down her front. "And you made me do that," she added.

I rolled my eyes. "Is it so you can dress up as Legolas for the next social?"

"No, it's because I'm a badass with a crossbow." She poked Sarah. "Cheer up, you. You start your new job tomorrow, right?"

Sarah nodded. "Breakfast shift at seven."

"On a Sunday? Good luck with that. I'll be up then, actually."

"Learning to fight off zombie hordes with your badass crossbow?" I said.

"You got it," said Alex. "Come on, Sarah, it won't kill you. You're not still having issues with that asshat boyfriend of yours, are you?"

"I…"

Unlike Alex, I was pretty good at telling when someone wanted to avoid being questioned. "Hey, is that Benedict Cumberbatch outside?"

Alex flew to the window so fast she'd have tumbled out of it if it had been open.

"What? Where's Sherlock?" She turned accusing eyes on me. *Crap.* Well, I'd kind of asked for it.

"Um… maybe it was just someone who looked like him?" I shrugged, innocently. "I saw a guy at home once who looked exactly like David Tennant."

"Did he have a blue box, by any chance?" said Alex.

"Sadly, no."

It helped that Alex was as easily distracted as a hyperactive child. Sarah looked marginally more cheerful. I wished I could offer her advice, but as recent events showed all-too-well, relationships weren't my area of expertise.

When we left Starbucks, my attempt to forget about last night went out of the window. Outside a local newsagents', the paper's headline read, *Blackstone Murderer Still Remains at Large.*

In the aftermath of the interrogation, it had slipped my mind that there was someone out there murdering vampires. I picked up a copy of the paper, pretending to be interested in a supplement on books they had featured.

"Weird, that," Alex commented, glancing at the headline. "I thought Blackstone was the safest place you could get. Nothing ever happens. Usually the headline's about a runaway sheep."

"It's scary," said Sarah. "What if it's a serial killer?"

"I doubt it," said Alex. "Still, we're safe on campus."

Safer than you think, I thought. The university, like the village itself, was under the protection of the Venantium's shield, which ensured no demonic creature could come within a ten-mile radius. But the killers hadn't been demons. The victims' energy had been drained, which suggested another vampire was responsible. A human.

Still. Why had Mr Melmoth attacked us? It made no sense. Apart from being Leo's guardian, he'd also been a former Venantium employee, vampire—and, according to Leo, the only person ever to invent a cure for the Vampire's Curse. *Maybe someone sent him mad. Maybe it was whoever killed him.* But why had he gone for *me*? I could see the sharp look in his eye as he'd said, *"You,"* just before he'd leapt at me. As though he'd seen me before. But how was that possible? And why would he want to kill me?

As if I needed anything else to worry about, one of the demons spoke to me as we left the newsagent's.

"You might want to reconsider your choice." I pointedly

ignored the cold voice that slid like ice-water down my spine.

"We can protect you, if you join us."

"I'm not interested," I muttered, quietly so no one else could hear.

"We know which shadow has your face."

I turned my head to stare at the demon. "What? What does that mean?"

The creature merely blinked, violet eyes vanishing into the blackness. I sighed. Only the fortune-teller could match demons for cryptic statements.

"We are on your side. You can't shut us out forever."

"Stay away from me," I said, and ran to catch up with my friends.

At first, when I'd started seeing demons everywhere, I'd been terrified of them. Whilst that fear had never completely gone away, I found them more of an annoyance than anything. They could appear anywhere, indoors or outside, and trying to ignore them was like avoiding my own shadow. Seeing them was, as Claudia put it, the curse of a connection to the Darkworld.

I just wished they'd stop trying to speak to me.

I skimmed through the newspaper as I sat on the bus back to Blackstone, but there wasn't anything substantial in the article, only comments from fearful locals. If the Venantium knew any more, I wasn't sure we could find out. I wondered what Leo was doing. God, I had to talk to him. Whatever he'd said, he had to be hurting. And those murderers were still out there somewhere, still targeting vampires.

When I got back to the flat, I found that I had a message from Cara demanding that I Skype her as soon as I got back. It was the most reliable method of communication here, since the mobile phone reception around campus was dodgy at best. *Crap. I haven't called my parents this week, either.*

"Ash!" said Cara, giving me a little wave on-screen. She'd recently taken the purple highlights out of her hair and as a result looked disarmingly plain, apart from her bright red t-shirt patterned with unicorns. "What do you think about those grave robberies?"

I groaned. I might have known Cara would pay attention to that particular story. "I have no idea," I said. "Are they still happening?"

"Have you been reading the paper?"

"Er…" I scanned the newspaper I'd bought again. Sure enough, on the second page was a supplement about the desecration of several graves in a cemetery in Blackburn. *That's the third place this week—and a town this time.*

"Creepy, isn't it? I have a theory," she said.

I rolled my eyes. "Let me guess," I said. "There's a wannabe-Frankenstein on the loose, re-animating the dead?"

"You think so, too?"

I had to laugh. Really, though, who was I to say reviving dead bodies was impossible, after everything else I'd seen?

"I think someone has a sick sense of humour," I said. "I'd say there's definitely a gang involved, judging by the graffiti."

That was what the picture in the paper showed, another gravestone defaced by words sprayed on in neon yellow paint. *The Ghouls Were Here.*

"You know," said Cara. "I've been researching. Ghouls are supposed to be flesh-eating demons that live in grave-yards. Maybe there's a connection?"

"Maybe it's a myth?" I retorted, though I couldn't

suppress a shudder. I didn't want any more to do with graveyards right now.

"Anyway, I'd watch out for yourself. I recommend carrying garlic."

"Thought that was for vampires, not ghouls," I said. "And I'm not dead, so I won't need to worry about anyone digging up my grave."

We talked like this for a while, but I got the impression my flippancy hadn't entirely convinced her that supernatural things didn't bother me. Maybe I used to be able to do that, when the world had made sense, like when we were twelve years old and borrowed her dad's camera to film our own horror movie in the woods near the park. But after the first time I'd seen a demon, everything I thought I knew about what was real and concrete had been thrown out of whack. Maybe there really *was* a murderous gang of ghouls on the loose.

Whatever my views were on the supernatural, my liking for walks at night had never quite diminished, and my room felt stifling after being out all day. Back at home in one of the less appealing areas of Greater Manchester, the threat of muggers and knife-wielding maniacs kept me confined to the house, but I felt safe enough to wander around at all hours here. So I grabbed my coat and left the flat.

The woodland path was fairly straightforward to navigate, even in the pitch-dark. In a way, I enjoyed the challenge of feeling my way forwards with my feet, treading a now-familiar path. I let my thoughts drift, enjoying the silence and the fantastical patterns the moonlight created on the frost-coated trees.

Then someone stepped onto the path in front of me, breaking my contemplation.

"Ash?" It was Leo.

"Hey!" I said, surprised. "What're you doing in here?"

"Same as you, by the looks of things. Walking."

I nodded. I knew he had as much on his mind right now as I did, if not more.

"I like walking in here at night. No one else is around." This was a pretty lame thing to say, but now I'd run into the one person I wanted to talk to, my mind had gone totally blank.

"Yeah," he said. "Are you okay? You haven't heard anything else from the Venantium, have you?"

"No, I'm fine," I said. "Um, how are you doing? I mean, have you found out anything…" I trailed off.

He seemed to guess what I was thinking. "I've been doing a little investigating of my own. Turns out Melmoth had a secret store room even the *venators* didn't know about. Should have known, really. He never trusted them after they ousted him from the Inner Circle. It's in our old house, I was gonna go check it out tomorrow. Want to come with me?"

"I—really?"

"It's okay if you don't want to. It's hardly a fun trip," he said. "Just thought it might take your mind off shit. And you might learn an interesting thing or two about the Venantium. But if you already have plans…"

"No, I'm not doing anything tomorrow. I'll come. Where are you living now, anyway? I mean, when you're not at uni."

"Cy's got a place in town. I'm over eighteen. I can do what I like anyway. Might go travelling over the summer."

"Do you have the money?"

"My dad gave me some. To make up for utterly failing at parenthood."

"Oh." I didn't know what to say to that. I knew I was lucky to have both parents, but I couldn't imagine how it would feel to be in Leo's position, without parents and now completely alone.

Maybe that was why he wanted me to come to the house with him tomorrow. He needed someone there.

"What about Cyrus?" I said. "Is he in on this investigation thing?"

"Cy thinks we should leave it to the Venantium. He and Melmoth never got on."

"Ah, right."

"He's an idiot. There's something seriously messed up going on here, and if Melmoth never mentioned it to the Venantium, he must have wanted me to find it before they could. I can't think of any other reason why he'd come to campus. It must be important."

"Yeah." I looked up, and was surprised to see fields ahead. Without realising it, we'd walked all the way to the other side of the woods, to the road leading to Blackstone. Fields lay on either side of us, like pits of blackness in the gloom; down the road, the village was a cluster of glittering lights. There was no one else around, but I had the sudden feeling of someone watching me.

I turned around in time to see a person duck out of sight into the forest. It happened so quickly, the only impression I got was of a girl with shoulder-length dark hair wearing a black coat, like I was. Then she was gone.

A shiver danced up my neck. I turned to Leo. "Did you see that?"

"See what?"

"Never mind. We should head back."

"Sure," he said. "So can I count you in for tomorrow?"

"Yeah," I said. "I'll come."

7

CROWLEY

We set off for Blackstone through a gale that threatened to whip us off our feet, under a slate-grey sky. Rain pelted down as we waited in the small station for the hourly train to Crowley, a village on the other side of Redthorne. I looked ruefully at the remains of my umbrella.

"Sixth one this year," I said, and I wasn't exaggerating. The north of England boasted some pretty intense weather.

"Get a wind-proof one next time," said Leo, who hadn't bothered with an umbrella, or even a coat, instead wearing a Pac-Man hoody. His curly hair soon dripped with rainwater.

"Is there a way to repel rain using magic?" I asked, curious.

"Probably, but you'd walk into things if you spent every second of the day willing raindrops not to hit you. It'd be funny to watch, though."

I rolled my eyes. "Magic isn't good for anything useful, is it?"

I'd been rereading *Harry Potter* the night before, for the hell of it, and I couldn't help but think their magical system was far more convenient. It wasn't as if I could bewitch my laptop to write my essays for me or anything—not that I, as a self-confessed workaholic, would ever do that. Lame, but true.

"Depends what you define as useful. I for one find the ability to become a human torch incredibly convenient. If there's a worldwide power cut, we're set."

"True."

His light tone didn't quite reach his eyes. He was silent as we got off the train and walked along a cobbled street similar to the one in Blackstone. I glanced at him occasionally, but his face was expressionless. I wished I knew what to say. I'd been lucky in my short life not to lose anyone close.

"Here it is," he said, as we came out of the other side of the main street and into an area where the houses were larger and more spread out. He pointed at a large, grand old house, identical to its neighbours. Arched windows looked out over a sprawling garden which was overgrown with weeds.

"You *lived* here, Leo?" I said. "This place is huge!"

"Yeah," said Leo, with a shrug, "But I wasn't allowed in half the rooms. Old Melmoth didn't trust me so he locked them using magic. But the *venators* broke through it easily. I'm pretty sure they'll have cleared everything out of there by now."

"I can't believe they broke into your house," I said. "They shouldn't even be allowed to do that!"

"The Venantium operate on their own laws," said Leo dismissively. "I have most of my stuff at uni with me, anyway. I'll be pissed if they broke anything, but it isn't that important. I wanted to get the hell out of there as soon as I could."

He pulled out a key and unlocked the front door. The wind followed us in, sweeping clouds of dust into the air. It got in my mouth, making me cough.

"Sorry," said Leo, "Melmoth never really cleaned the place. He practically lived in his study."

We stood in a grand entrance hall with walls panelled in dark wood and carpeted in blue. An old-fashioned chandelier hung above a wide staircase. The dust and lack of light accentuated the gloomy atmosphere; it didn't feel like anyone had lived there for a long time.

"Where's this hidden room?" I said.

"In the cellar. Typical Melmoth, really, he had to be boring. I was a bit disappointed in him to be honest."

"And the Venantium didn't find it?"

"Apparently not. Melmoth was more inventive than I gave him credit for. I just need to check upstairs, first."

We climbed the staircase onto a landing with more doors than I could count. I couldn't believe how many rooms there were. It seemed absurd that only three people could ever have a use for all of them. Leo opened a door at the end of the second-floor hallway.

"This was my room."

It was completely bare, save for a wooden bed, desk, and chair. No posters marked the walls, and there was nothing to suggest that a teenage boy had ever lived there.

"Like I said, I have most of my stuff at uni. It's not that I didn't trust Melmoth, but he had a lot of enemies and I didn't want to get dragged into anything. I don't think many people even knew he was my guardian. Cyrus never told anyone except Claudia and Howard. And Berenice found out, obviously."

I didn't know what to say to that. I was conscious that I wasn't being much help, standing there awkwardly whilst Leo paced the room, checking underneath all the furniture. A large window overlooked a back garden as overgrown as the front, backing onto a patch of trees. Behind that was a cluster of low hills, extending into the distance. I could see the shape of a cottage at the top of the one nearest to the house.

"There's Tombstone Hill," said Leo, noticing where I was looking. "That place almost beats Blackstone Cemetery for creepiness."

"Who lives in the house?"

"That's the old gravedigger's cottage," said Leo, in a spooky voice. "No one's lived there for years. It's the classic horror-story scenario. If I'd lived here when I was a little kid I'd probably have had nightmares about it."

"Creepy," I said. Then I frowned. "Wait a minute, isn't that a light in the window?"

"Yeah," said Leo. "Kids are always breaking in. Of course it started all kinds of rumours in the village. The locals scare easy."

"I can imagine," I said.

"Well, the demons seem to love the place, anyway," said Leo. "I think it might be because they can't get at Blackstone, so they go for the next creepiest-looking place."

"I thought demons were drawn to people," I said. "I always see more of them in crowded places."

"Generally, but they're also drawn to sites of strong magical activity. There are a bunch of sorcerers buried in the catacombs under the chapel up there—mostly Venantium members who lived a bit farther away from Headquarters."

I nodded. "I guess that makes sense, then. I was

wondering, can ordinary people feel demons? At all? You know you sometimes get that feeling of being watched?"

"Who can tell? Maybe," he said.

"They don't know how lucky they are," I said.

"Some people would say we're the lucky ones, because we can see the world the way it really is."

"That's exactly what the fortune-teller said when I first met her," I said.

"Yeah, it's her kind of thing. The woman's an enigma, almost as much as you are."

"*Me?*" I said. "Since when do I talk in riddles?"

Leo blinked. "I meant… I don't know. You always look kind of haunted. The demons are fascinated by you and no one knows why, right?"

"Right," I said. My heart started beating fast. I was on the cusp of confessing, there and then, why I was different. *Haunted* was a good word. But I said nothing.

Leo sighed and turned away from the window. "Ready to check out the cellar?"

After the tunnels under Blackstone, I wasn't at all keen to venture underground once again, especially in an empty old house. But I quashed the feeling that we were asking for a horror-film scenario and followed him down the narrow stone steps into darkness.

Light flared as he flicked a switch. The cellar was empty, but the deep markings in the floor indicated where several heavy objects had been. Nothing suggested a hidden door or passage; I was about to say so when he hushed me.

Then I heard it. A footstep above. Someone else was in the house.

We had no time to do more than step away from the stairs before we heard the unmistakeable *thud* of footsteps against the stone steps.

"*Shit,*" Leo mouthed at me.

A figure appeared on the stairs, a shadowy silhouette like a puppet dangling from above. Each step echoed. Heart thumping in fear, I moved closer to Leo as the figure reached the bottom of the stairs, and the light.

For a heart-stopping second I thought the figure was headless. Then I realised they'd had to stoop under the low ceiling. And it was Jude, the boy receptionist from the Venantium.

Leo recovered first. "What the hell are you doing here?" he demanded.

"I could ask you the same question." Jude's face was so serious, it almost looked comical, like a caricature. "The Venantium have marked this place against access."

"I used to live here!" said Leo. "In fact, legally, I still do. You, on the other hand, can bugger off."

"I'm authorised to enter here. I'm under orders."

"What the hell is there to see? Everything's gone."

"So why are you here, then?"

"Not that it's any of your business, but I came to see if I'd left anything behind in case your people decided to run off with my things."

"You know, I would believe you, were it not for the circumstances. I rather think you and your *friend* intended to make light of your guardian's memory by defiling his house."

"Huh?" said Leo, blankly.

"I think," I said, "he's implying we came down here to have sex."

For a second, Leo gaped at me. Then he laughed. "Yeah, that makes perfect sense. It's not like there are a dozen bedrooms upstairs or anything."

I couldn't help laughing at Jude's bemused expression.

Leo said, "So, what the hell are *you* doing here?

Looking for stuff to steal? There's a nice cockroach over there. You can have that."

"You really shouldn't be so arrogant," said Jude. "You are one step away from an official summoning by the Venantium, and besides, I don't entirely trust their verdict on your standing in the Melmoth case."

Leo narrowed his eyes. "Man, are you high? Melmoth made enemies of every sorcerer under the sun, and you think *I* killed him?"

"I think you and your brother are hiding something," hissed Jude. "Why was I not informed that Melmoth was your guardian beforehand?"

"Because you were too busy sucking off the higher-ups?"

Jude gave him a condescending look. "Don't assume that because I'm not in the Inner Circle I'm not aware of the secret discussions of the Venantium. It happens I know some rather incriminating information about your former guardian."

"Like what?" Leo took a step towards him. My heart dropped. Jude was far bigger than Leo; in a fight, it was clear who had the advantage. And there was something frightening about him, too, like he had a hidden temper that he worked to restrain, although there was barely a hint of evidence of this on the surface.

Jude plainly had no intention to rise to Leo's bait. "It's classified. Ask the Venantium yourself."

"Like hell I will."

Leo advanced on him. I saw fire flare at his fingertips and a chill swept through me, not because I was keen to fight, but because I'd never seen Leo look so angry, and it scared me.

"Do you want to be arrested?"

"Do you want me to burn off your ear? I know you righteous pricks are afraid of a real fight."

"Leo, stop it!" I said.

Leo looked at me. I couldn't explain why I felt so shaken. Didn't Jude deserve whatever he got?

"Ash? What's up?"

"Nothing," I lied. "Just… don't start fighting."

"I won't," said Leo, in a very different voice. He glared at the intruder. "You can go rot in hell, Jude. I'll find out the truth either way. I'll bet you don't really know a thing. You're just the front-boy."

"I know more than *you* do, you insolent traitor. You're a disgrace to everyone who fights against the darkness."

"Dramatic, much?"

Jude stepped forwards, his face taut with rage. The two glared at each other for a good minute.

"When are you going to get out?" said Leo.

"When you do the same," Jude retorted.

It was clear that no one was going to win the argument. Leo said, "Come on, let's leave him down here."

He started up the steps and I followed. Was he really going to lock Jude in?

Jude seemed to think so. A chill crept over my back, the unmistakable sign that someone had contacted the Darkworld.

"Don't you even think about it," he snarled from below the ladder. Leo sighed, and the chill went away. We climbed out into the hallway.

He waited for Jude to leave first, to make sure he didn't sneak back in. Then I followed, and Leo locked the door behind us.

"Well, I believe I may be seeing you at Headquarters soon," said Jude. "I look forward to it."

"Get fucked," said Leo.

Jude narrowed his eyes at him. Then he turned away. He strode off down the street without looking back.

Leo gave him the finger. "I really hate that guy," he said.

"Same here," I said. "So does Claudia. Is it true that he once dated Berenice?"

"Nah, even she has standards," he said. "That guy's a Class-A prude, anyway. He was always hanging about here when Melmoth was alive."

"Really? Why?"

"We're the same age—well, Jude's a year older—so he tried to pretend we were friends. I think he was about sixteen at the time, trying to get into the Venantium early—you normally have to be eighteen to join up. So he was sucking up to Melmoth in a really sickening way. And, um, I kind of set his hair on fire."

I laughed. "No way. You didn't."

"I did. At a meeting where three of the Inner Circle were present. I doubt they ever forgot him."

"Leo, you're terrible."

"Melmoth gave me a stern talking-to. I'm still not technically allowed into high council meetings—not that they normally let kids in anyway. It was only because Melmoth talked them into it, seeing as they needed to consult him on something. At the time, I think they wanted me to sign up when I turned eighteen, so they let me and Jude in. And then... yeah. I caused a scene and got us both thrown out."

I shook my head. "Wow. I have no words."

"That's why Jude hates me so much. He has this hang-up about unregistered magic-users anyway, but he's just parroting the more old-fashioned views. I've met some other *venators* who were almost human, apart from working for crazy despots."

"So, what's the plan?" I said. "I mean, we're coming back, right?"

"Course," said Leo.

"Today?"

"You've got it. Give it an hour, make sure he's actually gone."

8

MR MELMOTH'S SECRETS

The village's centre was two main streets of little businesses, from old-fashioned sweet shops to second-hand book stores. Leo and I shared a bag of assorted sweets whilst traipsing around the shops and market stalls. Leo looked amused at my agonising over whether or not to buy a particularly tempting book of ghost stories.

"Thought you had enough of that in real life," he said.

"Yeah, but it doesn't stop me reading it, even if it gives me nightmares," I said. "I seem to have an addiction to the macabre."

"You know, I've never heard anyone use that phrase before."

"Are you making fun of me?"

"No, I think it's cool."

"What, I'm cool because I'm an unashamed literary nerd?" I laughed. "That'd be a first."

"There are worse things you could be," said Leo. "So what else do you do in your leisure time, aside from reading gruesome tales of murder and ghosts?"

"Play Mario Kart and sleep," I said. "I'm not exactly your typical student."

"I think you're like a lot of students, actually," said Leo. "I for one value my sleep far more than early morning lectures. And Resident Evil is much more interesting than Wordsworth."

"I'm with you on that one," I said. "Have you made it to a single lecture all year?"

"You insult me. I've made every effort to *try* and get out of bed."

I grinned. "That's not very convincing."

We went on like this for a while. It was the first time I'd talked to Leo about anything unrelated to the Darkworld or the Venantium, and, as it turned out, it was as easy as speaking to one of my ordinary friends.

"What do *you* do?" I asked him, when we were in a toy shop and he was examining all the Lego models like a kid unleashed in Legoland. "I mean, do you have any career plans? I take it you aren't planning to join the Venantium?"

"Nah," said Leo. "I'm looking into journalism, actually. I might go travelling."

I nodded. I wanted to travel, too. I'd not been farther from home than Disneyland Paris, on a school trip five years ago, and I wanted to see the world. The only problem was being utterly skint. I could barely afford to look after myself on my student loan, and my parents weren't exactly rich.

We'd reached the end of the street by now. The village more or less ended there, bordering fields that gave way to rolling hills. A low stone wall marked the entrance to an old graveyard, and I saw the house we'd seen from Leo's bedroom window beyond. Close to, it looked abandoned and uninviting—a crumbling mass of moss-covered bricks topped with a slanted chimney. Roof tiles were missing, and the windows were boarded up.

Leo frowned. "That doesn't look good."

He pointed at an old tombstone. My heart plummeted as I realised it had been defiled by bright, neon paint. Almost without realising what I was doing, I moved in for a closer look.

The spray-painted message read, *The Ghouls Were Here.*

"This one wasn't on the news," I said doubtfully. "Was it?"

Leo shook his head. "This is recent."

I climbed over the wall. The graveyard was clearly abandoned. The graves were crumbling to pieces, covered with moss and lichen. Now neon paint covered several of them. Always the same message. The ghouls were here.

"I'm starting to think there's something more sinister going on than grave robberies," said Leo. "This place has been deserted for years. The last burial was in something like 1800."

"Weird," I said, my hand absent-mindedly moving to my pendant.

A sudden chill rushed through me, unmistakeable. I was near a dark space.

"You felt that?" said Leo, suddenly alert.

I nodded. I looked up at the old grade-digger's cottage, and for a second, I could have sworn an indistinct shape moved behind one of the boarded-up windows.

"If this was a horror film, we'd go into that house right now," said Leo, taking a step in that direction.

"But we're *not* in a horror film," I said. "And I think we should leave it. We don't want to get blamed for that graffiti. And what if Jude's still around?"

"Fair point," said Leo, turning back to me, away from the dilapidated cottage.

So we walked back towards the village. After the creepy graveyard, the last thing I felt like doing was going into Mr Melmoth's cellar, but I knew it was important to Leo to find what he'd left in the hidden room. After all, it was why we'd come in the first place. So we made our way back to the old manor house.

I was so on edge by this point, I half-expected to run into Mr Melmoth's ghost, but the house seemed as deserted as ever. Leo did a quick magic scan to make sure Jude or anyone else wasn't nearby, before we made our way once more through the overgrown garden.

"Go time," said Leo, holding up the key.

The cellar didn't show any signs of concealed doorways. I scrutinised every brick in the stone walls, but none looked like they might trigger any kind of mechanism.

"Melmoth was too smart to go for something so obvious," said Leo.

At that moment I tripped, stumbling into Leo. "Oops."

Glancing down, I saw part of the floor was slightly raised; that was what tripped me. An idea stole into my head. Could it be——?

Leo figured it out in an instant. "A cellar within a cellar. Kudos to Melmoth, I knew he wouldn't let me down."

The uneven bit of floor was a trapdoor, leading down to another staircase. Leo conjured a light, and I did likewise, as we descended into blackness.

The room below wasn't so much a room as a cave, with stone walls and a low ceiling. It resembled a study, in that it contained a desk, chair, and a large quantity of books and papers stacked all around us. There were several candles mounted on the walls, and Leo lit them with conjured flames whilst I looked around for anything remarkable.

Leo started opening the desk drawers and sifting through papers.

"This is where we'll find what he was up to," he said, pulling out a drawer and emptying it onto the desk. It contained a stack of newspaper clippings, some scraps of paper, and a leather-bound notebook that looked like a journal.

"I've had a look in this before; he used to carry it everywhere. He was really mad when he found me reading it."

"Is it his diary?"

"Yeah, it's a record of his experiments. I used to have this theory he was a mad scientist. Turns out I wasn't far wrong, if he was making cures for vampirism."

"This place doesn't look much like a laboratory," I said, looking around. It was more like a hermit's cave than anything.

"Now this is weird," said Leo, holding up a newspaper clipping. I came closer, squinting in the dim candle light.

The clipping showed a picture of a house, which, although faded and small, was unmistakeably the one we'd just been at, the gravedigger's cottage. The heading was, *Tombstone Hill: Haunted or Not Haunted?*

"Something about sightings of a ghost," said Leo. "I think I remember this one, actually. It was only a few months ago. Hmm…"

There were a number of other clippings dating back a few years—all centring on that old house and graveyard.

"That's weird," said Leo. "I've never heard Melmoth mention it before. Except to call the locals idiots for believing in rumours and superstitions."

"It mentions a gang called… the Ghouls," I said.

Leo looked at me. "Really?"

"Yeah. Aren't they the ones who are supposed to be behind all this grave-robbing?"

"Yeah. Melmoth was fascinated with them. I just wish I knew why."

He began flicking through the journal. "This looks like a record of meetings. And he's using codenames. I guess he thought someone might find this."

I put down the newspaper clippings and picked up a stack of what looked like newsletters.

"These are from the Venantium," I said. The top one read, *Former Inner Circle Head Resigns.*

"Born in Hull, Mr Melmoth joined the Venantium after graduating from Blackstone University at the age of twenty-one. He worked for ten years as a demon-tracker before applying successfully for a position on the Inner Circle. He became Chairman two years ago."

"Ah, that must be from when he resigned," said Leo, taking it. "This looks like a record of his achievements. I know about most of them... Before they knew his secret, he was pretty well-respected. He took down this sorcerer, Lucifer, twenty years ago. Yeah, the guy called himself *Lucifer.* People get up to some seriously weird shit. Oh, and he exposed a traitor within the Venantium itself. That stirred everyone up."

"Really?" I said.

"You'd be surprised how many crazies are ex-members, driven mad with power. I know for a fact some practice necromancy, and that's technically illegal."

"Creepy," I said. "What—raising the dead? What if..." I trailed off, staring at the clipping in my hand. "Wait a minute. The cults he took down. Look at that one. The name."

"The Ghouls?" said Leo, glancing over. "Interesting..."

I went through more of the collected leaflets, finding scraps of information here and there, but nothing concrete. Mr Melmoth seemed to have compiled a complete record of the Venantium's activity for the last thirty years. The stories of foiled attempts to summon demons and cults disbanded began to blur together in my mind. Leo continued to read the journal, until he looked up from the final page with a perplexed expression on his face.

"The journal just... ends," he said. "It's a record of his experiments with magical energy, though he doesn't really go into any details. From what I gather, the Venantium wouldn't approve of his methods. But this last bit's just plain weird. 'I have felt eyes watching my footsteps for some times. I have the knowledge he desires, but I am confident that the protection will endure even beyond my death. But he is not the only one. I cannot stop the others, but I must find the Death Child. I have to stop her...'"

He looked at me. "That's it. Man, I knew Melmoth could be pretty dramatic, but that takes cryptic to a whole new level. For God's sake."

He suddenly punched the desk, hard. The resulting *thunk* echoed around the room.

"Leo..." I said, hesitantly.

"Why did he do it? Why didn't he leave anything helpful? If he was doing something so important, why not leave even a record of his experiments? That Vampire's Curse cure could save lives!" He shook his head. "And as for that other crap, I've no idea. Let's get out of here. We've been down here for hours; it'll be getting dark soon."

"True," I said. I didn't much fancy walking past that graveyard at night.

"I'll take some of this," he said, taking off his rucksack. "Knew I brought this for a reason." He began shoving papers haphazardly into the bag. I helped, looking around in case there was anything we'd overlooked. Then I stopped dead.

"Look at that," I said.

There was a portion of the stone wall which seemed to

jut out marginally farther than anywhere else. I ran my fingers over it. It felt strange—not like stone at all.

Like metal.

Leo was at my side in an instant. "No way," he said. "Melmoth, you sly bastard."

My suspicions were right. There was a door concealed in the wall, although I could only see it if I tilted my head slightly. That struck me as odd, given that, being metal, it ought to stand out.

"Magical concealment at its finest," said Leo. "C'mon, let's check it out."

"Isn't it locked?" I said.

"Maybe, but if I know Melmoth, he won't have wanted his work to go to waste. Who knows, maybe he fixed it so that one trustworthy person could enter. You can be incredibly selective with that kind of magical protection if you know your stuff, and Melmoth sure did."

He braced his shoulder against the door, but it didn't give.

"Might be a handle somewhere?"

He ran his hands over the stone, then jumped back with a curse as a light flared out of nowhere, brief and bright.

"Shit," he said, holding up his hand. "I think that was the anti-demon defence."

There was a large burn blister already forming on his palm. My heart flipped unpleasantly as I realised it would have been a lot worse if it had been me who'd tried to open the door. I was pretty sure anti-demon defences extended to human-demons.

But the stones were moving aside, to reveal yet another passageway which sloped downward.

"Seriously?" I said. "We're deep enough underground already!"

"Best place to hide things," said Leo, holding up his conjured light. "Like the Venantium. Let's go."

At some point my own light had gone out, so I quickly summoned another one. I felt a momentary rush of claustrophobia as we descended, and the stuffy air filled my throat. My lungs screamed for fresh air, my eyes for natural light. But even as I forced myself to follow Leo, I couldn't restrain myself from groaning in frustration as we reached a point where several tunnels branched off in different directions.

"You're kidding me!" I said. "This is a bloody maze!"

Even Leo didn't look too pleased. "Really, Melmoth," he muttered. "Right... let's try this one."

We walked for an hour or more, along the flat ground, looking around in case another tunnel entrance presented itself. But the passageway was unbroken, unrelenting. I felt like crying. We were never going to get out of there.

"Ash?" said Leo.

I tried to say I was fine, but could only manage a faint, "Yeah."

"Ash, relax." He took hold of my hand, which made me jump before I realised it was him. "It'll be okay. There's bound to be something soon."

"And if there isn't? It'll take hours to walk back, and it's dark outside..."

And I couldn't help thinking of the Venantium's harpies, how they'd attacked me in the dark, the last time we'd gotten lost in a tunnel.

"I can see something," said Leo, and I wanted to believe him, although I knew he was probably trying to reassure me.

But then I saw it, too—a light. A blue light. The tunnel rounded a corner and suddenly I realised where we were. We must be underneath Blackstone, because on either side were the blue, flickering candles of the Venantium.

"Well, what d'you know," said Leo, in a whisper. I looked uneasily at the crone-shaped candle holders. I never could figure out if they were all harpies, or if only some of them were. Even so, I wanted the hell out of there.

Soon the tunnel branched, and we took the one that looked as though it sloped upwards.

"I know where we are. It's cool. We're out of here soon."

And he was right. Within ten minutes we were climbing stone steps and emerging into the fresh, cold night air.

I leant against him, dizzy with relief. "I never knew how much I hated tunnels," I said. "Sorry I freaked out so much."

"Don't worry about it," he said. "Lots of people would be worse. At least you're not scared of the dark. And you have good reason to be afraid of monsters."

"True," I said. "I was more worried about a cave-in, really. Or those harpies coming back."

"Sensible thinking," said Leo. "Man, I didn't know the tunnels went all the way to Crowley!"

We stood behind a patch of trees, on dew-wet grass. For an instant, I was confused as to where we were, then I realised the roaring in my ears wasn't the wind, but the sound of the sea crashing onto rocks. We were right next to the cliffs above the beach outside Blackstone.

"I guess we never found the secret lab," I said.

"No," said Leo. "Still, plenty of time to explore. You don't have to come," he added. "You'll get into more trouble than me if they find you down there, anyway."

"True," I said. "Should we head back to campus now?"

"Might as well go for a drink first," said Leo.

Sitting in the Coach and Horses, I felt as far removed from those tunnels as possible. I'd never appreciated *noise* quite as much as I did then. The chatter of the other people in the pub, even the yells of the football supporters crowded around the widescreen televisions, were a blessing to my ears, which had heard only the sound of footsteps on stone for too long. And even though I usually hated the smell of beer and sweat, it was a relief to no longer have to inhale the musty scent of the tunnels. It still astounded me that they were right beneath our feet, yet most people were oblivious to them.

"They have all sorts down there," said Leo. "Most of the main offices are underneath Blackstone, but I have a feeling they keep all the *real* secrets deeper underground. The machinery that runs the Barrier."

"What, they actually have a machine?" I pictured a huge hunk of metal, weaving a protective net. It was difficult to imagine something like that keeping the Darkworld out. The Darkworld was an ancient force, everlasting even.

"No, they won't have. Those Barriers have been there for five hundred years, and they were put up on the surface. From what I gather, sorcerers from all over came here and made some kind of shield. Don't ask me how."

"Who exactly runs it?" I said. "Who are their leaders?"

"The Venantium's leaders are known as the Inner Circle," said Leo. "There are seven members, but only they know who the Chairman is. It's a precautionary measure."

"So they do what, make all the decisions?"

"Yeah. Like politicians, and they're just as big a group of liars, too."

"So what do the other members do?" I asked.

"Maintain the Barrier," said Leo. "And hunt down rogue sorcerers and demons. There are also members in the government, working undercover to protect everyone in case there's a mass demon outbreak. It hasn't happened since the Demon Wars, but it's always a possibility."

"Wow."

"Most of them want to get into the Inner Circle," said Leo. "It changes every five years, and everyone goes power-mad around that time. It's happening again next year, I think."

"They sound like a crazy religious cult," I said.

"Pretty much," said Leo grimly. "They're usually too late to stop most things. I mean, we live in the safest village around, yet all it takes is one wayward sorcerer and you have total chaos. The Demon Wars started here, you know? Right under their noses."

"The guy questioning me at the Venantium told me the Blackstone family started it," I said.

"Didn't you know?"

"Well... no. I mean, I knew they were local, but I didn't realise they were actually connected to the Venantium. He said the girl, Melivia, was tricked into summoning a demon."

"That's one version of the story," said Leo. "The other was that she was seduced by a demon itself. An incubus. Or even a higher demon. There's a cult within the Venantium who believe it was Lucifer himself, leader of the higher demons, in human form, and that someday he will return to Earth again. Then again, a lot of that group also believe in the impending apocalypse, so I wouldn't take it too seriously."

"Does no one know what actually happened?"

"Well, there weren't any surviving witnesses close enough to know for certain, so the stories are pretty much based on speculation. I mean, the Blackstones are all dead, even old Marcus, who was out of town at the time and came back to help fight in the Demon Wars. He built that monument to their family and insisted on the village—what was left of it—taking their name. Died alone, about a hundred years ago."

"Did the sorcerer—the one who started it—die too? Wait." I frowned. "The guy questioning me said he did. But—he said his name was Lucifer."

"Really, now? A lot of sorcerers have used that name. Hmm. That's interesting. I always thought they knew more than they let on. But as I said, no one knows for definite, which is why all those stories about incubi and the like sprung up. And Lucifer, the higher demon. Not sure how he'd feel about sorcerers using his name, to be honest."

"The guy at the Venantium… he said Melivia burned herself alive to exorcise a demon."

"Did he now?" Leo frowned. "Who was he?"

"Mr… Priestley? I think that was his name."

"Oh God, he's one of them. That'd explain it."

"Who?"

"The crazy cult who think Lucifer the higher demon is the Second Coming, or whatever."

"He didn't seem crazy to me. He did let me off."

"Probably took it as a sign from Lucifer. I think he was the one who tried to lecture me about the state of my immortal soul."

"Really?"

"Yep. He's one of the okay ones, in all honesty. At least you had him and not Dr Philips or one of Jude's friends."

"Hmm. Why d'you think Jude was at the house, anyway?"

"God knows. If he tells his superiors that I was in Melmoth's house—and he will, there's no doubt about it—then they'll be watching me."

"I thought they were watching us anyway?" I said.

"This just complicates things. The real question is whether Jude was acting on orders, of if he just felt like nosing around Melmoth's house." He sighed. Then he grinned at me. "Well, at least it saved us paying train fare!"

Despite everything that had happened, I couldn't help grinning back.

9

THEORIES

Unsurprisingly, endless tunnels threaded my dreams, and I awoke with a brief flood of panic thinking I was enclosed in the Venantium's glass case again. I went for a walk to clear my head. After another cold night, every blade of grass and tattered fallen leaf wore a coating of frost.

I was going to follow the woodland path directly to town, but then I saw a flock of large black birds fly overhead, in that direction. I had no intention of doing anything to attract the harpies' attention, so I altered my course and walked in a loop around campus instead.

Unfortunately, it was early enough that the hard-core partygoers were only just returning from Redthorne's all-night bars, and the sounds of shrieks and laughter from the still-inebriated students returning from town punctuated my thoughts, keeping me from brooding. It was probably a good thing, I thought as I changed track back towards the student village. I had work I was supposed to be doing, anyway.

My phone buzzed in my pocket. Alex had texted me

asking where I was. My friends could never understand my habit of taking random spontaneous walks in the woods, although I suppose I didn't quite comprehend Alex's rampant enthusiasm for every sport under the sun, or why Sarah liked romance novels so much. It bothered me more that I had to tell them so many little white lies, like where I'd been yesterday, for instance. Alongside Cara, they were the best friends I'd ever had. They were my anchor to sanity.

I stopped suddenly, mid-step. I was about to walk into a frozen puddle, although that wasn't what made me pause. I saw movement in the trees ahead, and beneath the sounds of chatter carried from campus on the breeze, I was positive I'd heard a quiet voice nearby. It could have been my imagination——perhaps it was the sound of tree branches rubbing together, stirred by the restless wind. But it sounded more like a whisper.

There was a lull in the noise, and I heard a soft laugh.

I skirted the puddle, moving towards the source. Someone was definitely there, only a few metres away from me. The trees here were dense, but I caught a glimpse of the figure, between bramble bushes.

I remembered the girl I'd seen the other day. Was it the same person? I squinted through the trees, unease shivering down my spine.

Then she darted away. In a blink, she was gone, leaving only a blurred impression on my eyes.

What the hell was that?

I walked back in a daydream, wondering if it was a sign I was cracking up that, for a second there, I'd thought I'd been looking in a mirror, that the girl had looked exactly like me. But there were a lot of average-height girls with dark hair who wore black coats. I was being stupid.

"Ash!" said a voice behind me. "I thought it was you."

I turned to see Conrad beaming at me. *Oh, crap.*

"Hi," I said.

"Where have you been? Where are you going?"

Seriously? "I've just been for a walk. I'm going back to my flat now."

"Ah, cool. I love walking. I've just been in the forest myself, I thought I saw you earlier on the other side of campus, but it can't have been you, because you're here!"

I didn't even know what to make of his babbling. "Um, yeah," I said, lamely, wishing he'd stop staring at me. Didn't he ever blink?

"Did you have a nice weekend?" he said.

"Um, yeah, it was okay," I said. *Just the usual. Exploring underground tunnels and creepy old houses, and having a cryptic conversation with a demon in the middle of town. Typical student life.*

"Great. I'm glad. I know you get stressed out about stuff, right? Claudia told me."

"You've talked to Claudia?" I said, making a mental note to have stern words with her.

"Yeah, I saw her yesterday. I was coming over to see you and she said you'd gone out."

"Right," I said. *Jesus.* If I wasn't careful, I really would end up with a stalker.

"Where were you yesterday?"

Was there a nice way to tell someone to mind their own business? "Just around, with my friends. Why did you want to see me?"

"I wanted to ask if you'd thought any more about the dance."

"Huh?"

"The Valentine's Ball?"

"I don't do formal dances," I said. "I've no money, anyway."

"I'll pay."

"I'm really not interested, Conrad, sorry."

Surely, I thought, that would put off the advances of even the most eager guy. But not Conrad.

"But it'll be fun!" he insisted.

"I don't think so." I walked faster, keen to get as far away from him as possible.

He hurried to keep up. "It's okay, we don't have to go. We could go watch a film or—"

"Conrad." There really was no other way to say it. "I'm sorry, but I really don't have time for dating. I have a lot of work to do." Lame excuse, but I *did* have a lot on my mind at the moment.

"It's cool," he said. "But just so you know, I'm available—"

Doesn't he ever quit? I'd thought Pete was a walking turn-off, but Conrad's inability to take a hint astounded me—and I was hardly an expert in romance.

I walked as fast as I could without risking slipping on the wet ground. I kept glancing at the trees in case that figure appeared again, but with Conrad's constant wittering, I wasn't surprised they didn't. Even demons would stay away.

When we got back to the student village, I said, firmly, "I'm going to do some work now. Bye, Conrad."

Thankfully he didn't try to follow me into my flat. I made a mental note never to let slip that there were two empty rooms in the flat—as of yet, no one had claimed the rooms that David and Terrence vacated, though Alex said that someone was viewing them in the next couple of weeks.

I looked at Terrence's door. Someone had taken down the Dante quote he'd had up there, and if there had been any evidence of whatever illegal demonic summonings he'd been doing in his room, the Venantium had long since removed it. I never did find out if the screams coming from there had been coming from real people.

I shuddered and went into my own room. Best not dwell on it. Terrence was dead, and I wasn't sorry. He'd brought it upon himself by making a deal with a demon. And nobody had noticed until it was too late, not even David. Of course, David had been too busy investigating *me*...

My phone buzzed again. Leo had texted me asking if I wanted to meet in the library later. I replied in the affirmative, and an hour later, I left for campus again.

As I crossed the courtyard to the library, I spotted Leo waiting outside the doors. He waved at me. Just as I caught up with him, I heard raised voices behind me.

"The hell you don't know what's going on!"

Around us, everyone was stopping to stare at the altercation brewing in the middle of the square. At the centre was Howard, and another guy. Leo started towards them.

"Do we really want to get involved?" I said, following.

I stopped short as I realised it was Jude. I'd totally forgotten he studied here. *Okay. We definitely don't want to be involved.*

"Really, Howard," he said, in his usual condescending way. "You don't want to get hurt."

"I'll give you an injury. I'll break your fucking neck, *venator.*"

"Language," said Jude.

Howard moved closer, his fist clenched. "Give me a reason," he snarled. "I know you're not as saintly as you like to think. I've seen you skulking around that cemetery at night."

"I am employed by the Venantium," said Jude stiffly. "The entrance to Headquarters is located in the cemetery, which you should be well aware of by now. Wasn't that the last place you saw your parents?"

At that, Howard seized him around the neck and lifted him off the ground. Jude choked, flailing. Leo moved to intervene.

"Stop!" I shouted, at the same time as Leo yelled, "Don't be an idiot, Howard!"

Howard released Jude, breathing heavily, his face a mask of pure hatred. It scared me. My heart thrummed so fast I could feel it in my fingertips.

Passers-by gawped at him. Jude massaged his neck, his face tight.

"Mention my parents again and I'll smash your holy balls in."

"You need to learn to control your temper," Jude said, in a hoarse voice. Then he turned on his heel and walked off.

Howard let out a pretty impressive string of curses, and stormed off in the opposite direction.

"Leo," I warned, as he made to follow him, "I don't think he's going to listen to you right now."

"Right," said Leo. He looked troubled. "Man, and they call *me* reckless." He suddenly grinned at me. "'Holy balls,' though."

A second's pause, then we were both laughing. The tension of the moment eased, like the air had been let out of a balloon.

We walked to the library, talking of other things, although the confrontation between Howard and Jude wasn't far from my thoughts. Still, I had another distraction, as Leo and I found a free table and covered it with a bunch of newspapers and articles he'd pillaged from his late guardian's study.

"Let's see what he was up to," said Leo, taking a bookmark out of Mr Melmoth's diary.

It crossed my mind that this was a rather morbid pastime, but the fascination had gripped me as hard as it gripped Leo, like trying to solve a mystery. The cuttings constantly made references to the Ghouls and something called the "Death Child."

"God knows what *that* means," said Leo.

He paused at one particular newspaper article. A surprising number of the recent ones kept referring to the old abandoned house on Tombstone Hill.

"This is from December," said Leo, frowning at it. "It doesn't make any sense for people to suddenly be showing an interest in it now. I know the place has some kind of history, but I wish I knew what *happened* there. Melmoth's journals kind of skirt around it."

Apparently lights appeared inexplicably in the windows at night, and when anyone tried to get in, the doors were sometimes locked tight, even though no one had ever been seen to enter.

"Well, we know one thing for sure. The Ghouls and that old house are somehow tied together. Still, that doesn't explain why someone killed him. Or why he attacked you."

I could tell the lack of conclusiveness bothered him. After all, it held the clues as to what Mr Melmoth had been doing during the last hours of his life. Other than attacking me, that is.

I still couldn't puzzle that one out, either. I *knew* I'd never seen the man before. The only guess was that it had something to do with my being part-demon. But who else could possibly know that, besides the fortune-teller? I decided not to mention thinking I'd seen a girl who looked just like me, too. Sometimes paranoia was just that. Still, I wondered about it.

A shadow has your face. A shiver danced down my spine.

Did Jude—and the Venantium in general—really know something about Mr Melmoth that we didn't? But they'd already refused to tell Leo a thing about their former leader, not even what his old job had been like. Everything about the inner workings of the Venantium was classified.

All the same, Leo risked another trip to their library that night to search the archives. Whilst the Venantium didn't keep any employee information there, they did have a stash of all their old newspapers and leaflets.

"Some of it's pretty dramatic," Leo told me on Wednesday, when, once again, we were the first to arrive at the Games Room. "The ones from twenty years ago are all like, 'Beware Lucifer and his temptations. Surrender your life before you surrender your soul!' I gathered that it was when that sorcerer was causing trouble. The one Melmoth brought down."

"Have you found out what he actually did?"

"Melmoth? Tracked this lunatic down and burnt him alive. Killed both the human and the demon. Horrible job, but y'know, the guy killed like forty people with that demon. He'd done something to protect himself from possession. The Venantium had a nightmare with that one; they managed to convince the police that the deaths were a mass suicide, a cult thing."

"Sounds pretty horrible all around," I said, shuddering. "Was that the last time anything major like that happened?"

"Yeah, there have only been minor instances of possession since then. Most were kept quiet."

Possession. Now I'd seen it myself, I knew it was nothing like they showed in films claiming to be based on real events, although perhaps they did have some basis in reality after all.

"Well, it's freaky to us. Imagine what it's like to ordinary people," said Leo, when I mentioned this. "In old times they used to blame evil spirits for pretty much everything, but in modern days it's a bit trickier to explain. Usually it's put down to psychosis."

"What, the purple eyes, too?" I said.

"The Venantium use their mind-tricks, don't forget. They make people think they saw something else."

Mind-magic. Influence. I'd used it myself once, to make David forget he'd seen me using magic, not that it did any good in the end. It seemed like it could give someone permanent brain damage.

"Is that permanent?" I said. "I mean, could you make someone totally forget something, like, indefinitely?"

Leo looked at me. "I guess so. I've never really thought about it."

"Terrence used it on me," I said. "But it wore off as soon as he revealed himself."

And, I thought, the fortune-teller had used it, to fool me and my parents into thinking she was a relation. That was bigger than removing individual memories. The very idea of fabricating a whole person's existence like that creeped me out. It was so intrusive.

"Maybe he wanted you to remember then, and took it off himself. It's a good question. I'll ask Cyrus."

On cue, the door to the Games Room opened. Cyrus came in, along with Howard, Berenice and Claudia.

"Ooh, are we interrupting something?" said Berenice. "You two look awfully close."

A flush shot up my neck like a traffic light. Leo and I had unconsciously moved on the sofa so we almost leaned on each other. I shifted away, as the others came over and sat down in the empty chairs around the TV.

Berenice smirked as she shuffled her chair closer to Howard's. "Don't let me spoil your cuddling session."

"We're reading Mr Melmoth's diaries," I snapped, "trying to figure out why people are *dying*."

My harsh tone completely failed to hide my embarrassment, but Leo jumped in.

"I don't suppose any of you know what a Death Child is?"

"A what?" everyone said at once.

"That's what Melmoth's calling it here. Apparently he was after a demon called the Death Child."

"A demon?" said Claudia. "A real demon, or just a shadow-beast or ghoul?"

"Possibly a ghoul, but a shape-shifter. It took the form of a young girl."

"What did it do?"

"Just scared a lot of people by appearing out of nowhere, but Melmoth seemed convinced it was some kind of dark spirit."

"Death Child. Sounds lovely," I said.

"So now we have a demon child as well as the vampire killers?" said Claudia. "Great."

"It doesn't say whether he caught her or not," said Leo. "Just that he could tell she was a dark spirit, and she…"

He trailed off.

"What?" said Howard. Even he'd looked up from the Xbox to pay attention.

"She came here," he said. "He was following her to Blackstone. And that's where the journal ends."

He looked at me, and I knew he was thinking the same as me. "So when we ran into him… that's what he was doing."

"But he was right near campus!" said Claudia. "Does that mean the Death Child—they're somewhere around here?"

"Looks that way," said Leo, frowning.

"I found something interesting," said Claudia, waving a leaflet in the air. "Look at this. It's the latest from the Venantium."

"Where'd you get hold of that?" said Cyrus. "Don't tell me you've actually been sneaking into Headquarters."

"I may have a bit of influence over a certain young *venator.*"

"You're not dating one of them?" said Berenice, looking disgusted at the very thought.

"No, but someone has a bit of a crush on me. Or is possibly terrified of me. I never can tell the difference." She laughed.

"Not David?" I said, incredulous.

"You've got it." She laughed again. "Your face, Ash. You look like I just skinned a puppy."

"I just can't picture it. You and him." Strange, it didn't bother me at all, even though we'd used to be friends. Even though I'd thought I liked him.

"It's not like that. The poor fool." This time, her laugh bordered on evil. "What? We have to get our information somehow."

"So you're using an innocent young *venator?*" said Cyrus. "That isn't very nice."

"I'm not nice. Think he's under the impression he's spying on *me,* but I haven't given him any useful information. Anyway, check this out."

Ghoul Murder Site Feared as Next Target for Grave-Robbers, the leaflet read—and underneath was a photograph of the house on Tombstone Hill.

"A graveyard in the village of Crowley, located in the

vicinity of the Venantium Headquarters, is the latest victim of the graffiti used by the grave-robbing gang calling themselves the Ghouls," Claudia read aloud. "Experts fear an ill omen, given that a house near this cemetery was the site of a brutal triple-murder twenty years ago, during the terror campaign of the sorcerer Lucifer. A small group of necromancers were targeted by the sorcerer during his quest for information on illicit demonic activities, and were tracked to the house of one of their members, who was a grave-digger in the local area. The three were murdered following the extraction of everything they knew. Their mutilated corpses were discovered in the hallway of the house, which has remained uninhabited ever since."

An uneasy silence filled the room.

"Really," said Claudia, finally, "If there's a way to ensure that it *will* be the next target, it's publishing this. Morons. *Experts?*"

Leo shook his head. "So... well, that explains a whole lot. It explains Melmoth's interest, at least. He was after that sorcerer, Lucifer, too."

"But what do the Ghouls have to do with it *now*?" said Claudia. "I mean, all that stuff happened twenty years ago. It's not like there's any reason to drag it up again now."

"It's probably nothing," said Cyrus. "It's a graveyard like any other. They rob graves. It's an obvious target, right?"

"Still gives me a bad feeling," said Claudia.

"Maybe we should check it out," said Howard.

"Fat chance," said Berenice. "No more graveyards."

I looked at Leo. He seemed lost in thought. "Nah," he said. "If the *venators* are watching it, we'd probably attract a bunch of attention. It's not worth it. We're not going to Tombstone Hill."

"Agreed," said Cyrus. "Now, it just happens Claudia

isn't the only one who's been sneaking around. I decided to do some background research on the Vampire's Curse."

"You went to the library?" said Leo.

"Nah. I kind of hacked into the *venators'* computer system."

"You did what?" said Claudia.

"I didn't even know they *had* a computer system," I said, thinking of the dark tunnels. But I supposed even they had to rely on twenty-first century technology for some things.

"Yeah, it's a shocker. But they had Melmoth's notes."

He pulled out his laptop and switched it on.

"There wasn't much. Just a detailed analysis of the symptoms. I reckon he kept paper records of what he was really doing."

"Give me that," said Leo, reaching for the laptop.

"You don't know my password."

"Sure I do. It's 'your mother.'"

"How mature," said Berenice, snickering.

"Hey, we final-year students are a serious bunch. How long have you been using my account?"

"Since forever," said Leo. "Melmoth put an age-block on my laptop so I couldn't download X-rated films."

"Or porn?" Berenice said.

Leo ignored her. "Okay. So you decided to just leave their private files open on your laptop? You'd better hope no one else knows your password."

"No one else is as nosy as you, bro. I'll have to think of something more inventive next time. You see anything interesting there?"

"Apart from some very dirty pictures? No. I knew all this already. He wouldn't have told the *venators* anything important, just in case. He knew they were going to get rid of him in the end."

"So it's useless?"

"I guess so. It doesn't say what the cure actually *is*. Or who was giving it to vampires."

"I wonder why that Conrad guy didn't get it?" said Claudia.

"He thought he was going to be killed, remember?" said Leo. "Maybe he was about to go and get it, but heard about the murders."

"Any clue, Ash?" said Claudia. "You know the guy, right?"

"Wish I didn't," I said. "I've never thought to ask… I forgot he's a vampire."

That was stupid, I thought. A testament to the level of weird in my life that I'd forgotten.

"What, all the time you two have spent together…" she trailed off suggestively. The others all watched me now. *For God's sake, it's Alex all over again.*

"We're not friends," I said. "He's just an annoying guy on my course who can't take a hint. I've never been able to get a word in edgeways. He never shuts up."

Claudia laughed. "I thought so. You could do way better than that."

Berenice snorted.

"Hey." I shot her a glare, then turned back to Claudia. "Kinda harsh?"

"Just being honest."

Berenice laughed outright. "Yeah, Ash might rank five out of ten, but Conrad? No hope."

I turned my glare on her again. "No hope that you have any brain underneath all that hair. Congratulations. You rank ten for shallowness and stupidity."

Berenice's face reddened as Leo rolled around laughing. She looked at Howard for support, but he was too absorbed in some tactical war-based game on the Xbox to even notice the rest of us. Cyrus raised his hands in an *I'm staying out of this* gesture.

Anger blazed within me. It wasn't the fact that she'd insulted Conrad—or even me; hell, I knew I was no supermodel—but a culmination of the confusion and fear of the last week. Not that Claudia had helped matters by starting it all.

"Whoa there," she said. "Save the cat-fight for later. I'm just trying to figure out what's happening. So, did Conrad mention anything that's going on?"

"No…" I frowned. "Come to think of it, I don't think he's said a word about vampires, or anything. But we've only really spoken… once."

Idiot. You could have questioned him about it. But I'd been so busy trying to avoid him that I'd forgotten he was a potential link to what was happening.

"Seduce him," said Berenice, her smirk back in place. "Get him to tell you his dark secret."

I raised an eyebrow. "Seriously?"

"Yeah, I'm sure even you're capable of that. He's dying for it, anyway."

"Oh…kay," said Leo. "I'm taking that as my cue to leave."

"I'm not *seducing* anyone!" I spluttered. "How the hell did we even get on this subject? I don't think he's involved in this at all. He's annoying, whiny, and completely dense. That's why I don't like him."

"Okay, let's forget about Conrad," said Cyrus. "From what you told me, it sounds like he just wandered into this by accident. What we do know is that Mr Melmoth was chasing a shape-shifting demon, or ghoul. We don't know whether he caught it or not, but I'm thinking that he didn't. Either the person who's killing vampires happened to run into him then, or it's the same person—ghoul, whatever he was after, who's killing the vampires."

I nodded. "Good logic," I said, relieved that someone was willing to take a sensible approach to this. "So we just need to figure out the connection."

"Yeah, that's where I'm completely lost," said Leo. "Maybe we should check his study again. Fancy another trip into the tunnels?"

He was asking if I wanted to go with him. A flush crept up my neck again as I felt Berenice watching me.

"It's cool if not," he added. "It might look at bit suspicious to the *venators* if you're always lurking around their headquarters."

"Same with you," I pointed out.

"Nah, they know Melmoth had no control over me. I was always wandering where I wasn't supposed to be. Now he's gone… well, I don't know."

"I'll go with you," I said. "I always used to dream about finding a hidden underground laboratory."

"Ash, you're a terrible liar," said Leo.

Foiled again. "I want to… I want to know why he attacked me. He must have mistaken me for someone else."

I cringed inwardly. That sounded so selfish. But to *say* I wanted to go along so he'd have company sounded incredibly lame. Was lame better than selfish? *Ugh, I completely suck at this.*

"Sure," said Leo. "I was only joking. You're pretty hardcore. Meet me at ten on Sunday?"

"You got it," I said.

Okay. I can do this.

After the meeting broke up, Claudia and I ended up walking back through the student village together.

"So," she said, as though carrying on a previous conversation. "You and Leo looked pretty cosy in there."

"Oh, don't you start." I rolled my eyes.

"Hey, Berenice had a point, but I didn't think you'd appreciate it if I said it in front of everyone." She shrugged. "It's cool. I'm happy for both of you."

"Right." I could tell any arguing would get me nowhere.

"No, really. Someone deserves a bit of happiness. Even with supernatural monsters on our heels."

I laughed. "Well, that's one way of looking at it."

"Always look on the bright side, that's my motto," she said. "Have fun running around the secret underground passages together, anyway. And remember, if you need advice, I'm probably not the best person to ask."

Given what had happened with David last term, she kind of had a point. Still, romance was hardly my priority right now.

I had to help Leo find out who'd killed his guardian. After that—well, I wasn't sure there *was* a bright side as far as the Darkworld was concerned. But maybe Claudia was right. Maybe.

"We're going to Tombstone Hill," said Alex, firmly.

I spat out a mouthful of cereal. "You what?"

We were in the middle of discussing the literature society's postponed Halloween social over breakfast in the kitchen. What with everything going on, I'd totally forgotten about the LitSoc's quest to find a haunted house in which to spend the night.

"Why?" I said, feigning ignorance, although I'd instantly lost my appetite. "What's Tombstone Hill?"

"A creepy old house in a town over the hill," said Alex, tipping her cereal bowl to catch the last drops of milk. "Come on, they want something major. Apparently someone died there. It's near a graveyard. It's perfect, right?"

"Isn't that where the grave robbers have been?" I said, cautiously.

"I haven't heard," said Alex. "Is that the latest?"

"I think so," I said. Not that I had anything against

lucky normal people seeking a scare, but there was no way in hell I wanted to go near that house. More to the point, I didn't want my *friends* going near it either.

"I'll ask Rex to check it," said Alex. "He wants to go for the social organiser position next year."

"Why not ask him to think of a better idea for a social?" I said, clutching at straws. "Besides, isn't it on Valentine's Day?"

"So?"

"Won't you and Rex be busy?"

I looked to Sarah to back me up, but she had her head down on an open textbook, totally spaced out. Her new job was so exhausting she kept falling asleep in lectures.

Alex flushed bright red. "No. Sarah, you in?"

"In what?" Sarah yawned, knocking her cereal bowl off the table. "Crap."

"Tell them to stop giving you so many early shifts," said Alex. "You'll fall behind with your work if you're not careful."

"I'm okay," Sarah insisted. "I just didn't get much sleep last night."

"Well, are you in for the social? Or—wait a minute, are you doing something with Liam instead? On Valentine's Day?"

Sarah just shook her head.

"You need to be more assertive, girl," said Alex. "Honestly, just *tell him* if there's an issue. You're as bad as Ash."

"Hey!" I said.

"Well, you let that David guy push you around for ages…"

I shrugged, not willing to go into the topic. David and I had danced around each other for months, but it had been during the time I was finding out about demons and the Venantium and it had started making me paranoid about everyone. In the end, of course, my paranoia had turned out to be dead-on, but I doubted Sarah's boyfriend was spy for a secret organisation.

Sometimes I wished my own problems were that simple. But I felt bad for Sarah all the same. I'd only been able to stand up to David in the end because after fighting shadow-beasts and nearly getting killed, confrontation had gone way down on the fear scale. A year ago, I couldn't have done it.

"You know what you need?" said Alex. "A night out."

"Not in a haunted house," said Sarah, shutting her textbook.

"Nah, there's a karaoke night on at Franklin's Bar this weekend. A bunch of the LitSoc guys are going."

"Um, sure, I don't have work Sunday morning," said Sarah. "But I might have to have a nap before we leave."

"Come on, have some enthusiasm!" said Alex. "Life's too short to waste it stressing about crap you can't control. So *take* control. Tell the boss to cut your shifts, and for heaven's sake put your dickwit of a boyfriend in his place."

Sarah shifted uncomfortably. "Um. Sure."

Alex raised an eyebrow. "Not convincing enough. God, it's like living with two doormats."

"Hey," I said, again. "Not helping."

Alex shrugged. "I'll find a way to make you more assertive. You wait. Tell you what, you're coming on the social to Tombstone Hill."

"This again?" I said.

"How's throwing us in a haunted house meant to help?" said Sarah.

"Fear," said Alex, in her approximation of a wise-professor-voice. "You conquer your fears one at a time, right? So after spending the night hanging out with ghosts, standing up to your boyfriend'll be no problem."

"Not sure of the logic there," I said.

Alex gave me an evil look. "Don't question the words of the wise master."

Right. Who knew, maybe it was just Alex's version of exactly what had helped me stand up to David—but there had to be a better solution than spending the night in a house where three demon-related deaths had occurred.

Like I needed anything else to give me nightmares. I kept dreaming I was on fire, and waking with the scars on my arms ablaze with pain. I blamed the two stories of people burning alive I'd heard lately. Really, I deserved a break, something to take my mind off all the craziness.

"I'm totally up for going out," I said.

"Awesome," said Alex. "Oh… crap. We're running late."

I checked my watch, picking up my bag. We had ten minutes to make it to campus. *Oops.*

"And it's raining," said Alex, gesturing at the deluge outside. "Want to skip?"

Sarah shook her head. "I can't afford to miss any lectures, really. And it's on our essay topic, anyway."

"True," said Alex, pressing her palms to the window. "Hey—Ash's boyfriend is outside!"

"Oh God." I groaned. "Yeah. I think I'm skiving."

"Not today, missy. What did I say about being assertive?"

And she grabbed my arm and all but dragged me through the corridor, out of the flat, Sarah following.

Conrad stood outside the door, dripping wet. *Great.*

"Ash!" he said.

"Hi," I said. That guy really didn't know the meaning of subtlety.

Snickering, Alex pulled Sarah away, leaving me alone

with my vampire stalker. I hurried after them, Conrad half-jogging to keep up.

"Ash," he said, as we aimed for a sheltered walkway to avoid the rain. "Did you know tickets are on sale today?"

"For what?" I said, pulling my hood up. The wind promptly blew it down again.

"The Ball."

For God's sake. Like I need this right now. "I said I wasn't going, remember?"

"But you said last night you'd love to come."

I frowned. "Conrad, I didn't see you last night. I was in my flat."

"But I saw you at Tanner's Wine Bar. You kissed me!"

I stopped dead in the middle of the student village. "What?"

"Ash, don't you remember? I was a bit drunk, but I do!" His eyes shone as he re-lived God-knew-what vision.

"Honestly, I wasn't out last night," I said.

"But you were wearing that really pretty black dress and the purple necklace! You really don't remember?"

My insides turned to ice. *How can he know about the pendant?*

"Conrad," I said hesitantly, "Are you *sure* it was me?"

"Positive."

"That's… freaky," I said. "I really wasn't out last night. Ask my flatmates. We were watching a film."

"You sure?"

"Positive. Guys!" I called to Alex and Sarah. They ignored me.

I sighed and got out my phone. "I sent this text last night," I said, holding it up. The message asked some of the Lit Soc people to join us for the film night.

"I don't understand," said Conrad. "Can I——?"

I reluctantly handed my iPhone over. His fingers raced

over the touch screen. In the end, I had to practically prise it out of his hands. I had a bad feeling he'd been memorising my number. *Brilliant.*

"Look," I said. "It's not that I don't think you're a nice guy, I'm just *really* not interested in dating anyone right now."

"It doesn't have to be a date. The ball sounds like fun."

"I don't think so," I said. "I already have plans with my friends, anyway."

"Oh. How about…"

I tuned him out, trying to think of a way to ask him about the Vampire's Curse, and the cure. Maybe he'd only respond to a direct approach.

"Conrad," I said, interrupting his babbling. "Can I ask you something? About the——about being a vampire? I hope I'm not being rude." I cringed inwardly at how overly-polite I sounded.

Conrad turned earnest eyes on me. "You can ask me anything!"

Well, that was easy. "Um, I just wanted to know if you'd thought about getting the cure."

"There's a cure?"

He doesn't know?

"Um, that's what Mr Melmoth was working on, right?"

"I haven't heard about it." He blinked those owl-like eyes at me. "Maybe it's because I'm not in the Venantium?"

"Maybe."

But it gave me an uneasy feeling, all the same. I remained lost in thought, ignoring his yapping, all the way to the lecture theatre.

He started up again the instant the lecturer stopped talking and everyone started to leave.

"Maybe I could take you out tonight?"

"Seriously!" I said. "I *don't have time for this.*"

"Okay. Well, if you do…"

Unbelievable. I finally extricated myself from the conversation by pretending I had another seminar, then skirting around the quadrangle and re-joining my friends after making sure he'd gone the other way.

Alex raised her eyebrows. "Okay, I take it back. You should report that guy for harassment."

"I don't think he realises how annoying he's being," I said.

"Tell him," said Alex. 'Seriously."

"I turned him down ten times in as many minutes, what more do you want?" I said.

"You're too nice. Both of you."

Nice wasn't a word I usually used in conjunction with myself, but maybe she was right; maybe being mean was the only way to get rid of him. And it would help if girls who apparently looked exactly like me didn't come onto him. If that had really happened.

"Anyway, you'll never guess what Pete's done," said Alex.

"What?" I said.

"He's covered the library with Lonely Hearts posters, asking for a date for Valentine's Day. Rex told me."

"Seriously?" I said.

"It's sickening. He's described himself as a handsome bachelor." She snorted.

"Has he mentioned he showers once a month?" I said.

"I pity whoever responds," said Alex. "He photoshopped his picture, trying to make himself look like a cover photo guy."

I laughed.

"He looks more like a miniature troll. He said he was

going to put an ad in the paper, too; they're running a Valentine's Day special."

She pulled a rather sodden copy of the local paper out of her bag.

"I haven't looked yet…"

She flipped the page over, but not before I'd seen the headline. It read, *Body of Local Man Found in Lake.*

For some reason, this made my heart jolt unpleasantly. Was it another vampire death?

I waited impatiently for Alex and Sarah to finish laughing at Pete's inept advertisement, before taking the paper myself when we got back to the flat and settled down in the kitchen. The ink had run so the words blurred together, but I could still make out phrases. "Mysterious death… throat cut… suspected drug abuse…"

Just then, my phone buzzed.

I pulled it out of my bag and stared at the screen. *Stay indoors.* I blinked at the strange message. There was no name or number. *Weird.*

It gave me the creeps. Who had my number? Was it a warning, or just a prank? Was it the same person who'd sent me that other message a few weeks ago? Who else wanted to screw with my head?

"Who're you texting?" said Alex, peering at my screen. I quickly stowed it back in my bag.

"No one."

"Conrad?" she smirked. "Or have you got another admirer?"

Alex really was too curious for her own good.

"No. It's just Cara."

"Your imaginary friend?"

I blinked. "No, my real friend. From home?"

"Uh-huh. What about all those GameSoc people? Rex

says he's never met that Claudia girl, and he hasn't seen you in meetings the last couple of weeks either."

Oh, hell.

"Yeah," said Sarah. "Come to think of it, you were with us when the last meeting was on, weren't you?"

Busted. "I haven't felt like going lately," I said.

"...because?" Alex prompted.

Damn. Quick thinking wasn't my specialty. "There may be an admirer," I admitted.

"Aha!" Alex exclaimed, loud enough to draw a few curious stares in our direction.

"Will you drop it now?" I said, my face heating up.

"Oh, no, you're not getting off that easily. Who is it?"

"Not telling," I said, with a childish tone to match her own. "Seriously. It's probably nothing. And I'm not getting my hopes up after what happened...last term."

"Oh." Alex nodded, understanding. "Sure. I get it. But if anything changes, you have to tell us!"

"Yeah," said Sarah. "Give us an update. Someone has to have some good news!"

"You," said Alex, "need to cheer up. Disney night?"

"Hell, yeah," I said, jumping on the distraction. "But I've gotta catch up with my reading first."

I dug back into my bag and pulled out the hefty door-stopper of an anthology, as another buzz from my phone made me jump.

It was from Leo, asking if I was okay.

"Someone's smiling," said Alex, rocking forwards on her chair in an attempt to peer over my phone screen. "I'm guessing it's from Mr Mysterious Guy?"

"Perhaps."

"Ash, getting answers out of you is like hammering at a brick wall."

"Drop it," I said.

"Well, for all we know, you're secretly a ninja or something."

"Yeah, you found me out," I said. "I just returned from an undercover mission. Those strange noises during the night are me running over the rooftops."

"Well, you do sneak out a lot," said Alex.

"And wear that black coat," added Sarah.

"What's wrong with my coat?"

So, instead of writing notes on poetry, we ended up concocting undercover ninja names. A typical productive evening in Flat One. And more than welcome, considering all the drama in my other life. Sometimes I wished things were simpler. I wouldn't need to lie, sneak around, put on a front, pretend there weren't murders being committed under my feet. Yet it was difficult to imagine things being different when both lives were a part of me. Sorceress and student.

I FELT MORE and more uneasy about going out Saturday night, but I'd promised Alex, and I didn't want to lose that part of my life. I deserved a night out. And more to the point, I owed it to my friends. I reasoned that nothing strange had happened recently in Redthorne... *yet*, a voice in my head told me. *It's not like it's Tombstone Hill.*

Typically for a student town, the streets blazed with light on Saturday night. Students crowded the streets, waiting for buses, queuing outside take-aways, and waiting to get into night-clubs. The thud of club-house music throbbed through the air, and even the pavements seemed to vibrate with it.

Volcano Bar was packed. It took several minutes of determined pushing to get near the bar. Alex grabbed

Sarah and me by the arms and steamrollered her way through the crowd, paying no heed to anyone she accidentally knocked over. It was pretty impressive since she was a head shorter than a good three-quarters of the people here.

She shouted for three vodka and cokes over the clamour of drunken voices and the deafening music.

I took my drink and got away from the bar sharpish, before any of the leering guys who had been eyeing us up had a chance to come over.

"I have to say I prefer Satan's Pit," remarked Alex. "This place seems to have the same song stuck on repeat, and I don't think it actually has words. It sounds like an alien language."

"It's giving me a headache," said Sarah, who hated clubbing.

"We're heading to Franklin's soon for the karaoke night. Where the hell are the LitSoc people?"

I couldn't see anyone I recognised, although the rotating strobe lights made everything look distorted. It was incredibly disorienting, like that tunnel I'd once run through at Edinburgh World of Illusions where it seemed as though the floor was tipping up as you ran through circles of rotating lights.

I sipped my drink, knowing it wouldn't help the dizziness, as I scanned the crowd.

"I think Jake and Rex are over there," I said.

We made our way over to the other side of the room, skirting round the staircase in the centre. Sure enough, our other friends from LitSoc sat crowded around a table. Becky, Louie, and Christine were crammed onto one of the sofa-seats; Jake and Rex were on the other side.

"Hey guys," said Rex. "We were thinking of making a move in a bit. It's way too crowded in here."

"Good idea," said Alex, attempting unsuccessfully to squeeze onto the seat beside him. Rex tried to make room and succeeded only in knocking his drink over.

"Way to go, Rex," said one of the other guys, as everyone jumped up to avoid getting splashed with neon-blue WKD.

"I think that's our cue to move on," said Sarah. "Why's that girl staring at you?"

I looked where she was pointing. "I don't see anyone," I said.

"Just there…"

But the lights were so dazzling I could barely make out any people more than a few feet away; everything else was a hazy blur.

I turned back to my friends to see Alex apologising to a red-faced Rex, who was drenched in WKD.

"Don't worry about it!" he said. "Really, it's totally cool!"

Sarah and I rolled our eyes. Ever since they'd discovered a mutual love for *Lord of the Rings*, it had been obvious that they liked each other, but neither seemed aware of the other's affections. Sarah and I were still waiting for realisation to sink in.

My phone buzzed in my purse. I pulled it out. An unknown number. Not again.

R u out tonite?

I frowned, and texted back, *Who is this?*

Conrad. I'm in the Volcano Bar. Where r u?

Oh, crap. Whether it was really him or just a prank, I didn't want to stay here.

"Can we head somewhere else?" I said.

"What's up, Ash?" said Becky.

"It's way too crowded in here."

"I agree. And there's WKD everywhere now," added Jake, gesturing at what remained of Rex's drink.

"Shall we make a move?" said Alex.

Everyone started downing the rest of their drinks and getting up. Shaking my head to try and clear another bout of dizziness, I followed my friends back outside, thankfully not running into Conrad on the way out.

We made it to Franklin's Bar unscathed, though every shadow made me jump and my thoughts kept turning back to that night a shadow-beast had attacked Claudia and me, right here.

But once we were inside, the sounds of drunken singing drowned out my thoughts. The karaoke was in full swing, and the neon-lit dance floor was packed out. I offered to buy drinks to avoid the microphone—singing was not one of my talents. Alex dragged Sarah over there instead.

I ordered three more vodka and cokes, having to shout over the cat-strangling sound of someone butchering a Lady Gaga song. Glancing back at my friends, I saw that Alex and Sarah were next in line. *Anything'll be better than this.*

Their turn came. Alex actually had a nice singing voice, but Sarah totally took me by surprise. She was so quiet, she faded into the background half the time, but now her voice was more powerful than Alex's, and she hit the high notes dead-on.

"Way to go, Sarah!" I said afterwards, handing her a drink. The guy running the karaoke gave her a free shot, which she downed in one, surprising both Alex and me.

"You've been holding out on us," said Alex. "Where'd you learn to sing like that?"

"Um, I was in a choir at school."

"Not good enough. You, missy, are joining the Singing Club."

"I don't really have the time…"

"No excuses. Come on, you're freaking amazing." She turned to me. "Isn't she?"

"Yeah," I agreed. "That was something else."

We ended up staying until the karaoke finished, at which point the usual club music took over. Time passed strangely, as it always did when I went clubbing; an hour could pass in the space of a minute and I'd barely be able to recollect it afterward. It simply disappeared in a haze of dubstep and hands waving and trying to avoid walking into people.

All that I could recall afterwards was narrowly avoiding the path of a girl who was projectile-vomiting, Sarah being hit on twice by guys who'd heard her singing, and having to get out of the way of a lip-locked couple who turned out to be Alex and Rex. Their arms were entwined around each other, and neither seemed to notice that they were creating a pile-up on the dance floor where people couldn't get around them.

A bit later, Sarah and I realised we'd been separated from the others. We circled the room, trying to find them, and out of nowhere someone grabbed my hand. Before I knew it, Alex was dragging me towards the stairs, saying we had to leave if we wanted to get the 2 a.m. bus back.

"I think you're drunk," she added, as I stumbled through the crowd.

"Maybe," I said, swaying. It didn't make any logical sense that several hours dancing in a sweaty cellar made you feel revitalised, but it seemed to have happened to me.

Then I stumbled over my heels and almost walked into Conrad.

Shit.

"Ash!" he said, and, to my utter consternation, tried to *kiss* me. I backed away sharpish and he almost face-planted on the drink-soaked floor.

"Go away," said Alex, before I could so much as say a word.

Conrad didn't seem to hear her. "Ash, d'you wanna dance?" he slurred.

Good grief, he was even worse than I was.

"No thanks," I said. "I'm leaving."

"C'mon."

I slapped his hand away as he made to rest it on my arm. Maybe it was the alcohol, but I'd just about had it.

"Ash," he somehow managed to stretch my name out to several syllables. "I really, really like you. I think you're stunning. You want to dance?"

"Can you leave me alone?" I snapped.

He looked at me like a kicked puppy. "Ash…"

But before I could apologise for snapping, I heard myself saying, as if it was someone else speaking: "I don't want to go out with you. I don't even like you. That clear?"

He sank down to the floor, like his legs had collapsed beneath him. "But… I…"

"Get a clue," said Alex. "Girl doesn't like you. Stay the hell away. Got it?"

"Alex, that's enough," I said. "Sorry, Conrad."

I walked away before I could make the situation worse —if that were even possible. And then there was a dark space right in front of me, a small patch of blackness. Not unusual in itself, but the girl standing next to it… she had dark brown hair of around shoulder-length, and was so pale she seemed to gleam under the strobe lights. Her black dress looked identical to mine, but it wasn't that which made me stop and stare.

A violet crystal hung around her neck, and it glowed softly.

I glanced down at my own pendant. The amethyst gleamed bright. I looked up at the girl again, and—it could have been a trick of the light, but she appeared to catch my eye and smile.

Then she melted back into the crowd.

11

TOMBSTONE HILL

Mist surrounded me, wrapping around my body like a cocoon. Even the ground beneath my feet was masked. I moved forwards, shoes crunching like I was walking through snow, but I couldn't see where I was going. Shapes appeared behind the mist, hazy and unclear. They could have easily been shadow-beasts, or harmless objects like trees.

The demon heart around my neck burned against my skin.

"Ashlyn."

I shuddered at the death-cold voice. It cut through the mist, making the shapes take on a sinister familiarity. I saw figures, appearing for a second before being swallowed up by the mist again. Cara, Alex, Sarah. My parents. Aunt Eve. Leo, Claudia, Cyrus, Berenice, Howard… all appeared, yet as soon as I drew closer, vanished like shadows.

"You think you aren't like us. You think you're above us. But you don't know what you are capable of, Ashlyn. You've barely tapped into your power. We can help you."

"What does that even mean?" I said, aloud. The mist caught my voice and smothered it. "You've done nothing but try to ruin my life. And I told you. I'm not like you."

"You think that because you haven't used your power, it doesn't exist?"

"You think you've never done anyone harm?" Another voice joined the first, and this was familiar, human. My heart turned to ice.

Terrence stepped out of the fog. He glared at me, grey eyes narrowed. Scratches marked his face, four of them from forehead to chin, deep red cuts.

I looked down in shame, remembering how my own nails, strengthened with ice, had ripped open his skin like paper.

The mist began to swirl around me, violently, changing from white to thundercloud-grey, then to black as shadows. Horrible, hissing laughter echoed in my ears, and another demon's voice spoke. I couldn't pinpoint what was different about it; only that it wasn't the same. It was lower, more menacing-sounding, if that was possible.

"You set so much by the so-called virtue of your humanity? You don't even have a heart. You can't love. You can't be loved."

The black smoke cleared slightly, just enough to reveal Terrence. His grinning face, forehead pierced with a demon's heart, violet light shining from his eyes.

"I am you, Ashlyn. You are a part of us now."

I shook my head. "No."

But the form of Terrence was changing before my eyes—next second, I looked at my own reflection. The girl resembled me in every way, from her tangled dark hair and pale features down to the black trench coat, jeans, and Converse I wore myself.

The girl grinned at me. I put a hand up to my own

face, convinced I'd feel my own expression mirrored. *It's a trick*, I thought.

The demon laughed again, and so did the girl.

"Ash," she said, softly. "Poor Ash."

"What?" I said, staring right into her eyes. I saw the tell-tale violet light appear, briefly.

"You have no idea what you're up against."

"Care to tell me?" I said. "I'm dreaming, anyway."

The girl and demon laughed again, their voices becoming one.

"You're fascinating to me, human-demon. You think you're safe in your little university house? I can find you, Ashlyn. Or you'll come to me. You think that you're safe because you can't see us in the waking world? We can get into your head in all kinds of ways, Ashlyn. The Barrier might contain us, but we're here. We're always here."

The girl threw back her head and laughed, and her outline blurred, the demon beneath grinning at me.

"You're in an interesting position. Not many people get to pick sides."

"So you and your little friends had better choose wisely."

And the smoke cleared completely. I recognised my surroundings: the cemetery in Blackstone. I stood right next to the Blackstone memorial.

"The Blackstones thought they could escape their calling. Now it's up to you to decide whether you want to face the same fate. Otherwise…"

The Ash-demon pointed to the tombstone and names appeared, etched against the black stone: *Ashlyn Temple. Claudia Delaney. Leo Blake…*

"No!" I shouted, and awoke in a cold sweat, tangled in my bedcovers.

My alarm blared, far too early for a Sunday. I groaned, glad I'd had the presence of mind to drink a litre of water when I came in last night to stave off a hangover. It had totally slipped my mind that I'd promised Leo I'd accompany him into the tunnels again today.

I switched off my alarm, catching sight of my own reflection in the wardrobe mirror. My eyes were bright, but their hazel colour was clear. There was no violet demon light there.

I'm not a demon, I thought. Right then, I wished I was fully human.

How could the demons ever think I would side with them, knowing what cold-hearted killers they were? True enough, humans could be equally selfish, but given powers like the demons had, nobody would enter a person's mind and cut off their life in an instant.

I didn't like to lament about how I wished things were different——God knows I'd wasted enough time on that in sixth form. Back then, I'd woken every day wishing that on that cold December day in assembly I'd tilted back and seen nothing watching me from the shadows, that no cold eyes haunted me everywhere I walked, that I faced an ordinary future, free from the darkness I didn't yet have a name for. In another life I might never have come to Blackstone and never met Claudia, never spoken to the fortune-teller. I might have…

But that was wrong, I thought. There was no possible future in which this didn't exist, because it was a part of who I was, whether I liked it or not. I wouldn't exist if I wasn't tied to those creatures and the Darkworld.

You don't even have a heart. You can't love. You cannot be loved.

"Bullshit," I whispered. I loved my family and friends, and that was more than any demon could claim.

This was just my lot in life. I'd always wanted something more than the ordinary. I wanted to *live*, to learn, to love, to travel the world. Losing everything had made me all the more determined to fight for what I could get.

And there were some advantages. For fun, I conjured a small light and watched it fly around the room like a butterfly, changing colour as it went. I'd *never* use magic to harm another person. With David, I hadn't known what I was doing, and with Terrence it had been self-defence...

Sure you're not just making excuses?

Quiet, I told the voice in my head. *I was just dreaming.*

But what if it was true? What if the demons could somehow get into my head, even from behind the Barrier? It would explain the vividness, not to mention the recurring nature, of my dreams...

I shook my head. Even if it was true, they couldn't hurt me from that side of the Barrier. Could they?

LEO and I caught the train to Crowley at ten in the morning, to avoid ending up stuck there after dark. The little village cowered under heavy rainclouds, promising a storm later. I hoped we wouldn't get caught in it, but I supposed we could always take the underground path back to Blackstone if need be.

Mr Melmoth's house was deserted and even dustier than before, suggesting that no one had been there since we last visited. We made our way down to the cellar in silence, and Leo found the hidden trapdoor to the secret room.

Even though Leo had pretty much cleared it out last time, we still did another search of the study. I shone the light into every crevice, searching for more hidden doors and clues as to where this laboratory—if there was one—was hidden.

"I think we can assume there was," said Leo. "There's got to be something I haven't thought of. That place is a labyrinth, and I don't remember Melmoth ever being particularly good with directions. I think he must have marked it in some way so he could find it. Unless it disappeared when he died."

He returned to searching the store of newspapers and articles. Melmoth had been quite the celebrity, by the look of things.

"He was pretty modest," said Leo. "Like he wanted everyone to forget about him really. Can't blame the guy. He was cursed. He even got hate mail from other *venators*."

"Shit, really?" I said. "That sucks."

"Yeah, especially the Righteous Cult. They died out a few years ago. His own brother was the leader."

"Seriously?" I shook my head. "That's messed-up."

"Tell me about it. He and his brother never got along, but I don't think even he thought his own sibling would head a cult that would commit mass suicide. They offered themselves up to defend humanity against the Darkworld."

"How... how did they do that?"

"By giving themselves up as demon hosts. In other words, they were filthy hypocrites. It was around the time... twenty years or so ago, demon summonings were really common. So the Righteous had this bright idea of stealing a demon heart of their own—a piece of crystal, I guess, from some dodgy wannabe-magic-users who collect that kind of thing—and using it to draw all the demons into one place. What happened was that they succeeded, but the demons they summoned killed all of them, and other sorcerers had to clear up their mess."

"Jesus."

"Tell me about it. Melmoth didn't really talk about his brother. Can't say I blame him."

He sighed. I followed his gaze to the hidden door in the corner.

"Want to go and look for that laboratory?" I said.

"You sure you wanna go into the tunnels again?"

"Um." *Not really.* "That's where we're most likely to find answers, right?"

Maybe it was because I'd been dreading the moment when the sunlight cut off, but the tunnels seemed darker than I remembered. I conjured a small light and shifted it until it rested in the centre of my forehead, like a head torch. Leo showed me that I could adjust the brightness to my liking, so I experimented until it was at a level that showed every stone beneath my feet, yet not so bright it dazzled either of us. I was fully prepared to switch it off if need be.

"I came back the other night and marked the tunnels I've been down," he said, as I followed him down the stone-walled passageway.

"Really? You came back alone?"

"For the funeral."

I stopped. *Of course.* "I'm sorry. I forgot…"

"It's fine, Ash. Don't worry about it. The guy had a time-limit on his life anyway and he'd planned for it. It was a really quiet thing. He's buried in the catacombs, and I got totally lost trying to find my way. They're under the old graveyard."

"Like, around here?"

"Yeah. I marked the tunnel. I'll show you."

We walked in a straight line until we reached a fork. He pointed to the ground, and I shifted the light so that it shone on a cross carved into the floor by the left path.

"That one's a dead end," he said.

We took the right path, which led us to a wider tunnel, almost a chamber. Multiple other tunnel entrances greeted us. At least half were marked with crosses.

"Which do you think?" said Leo. "I got about halfway down that side last time."

I picked one at random, and held up my light, ready.

One long walk later and we were back where we started.

"Dammit!" said Leo, when he saw the familiar lines of tunnel entrances.

We moved onto another path. Most either ended in dead ends or led back towards Blackstone, which we wanted to avoid in case we accidentally stumbled into the Venantium's headquarters. We might be several miles away from the town, but neither of us knew when we were walking on the Venantium's ground. It wasn't like they'd marked it.

The trouble was, it was all too easy to end up lost, and despite our best efforts to mark the paths, after one particularly winding passage, we found that we weren't sure which way led back. I let Leo take the lead, trusting him to have a better memory than I did, but I felt the first fluttering of panic in my chest as we encountered one unmarked branching pathway after another.

"This one looks like it leads aboveground," Leo said, scuffing the floor with his heel. "See? It's earth, not stone. We can get our bearings."

"Yeah."

The tight sense of claustrophobia was doing nothing to ease my misgivings, so I quickened my pace. The tunnel did indeed slope upwards. We had to stoop our heads to avoid brushing the ceiling. A set of stone steps, like the ones that led into Mr Melmoth's cellar, appeared before us.

"Are you sure we aren't going in circles?" I asked.

"Hmm." Leo studied them. "I'm positive I haven't been here before... Let's have a look."

Our footsteps echoed sharply on the stone. Above was

a trapdoor, which opened when Leo pushed on it. Our conjured lights threw eerie shadows on the walls of the small room we emerged into. It was definitely a cellar of some kind, although it wasn't Mr Melmoth's.

"I think we're trespassing in someone's house," I said in a whisper. "Let's head back."

"One minute," said Leo. "This doesn't make sense... I thought I had my bearings right..."

He made for the wooden stairs in the centre of the room, leading to another trapdoor.

"Leo, wait!"

Heart beating fast, I followed him up the stairs. "Seriously! We could get into trouble—"

"Don't you think most people would know if they had a tunnel in their cellar?" said Leo. "Trust me, we aren't about to give anyone a shock here."

All the same, I didn't like it.

As he lifted the second trapdoor, a cloud of dust flew into the air and I sneezed violently. We were in a hallway, one that reeked of neglect. There was no carpet; several tatty, worn rugs concealed holes in the wooden floor. The wallpaper had once been white, but had faded to grey. A cracked mirror hung on the wall to the left. A rickety wooden staircase to the right led upstairs. There were several doors leading off the hallway. Leo pushed one of them open. It led into a living room which was just as derelict as the hall.

"Shit," said Leo, peering out of the grimy window. "We're inside that old house near Tombstone Hill."

My heart gave an unpleasant lurch. He was right.

"We definitely don't want to be here," Leo said.

"Agreed," I said.

Back in the hallway, Leo tried the front door. The bolts moved easily.

"You want to go out this way?" I said, surprised.

"Yeah, why?"

Because that way leads through a graveyard? Not that it made much difference; the tunnels were just as bad.

Outside, the storm hadn't yet broken, but the sky was a mass of cloud. Grey stones jutted from the ground between frosted clumps of grass. Twisted, leafless trees swayed in the breeze. I looked back at the cottage. It looked sad and lonely more than anything, but I wouldn't go back in there by choice.

Leo swore, pulling me into the shadow of a tombstone. There was someone else here. A man walked past, a tall spindly man wearing the uniform of the Venantium. He didn't glance in our direction, but the hairs rose on my arms.

"Mr Priestley?" said Leo, frowning. "The hell's he doing here?"

"Investigating?" I said.

"I guess they must be taking this thing more seriously than I thought. That, or—"

Cold rushed through my whole body, like a shower of ice-water down my spine. Someone was contacting the Darkworld.

"Shit," Leo whispered.

A figure stepped out from behind a grave, to stand directly in front of Mr Priestley. With the general gloom of the cemetery, I couldn't make out anything other than her black coat—it was definitely a girl, but a tree stood between us and her.

"You again," said Mr Priestley, to the girl.

"Hi," said the girl. I shivered. Her voice was hard to pin down; it was both cold and playful, like a demon's yet also like a child's. An image flashed into my head of the night before, in Satan's Pit. The girl who'd looked at me with demon eyes. The girl who'd looked like me.

No. Impossible.

"Why are you here? Why won't you leave?" said Mr Priestley.

"I like it here."

Strange, thought the part of me that wasn't paralysed with dread. Surely a senior member of the Venantium could easily banish a ghoul, or spirit, whatever she was.

"You can't make me leave!"

A sudden strong breeze whipped through the trees, making the branches rattle. Mr Priestley took a step back. It didn't seem worth risking being spotted to move closer, but something about that girl's voice... sounded oddly familiar, in a way.

Holy hell. It was *my* voice. Like listening to my voice recorded, I hadn't recognised it before. But there was no doubt. The fear bit deep, rooting me to the spot.

"You are a spirit who does not belong in this world. I can send you back to the Darkworld, but I would rather you chose to return of your own will."

"I don't belong in this world?" she said, her voice—*my* voice—now distorted, an inhuman snarl. "And you saw to that. You *venators* all saw to that. But I have power none of you could guess at. Now I can kill you. And I will."

She stepped forwards, the wind kicking up leaves around her. I instinctively moved closer to Leo, my heart beating fast in my ears, the amethyst pendant burning against my chest from where it hung around my neck. I felt the unbearable urge to hold onto it, but I couldn't do that, not with Leo here.

Mr Priestley stepped back. The girl raised both arms, and moved out of the shadow of the tree to advance on the old *venator*.

"You weren't there that night, were you?" she whispered. "You chickened out and sent your understudies in your place. But I know you were behind it, *venator* scum."

Mr Priestley started to speak, but the wind snatched his voice away. Leaves danced around him, the trees creaking and swaying.

"What's that?" said the girl. "You think I'm powerless? I'm more than a spirit, *venator*. I know all your secrets."

He stepped away, and even from here, I saw his face convulse. Whatever he saw scared the living daylights out of him.

I clapped a hand to my mouth as his body began to shake. Instinct pulled at me, screaming at me to run away before I saw something I really didn't want to see.

Mr Priestley screamed. He shook all over, and a wrenching crack split the air. The trees in the cemetery began to fall, each split into two neat halves. And Mr Priestley...

Leo pulled me back, turning me away from the sight of the *venator's* body falling as though struck by a heavy object. Blood streamed out, soaking into the grass. My legs gave out from underneath me, and I dropped to the ground. *Oh, God. That didn't happen. I didn't just watch that happen.*

And Leo was shaking me, saying something, but I couldn't hear a word.

"Ash. Ash! We have to go!"

I didn't even have it in me to protest as he pulled me back towards the house. I trembled and held onto Leo's arm for support as we made our way down to the cellar, then lifted the second trapdoor and let the darkness of the tunnels close over us once more.

"Okay. Ash, it's okay. Breathe."

Wasn't I breathing? I sucked in stale tunnel air. It helped my light-headedness a bit. A bit. I'd just seen a man die in front me me. The sight was etched on the back of my eyes. A vice clamped around my lungs, squeezing at my chest, and my racing heart sounded like it belonged to someone else.

"Ash. You're not going to pass out on me." Leo. Leo held onto my hand, firmly. Warm. Secure. I looked into his eyes. His face was grey-white, but no longer swimming before my vision.

I breathed in and out, in and out. My head refused to clear.

"Ash. I'm going to take you back to my house and you're going to sit down, okay?"

I nodded, or I thought I did. It took every ounce of willpower to make my legs move. I concentrated on Leo's presence beside me, leading me through the endless darkness.

Back in Mr Melmoth's study, he pushed open the secret door. The room was just as we'd left it, a mess. He held onto my hand as we made our way out of the cellar and into the hallway. Leo steered me into a living room and sat me down on a sofa. I instantly fell back into the seat as my legs gave way. My breath came out in short gasps. I hadn't had a panic attack in *ages*.

"Ash. Breathe. Drink this."

"What is it?" I asked, taking the glass in a trembling hand.

"Just water. Calm down. You're in shock."

"No shit." The glass trembled in my hand. "I think I'm going to faint."

"You're sitting down. It's okay. Fuck." He pressed his hand to his forehead. "I think I'm in shock, too."

"Leo," I said, dizzily. "Talk to me."

"Huh?"

"It'll stop me forgetting how to breathe. Give me something to concentrate on. Just talk. About… something. Anything."

"Like what?" Leo stood, and started pacing the room. "Crap. You know, it's kind of hard to think about anything else right now." He walked over to a dusty oak bookcase on the other side of the room. "I could read to you? Or is that weird?"

"Sounds perfect," I said, sipping water. The fog in my head had begun to clear, the knot in my chest loosening a little, but my mind kept threatening to send me down a path I didn't want to face yet. I didn't *ever* want to face it.

The girl with my voice, my face. My demon heart. The murderer.

"You like Milton, right?"

"You're going to read me *Paradise Lost*?"

"If you like. Or Shakespeare. Melmoth doesn't have much besides the classics here."

"Classics are cool," I said. "Don't call me a nerd."

"Wasn't planning to. I'm studying English too. I can't talk. Okay. *A Midsummer Night's Dream* is good."

And he actually started reading it. Even doing the voices. I shook with laughter that sounded half like sobbing, but it didn't matter. Nothing mattered except sending the terror away to a place where it couldn't touch me. Leo gave me that.

He glanced outside. "It's gonna get dark soon. Want to get the train?"

"Definitely," I said.

He held my hand all the way to the station. I no longer felt like I might pass out, but the world retained an odd, surreal quality.

"You're okay, Ash," said Leo. "You can come back to mine, if you want?"

I shook my head. "I'll have to get to my flat. My friends will be wondering where I am."

Hopefully, I wouldn't run into them. I couldn't act normal, not after what I'd seen.

"You sure you're okay?"

I nodded. "Thanks for reading to me."

"Any time."

Words came back to me then, from when we'd discussed Mr Melmoth's journals. *The Death Child... it took the form of a young girl.*

The Death Child looked just like me. That was why Mr Melmoth had tried to kill me. And it was still out there.

Like anything was going to be okay now.

A noise woke me from a fitful sleep. Leo had messaged me late into the night, sending me reassurances I appreciated even if I didn't believe them. Blinking awake, I winced as the first image to hit me was Mr Priestley's death. It felt like that had been the dream. Things like that didn't happen. Not even in my crazy world. I'd never seen someone murdered in cold blood before.

It took a while for me to realise the sobbing I thought I heard wasn't coming from me, but from outside my room. I jumped out of bed, moving swiftly towards the door. Pulling back at the last moment, I pressed my ear to the wood. The noise didn't come from the corridor, but from the room next to mine. Sarah's.

It's okay. It'll be something ordinary. But my heart beat fast all the same, my pulse racing, my mind conjuring up images I didn't want it to.

I opened the door. The fluorescent hall lights snapped on automatically as I stepped into the corridor, but no human presence was evident. Terrence's empty door stared at me; it still had the faded white-tack marks where he'd pinned up his poster. Abandon all hope.

I turned away and knocked on Sarah's door.

"Sarah," I called, my voice echoing in the deserted corridor. "Are you okay?"

Silence answered, and a shiver danced up my arms. *Stop jumping at shadows,* I told myself.

"Sarah?"

The door at the other end of the corridor opened, and Alex appeared, yawning. "What's going on?"

"I thought I heard…"

The sobbing sound again.

Alex crossed the corridor and knocked on Sarah's door, too. "Sarah!"

This time, the door opened. Sarah leant on the door frame, face streaked with tears. "Hey, guys," she croaked.

"Hey—what's up?" said Alex.

Alex hugged her so tight Sarah let out a squeak of surprise. I hovered awkwardly on the side, before turning it into a group hug.

"What's this about?"

"I can't breathe?" said Sarah.

Alex stepped back. "Don't tell me. You broke up with Sir Cockwomble?"

"Yeah." Sarah nodded, and her eyes filled with tears again. "You were right, but I…" She sank down to the floor, sobbing.

Alex scooted down beside her. "Hey. It's okay."

"Doesn't feel it."

"It will. Honestly."

Just as I sat down, my gaze fell on Sarah's window, and my breath caught. Someone stared at me through the glass.

I stood, swiftly. "I'll be back in a mo'," I said.

Alex glanced at me. "Sure. But be quick. You're needed."

I nodded absently and rushed to my own room, letting the door swing shut behind me. I pressed my palms to the glass, peering at the field. No one there.

But I'd been positive for a moment that I'd seen my own reflection—even though I was nowhere near the window. Or another girl who looked like me, peering in. *No. It couldn't be. Not here.*

That girl in the bar, though... it could have been a trick of the light. Or she'd worn an ordinary pendant from the market, not a demon heart.

Not a demon heart... I still wore it now. It was ice-cold to touch. No burning. No danger. I'd just imagined it.

You think that you're safe because you can't see us in the waking world? We can get into your head in all kinds of ways, Ashlyn. The Barrier might contain us, but we're here. We're always here.

Shivers danced up and down my arms. My chest felt tight, like a corset squeezed the breath form my lungs. *No panic attacks,* I told myself. *Go out. Go back to your friends. If someone is trying to screw with your head, don't give them the satisfaction.*

I pulled on my hoody, even though the chill had nothing to do with the cold, and went back into the corridor to find Alex in full-flow.

"Alex," I cut in, "Quit harassing the poor girl."

Sarah gave me a grateful smile. Really, I appreciated Alex for being willing to stand up for people, but there was a limit. Some things were best left alone.

"Hey, just trying to help," said Alex. "Well, Sarah, you handled it better than Ash did. Congratulations."

"Um... what?" I said. "You mean Conrad? Was I really that harsh?"

"Er, yes," said Alex. "But it was probably the best way to do it."

I sighed. "I feel like a total bitch," I said, and I did. I'd never spoken to anyone like that before—at least, not anyone who'd not done anything to deserve it other than being annoying.

"You had to say it. He'll leave you be now."

I hoped she was right.

"Anyway," said Alex. "I know how to cheer you both up. A night in a haunted house."

For God's sake. "Really?" I said. "How's that meant to cheer us up?"

"You really have an issue with this Tombstone Hill thing," said Alex. "You know what? I think you have a phobia."

"Of catching pneumonia from spending a winter night in a house without heating? Yes."

"That's what sleeping bags and blankets are for. Come on. Say you'll come."

"You'd really rather spend Valentine's Day doing that than going out with Rex?" I said.

"Did he ask you out?" said Sarah, rubbing her eyes.

"Yeah!" said Alex.

"He finally did it?" said Sarah, brightening. "Where's he taking you?"

"Just for a meal in Redthorne at an Italian restaurant. The night *before* Valentine's Day. We don't do tradition."

"Not a movie night?" said Sarah. "Nice going." Sarah and I had been joking that their first date should be a four-teen-hour movie marathon of the Extended Editions of *The Lord of the Rings*.

"Pretty fancy, considering he's a student," I said. "I thought you were going to say he asked you to that Valentine's Ball for a moment there."

"Nah, he hates stuff like that. So do I, come to that. And the social's the same night."

"You'd really rather sleep on the floor of an old house in a cemetery?"

"Ah, so it's the graveyard thing that's bothering you?" Alex nudged Sarah. "I think Ash is scared of the Grim Reaper."

Jesus. She really won't quit it. I rolled my eyes. "Whatever. I think Sarah should join the singing club."

My attempt to distract her worked; Alex launched into another plan for Sarah's life. At least this one didn't involve drop-kicking anyone.

"Come on, girl, you took control of your life when you told Liam to get stuffed. Just carry on!"

I needed to do the same, but it was difficult to take control of something that by definition was uncontrollable. A girl who looked just like me. Maybe I *had* seen her outside. Maybe she'd come to kill someone here.

I stood up so fast Alex and Sarah stared at me. "Anyway. We have a lecture in an hour. I'm going to get ready."

"Sure," said Sarah.

Back in my room, I pulled clothes on without really paying attention. I felt hot and cold both at once, and I recoiled as another strange sensation brushed against my chest, like a mild burn, but freezing cold. I looked down and sat that the amethyst crystal around my neck was vibrating, pulsing from one shade of purple to another. As I watched, it went jet-black.

"Ash! Ash!"

I pulled back my curtains to see Conrad waving from outside my window.

"What?" I said, trying to keep my voice even. "I'm trying to work in here!"

"I think someone's been hurt down here!"

I was out of the flat in a heartbeat. I caught up with Conrad at the foot of the hill. My stomach lurched as I saw that the frost-streaked grass was marked with dark red patches.

"What the—?"

I looked around wildly at the trees, the student flats. No one was around. But the blood was unmistakeable. *No. Not again. Not here.*

"Do you think someone got attacked? Do you think it was like Mr Melmoth? Do you—?"

"I don't *know*, Conrad!" I snapped.

I started back up the hill. "I'm going to get help. Why didn't you speak to the college porter or someone instead of running to me?"

"Because I felt a demon!" Conrad wailed.

I paused. "You know anyone might have heard that, right?" I said.

"Sorry," said Conrad, his gaze on his feet. He was trembling.

"I felt it too," I said. "Sorry. I just… I've had to deal with enough crap lately… never mind. We have to do something about this."

I looked up at the flat again. Claudia and Leo were better at dealing with a crisis than me. I sent Claudia a quick text, hoping that she was in and wasn't at a lecture. Then I texted Leo.

A reply came instantly, "I'm coming."

I knew Claudia lived on the first floor of the same block as me, but she took less than a minute to appear, breathless, at my side.

"What the hell?" she said.

"I know," I said. "This looks bad."

"Leo's coming," she added. "He's on his way."

She moved farther into the forest. I followed, keeping one eye on the thickening trails of red, even though they made me feel lightheaded. It was as though I walked through a dream. Hell, everything in the past twenty-four hours felt like a dream.

"Someone came through here from that way…"

Judging by the trails, the person had dragged themselves uphill through the woods—quite an achievement, considering all the blood.

A moan sounded behind me. Conrad had fallen to his knees. "Look," he whimpered.

One of the Venantium's harpies hung, limp, from a tree. Its head had been torn off completely, leaving a bloody mess of black feathers. The awful crone-bird head lay at the foot of the tree, beak gaping open, eyes gouged out. I gagged.

I'd thought those creatures were otherworldly, incapable of being injured in a physical sense, but here was one, dead, right in front of me. *What did this?*

"Something seriously twisted is going on here."

There was a rustling behind us, the sound of hurried footsteps. Leo came running down the hill. He stopped short at the sight of the dead harpy.

"Shit," he said.

"I know, right?" said Claudia, her voice rising an octave.

"I thought they couldn't be killed," I said. "I thought they were from the Darkworld."

"Harpies are a special case. The Venantium have held them in this world for so long that they're pretty much corporeal. Unless—well, unless you hit them with magic fire."

"Oh." Pity and revulsion seized me in equal measure as I looked at the hideous swinging form in front of us.

Claudia sighed. "I hate to say it, guys, but we're gonna have to make a move."

"She's right," said Leo. "I've never known anyone to attack one of the Venantium's minions before. This could get nasty. We don't want to be involved."

"Why is it *here*?" I said, glancing back at the student village, still visible through the trees. "I mean, why leave it right next to the university?"

"God knows. Maybe there's another Terrence," said Claudia.

Leo and I looked at each other. "Or maybe it was her," I said.

"Who?"

He hadn't told Claudia yet. I took a deep breath. Did I really want to bring up the subject now, with a dead harpy hanging above us?

"What've you two been keeping from me?"

"It's… yesterday," I said, suddenly feeling very tired, almost faint. "We went into Mr Melmoth's study again, and…"

I couldn't say it. Leo took over and told her what had happened.

Claudia swore. "Hell. That thing took down a *venator*? For real?"

"Yeah. It's sick," said Leo, shaking his head. "That thing has consciousness, a will of its own. But it wasn't a true demon. It said something about finding some source of power. It seemed to want revenge on Priestley. But I've never heard of demons holding grudges before. They don't have emotions."

I shivered. The girl's anger had been pretty apparent. "She did," I said. "Whatever she is, she's as close to human as I've ever seen a demon."

"That sounds bad," said Claudia. "And she looked just like you?"

"Identical."

"Has to be a shape-shifter. But someone must have summoned her."

"Yeah," said Leo. "That's the thing. She really sounded like she was acting alone."

Claudia shrugged. "Well, I've never heard anything like it. So this is the Death Child Mr Melmoth was after?"

"Yeah," said Leo. "She must be the one. But I'm guessing even she couldn't come near campus. Mr Melmoth thought Ash was her, that's why he followed her."

"That doesn't explain why she looks like me," I said. What reason would a demon have to imitate me? To get me arrested by the Venantium, or killed? I didn't have any enemies, demons aside.

"Do you reckon she did this?" Claudia gestured at the harpy.

I swallowed. "I could see her doing this, but I can't see the point…"

Claudia's expression changed as her gaze fixed on a spot just behind me.

"Oh, God," she said softly.

At first the bush she pointed to looked innocuous, then I saw, in the shadows beneath it, the unmistakeable shape of a human hand.

My demon heart throbbed again, and I clapped a hand to it instinctively. It burned, but with coldness, not heat.

"I can't touch it. Don't make me touch it!" Conrad was rocking back and forth, a wild look on his face.

Claudia made an impatient noise and stepped forwards. I watched, transfixed, as she pulled the body out of the bushes by one leg. Letting it go, she came to stand beside me, gripping my arm so hard it hurt.

It was a skeleton. There was no flesh on its bones at all—those that were still held together. One arm was gone, and the left leg was missing a foot. It looked as though it had been pulled from a hundred-years-old grave. The smell of earth caught in my nostrils.

"Is it—?"

Claudia picked up a stick and poked it tentatively, flipping the skeleton over. The bones were cracked, covered in moss and dirt. The skull stared sightlessly at the canopy.

"I don't understand," I said.

"Me neither," whispered Claudia.

Conrad let out another moan. He had his hands pressed over his face.

"There's an evil shadow around it," he said.

It just looked out of place to me. We stared at the skeleton a few moments more, as if expecting an explanation to present itself.

Then it moved.

13

SKELE-GHOUL

The skeleton's hand clenched. Its bones creaked against each other as it shifted to a kneeling position, flexing disjointed, earth-stained arms. Slowly, wobbling, as if lifted by unseen hands, it stood, facing us, limp as a puppet on strings.

Conrad was the first to scream, a high, keening wail of pure terror. My feet locked in position, frozen to the spot, as if caught in one of my sleep-paralysis dreams. This wasn't possible. It shouldn't be possible. I could hear every creak and pop as the fragmented bones unfolded. Last of all, its skull lowered to face us with empty eyes.

But the eye-sockets weren't entirely empty. A violet, alien light gleamed within, and a familiar coldness swept through me like a sudden shower of icy water. The demon's eyes stared at me through the living corpse with a malevolent intelligence. The skeleton raised its one trembling hand. The bones were stained dark red, and with a rush of horror, I knew what had killed the harpy.

Claudia reacted first, stepping forwards and whipping out the fan I'd seen her use against the shadow-beast we'd encountered outside Satan's Pit the first time we'd met. Fire flared along its edges. Leo moved to stand beside her, his hands burning, although the skin was undamaged. It looked absurd, two fire-wielding teens staring down a skeleton.

"Ever taken down a Skele-Ghoul before?" Leo said. "I admit it's a new one on me."

Skele-Ghoul. A hybrid, dark force and human corpse. I'd thought a person had to be living to be possessed...

But it wasn't alone. Somehow several other walking corpses had gathered behind the trees, unseen. Their violet demon eyes gleamed.

"Oh, *shit*," said Claudia.

We were surrounded.

Fleshless feet swept up decaying leaves as the skeletons advanced on us, arms held out as if to keep balance. I was reminded of the skeletons from the first *Pirates of the Caribbean* film and felt the displaced urge to laugh. A six-foot high, shadowy monster with teeth like daggers could inspire fear. A walking skeleton, not so much. They would have looked more comic than threatening, were it not for those deathless eyes.

Then one of them threw back its head, and a horrible, shrieking cry rent the air. It went right through me like a blade and I almost cried out myself as a pain pierced me somewhere behind my eyes.

"Come with us, Ashlyn," a voice whispered in my ear.

No, I tried to say, whilst coldness wrapped around me, suffocating.

"Now you see what they can do to us. Side with us before you have no choice."

I won't, I cried.

My thoughts, and the demon's whisper, dissipated as a yell shocked me back to reality. Claudia was on fire—or at least she appeared to be. She lashed out at the nearest Skele-Ghoul, which withdrew. Like all demons, fire was clearly their weakness.

Flames also flared from Leo's arms; like a human fire-ball, he threw himself into the fray. One by one the violet lights winked out, until the four of us were left surrounded by a mass of blackened bones.

"Well, that was hardly a challenge," said Leo. He looked back at me. "You okay, Ash?"

"I'm fine," I said. He hadn't heard the demon speak to me. It must have connected directly to my mind.

Conrad was hunched over on the ground, moaning.

"Get up," snapped Claudia. "Was this *you*? You led us here, you snivelling idiot."

"Claudia!" I said, shocked at her sharpness. "He…" I trailed off as Conrad looked at me.

Something strange was happening to him. His face was oddly stretched, as if an invisible force pulled it in two different directions. He moaned, hands gripping his face as if trying to hold himself together.

Leo said, "Well, let's add a vampire to the mix. Why not?"

Was this what it looked like to see a vampire's true form revealed? Conrad's face spasmed and twisted into unnatural expressions. Leo had said it was like being possessed…

Then Conrad lunged at me at a speed I wouldn't have thought he was capable of. His teeth were bared in a snarl that bordered on painful. I had no time to get out of the way, but the Darkworld answered my call regardless, ice spreading over my arms. His teeth glanced off the smooth surface and he fell to the ground.

Roaring like a rabid animal, he leapt up again, hands reaching out. I let ice fan out from my palms, catching his outstretched hands and coating them in an instant. When his arms and legs were locked to his sides, I let go, panting.

"I really need to find a better way of dealing with problematic guys," I said.

"Why, which other guys have you used it on?" said Leo.

"That David creep," said Claudia. "Sorry I didn't help. You just looked like you were handling it well enough on your own." She nudged Conrad's prone form with her foot. "Come on, Ash, take it off."

"You sure he won't attack me again?"

"We'll be here if he does."

Tentatively, I contacted the Darkworld and then withdrew it. The effect was like a fan-heater switched on without warning. The ice retracted; Conrad rocked back onto his heels, then collapsed face-first onto the ground.

"Conrad?" I said uncertainly.

"Oh, just leave him," said Claudia. "We need to get the hell out of here. Dead harpies and now this. I need a drink."

"I second that," said Leo.

"It's the middle of the *day*," I said.

They both gave me a look. Oh, right. Walking skeletons, headless harpies, and frozen vampires kind of eliminated any chance at salvaging normality from this.

"Just saying," I said. "Are they even serving at the Union Bar now?"

Claudia shrugged. "Let's go anyway."

"We can't leave him here," I said, indicating Conrad. "What if there are more of them?"

Claudia sighed. "Fine. We'll leave him outside his flat. Let's go, already!"

We dragged Conrad up to the student village and deposited him in the middle of the lawn. That would have to do.

"I hope nothing attacks him."

"I personally don't give a crap," said Claudia.

We ended up in the common room, sitting on the sofa whilst some people played *Left for Dead* on the Nintendo Wii. Watching hordes of zombies was hardly what I'd had in mind, but no one felt like talking much. It was as though by not mentioning it, we could forget it even happened. Like yesterday. Leo lay in a stupor beside me. He kept dozing off on my shoulder, and I didn't have the energy to move. On my other side, Claudia fiddled with her nails, occasionally getting out her phone and surfing the net. I had no idea what to say to either of them. The demon heart kept pulsing randomly, like it had a life of its own; I held my hand clenched over it in case anyone noticed.

This made no sense at all. Had that ghoul I'd seen yesterday—the one that had looked just like me—sent those walking skeletons after us, or had we just happened to be there? I'd seen *her*, too, that time in the woods. But no demons could come onto campus. It was impossible. The Barrier was extra-strong over Blackstone and the immediate area, so strong that no one could summon a demon —not even close.

And if it *had* been her, why had she left me alone? She'd killed Mr Priestley over nothing...

Too many questions. My head hurt. I took another drink from my bottle of cider, even though I wasn't thirsty.

We stayed there until long after the GameSoc people had left. Finally, Claudia said, "It was too easy."

"Huh?" I said. My voice was hoarse from lack of use.

"Those creatures were pathetic, even more so than general shadow-beasts. They certainly weren't capable of killing anyone, or of doing any real damage."

"But they killed the harpy," I said, trying to block out the image of the bloody feathery mess hanging from the tree. I wondered if it was still there—and the skeletons, come to that—or if the Venantium had cleared the evidence away. For the sake of the next poor soul to go for a walk in the woods, I hoped they had.

"Harpies are stupid," said Claudia, with unconvincing bravado. "They're instinct creatures, essentially. It wouldn't occur to them that trying to attack a skeleton is pointless. Not to mention they were attacking one of their own."

"Technically," slurred Leo, "The harpies' first loyalty is to the Venantium, not the Darkworld."

"True," said Claudia, frowning. She downed the last dregs of her glass of cider. "I don't get it. The Venantium's protection around campus is supposed to be faultless. Nothing's *ever* got past it, as far as I know."

"What would happen if you tried to summon something from the Darkworld here?" I said.

"Nothing," she said. "Demons can speak to you here, but they can't come close to the edge of the Barrier. That's why the only dark spaces are the ones spirits use for communication, and the only ones I've seen are by Madame Persephone's tent."

"We need to talk to her," I said, wondering why I hadn't thought about that before. "This has gone beyond weird."

"Tell me about it," said Claudia. "I'm off to get another drink."

I took the opportunity to shift to a more comfortable position. Leo leaned on my shoulder, and my arm started to go numb.

"It's them," he said, so softly I barely heard him. "They're the Skele-Ghoul grave-robbers. The Ghouls."

So that's why they dug up graves. Though what they hoped to achieve by setting demons to possess skeletons, I couldn't imagine. I thought of the shape-shifting ghoul, wondering what vital clue I was missing.

"How'd they do it?" I said. "I thought the person had to be alive to be possessed..."

I broke off. Leo had begun to snore softly again.

I sighed. I didn't understand any of it, and I was scared. If someone had summoned demons on this side of the Barrier, did it mean that the Venantium weren't as all-powerful as they claimed to be? *Had* someone summoned them? I struggled to make sense of what the demon had said to me. *Now you see what they can do to us...* Who were *they?*

What had happened to make the demons keep trying to get me on their side? My mind whirled. Maybe I should just drink myself into oblivion, like Leo...

I'd half-risen out of my seat to join Claudia at the bar when I saw someone approaching me. My heart sank.

"Hey, Ash," said Conrad.

"Conrad." *Well, this is awkward.* "Sorry we left you outside; I didn't know where you lived."

"Never mind that. I'm so sorry I attacked you."

"Don't worry about it. You didn't know what you were doing."

"I mean it!" he insisted. I practically expected him to fall to his knees and beg forgiveness.

I got up. I didn't particularly want Leo to wake up and witness this. Steering Conrad to the other side of the room, I whispered. "Look, it's fine. Do you... I mean, do you have any idea who could have summoned those... things here? I thought the Venantium's Barrier was supposed to be impenetrable."

"It is," he said. "I dunno what's happening. I'm so scared. I think they're gonna kill me."

"I don't see why they would. You don't have any enemies, do you?"

He shook his head.

"Then you're fine," I said, with more conviction than I was capable of letting myself feel. Everything I'd taken for granted was in free-fall, even in my admittedly already tenuous re-construction of my world-view after learning about the Darkworld. "Seriously. The Venantium will sort it out."

"If they haven't been betrayed," said Claudia from behind me.

"Huh?" I said. "Why would you think that?"

"The only way for a demon to get to this area is if someone lets it through from outside—someone who knows how the Barrier works. So, someone who either is or was a member of the Venantium."

Conrad's already pale face went the colour of off-milk. "Can that happen?" he said, his voice high-pitched with terror.

"I really don't know, Conrad," she said, returning to her spot on the sofa.

I couldn't get another word on the matter out of her, and I ended up leaving, tired of Conrad's anxious questions. I had enough questions of my own.

And there was, once again, only one person I could think of who might be able to give me some answers.

14

BAD FORTUNE

"You what?" I said to Leo, at the next meeting. "She's gone?"

Leo looked up from Mr Melmoth's journal. "Yeah. Madame Persephone's buggered off."

"Picked a fine time to ditch us," snarled Howard, who gripped the Xbox controller so hard I was surprised it didn't break. "Like any of us know what crazy shit's going on!"

We'd updated Cyrus, Howard, and Berenice on recent events at the start of the meeting. It hadn't gone down well.

"We know someone thought making demonic skeletons was a good idea," said Berenice scornfully. "I could have taken a hundred of them with my eyes closed. They'll have to do better than that."

"Believe it or not, Berenice, the world doesn't revolve around you," said Leo, from behind the journal.

Berenice tossed her hair. "Whatever. It was a stupid idea, anyway."

"I think there's more to it than what we saw," said

Claudia. "What were they doing at the uni? They can't have been looking for us."

"Unless that little rat really did sell us out," said Berenice. "Wouldn't surprise me."

"I told you, it was just a theory," said Claudia. "He was terrified himself, anyway. I don't think he was faking."

"And now Madame Persephone's decided to go on holiday," said Howard. "Well, I for one don't plan on dying because the only sorcerer who's actually on our side has decided to desert us. I say we strike first."

"You're overreacting again, Howard," said Cyrus. "But I do think there's something the Venantium aren't telling us. Not that that's anything new. I'll go and hang about the Headquarters, see what I can find out. No," he said, as both Leo and Howard attempted to cut in. "You two are in enough trouble with the *venators* as it is. Trust me. I know what I'm doing."

Cyrus turned back to the Xbox and started punching Howard's onscreen character in the head.

"Hey, I thought you said no fighting!" yelped Howard.

"I didn't say it applied in the gaming world," said Cyrus.

That was how the guys dealt with a crisis. Gaming. Never mind the ghoul walking around wearing my face, and dead harpies, and walking skeletons. Rolling my eyes, I turned to look at Leo.

"Found anything?" I said.

"Only that even in his diaries Melmoth's as cryptic as hell. Man, he won't *say* what any of his experiments actually were!"

I thought of the Skele-Ghouls. "You don't think he might have known what was going on? With those creatures?"

"Maybe," said Leo.

"How could a demon possess a corpse?" I said. "I thought it was the life-force of a person they fed on."

"Magic energy," Leo corrected me. "And I've been thinking about it. I don't think the person has to be alive to still have magical energy. Usually a demon stops possessing someone after they die to find a better host, but sometimes they stay. Really twisted sorcerers sometimes sic them on an enemy's family. Imagine being slaughtered by someone you think is your own mother or sister, or——"

I shuddered.

"Anyway, magical energy must linger after death. It's the only way those things could exist."

"So someone's digging up graves to collect corpses to make a demon army?" said Howard sceptically. Then he paused. "Shit. That might actually be true."

"We don't know anything yet, really," said Cyrus. "Like how those vampire killings come into it."

"It's all one big conspiracy!" exclaimed Howard. "The Venantium want to distract us so they've come up with this bullshit story about vampires being killed, when they're really planning on raising an army of——"

"Might I remind you that my own guardian was murdered the other day?" said Leo quietly. "You think that was bullshit?"

There was a very awkward silence.

"Nah," said Howard. "But the *venators* are up to something."

"I agree," said Berenice, to no one's surprise.

"Well, whatever it is, it's probably an accident we got dragged into it," said Cyrus. "Look, we're just a group of nonconformist undergrads hanging out here. What would anyone want with us?"

"They sure seem interested in *her*," said Berenice, pointing to me.

Here we go again.

"What's that supposed to mean?" I said, meeting her glare evenly. I'd had enough encounters with bullies and general hostility when I was at school to be pretty much impervious to it now.

"Well, two vampires have attacked you now, and that Conrad guy won't stop following you around."

I sighed. "Yeah, it's the pheromones in my blood. It sends vampires crazy, didn't you know?"

Berenice blinked. I don't think she got the sarcasm instantly. Leo, on the other hand, was hiding a grin behind the journal. For some reason, this riled me up even more.

"Fine, I won't hang about here if you think I'm going to get you all attacked." I stood up. "In case you've forgotten, there's a monster out there who looks exactly like me, and she *killed* someone the other day. I have bigger problems than your petty mind-games."

"Berenice, stop trying to pin the blame on Ash!" said Claudia. "I think those Skele-Ghouls were there to leave a warning for the Venantium, actually."

"What gives you that idea?" said Berenice.

"Think about it, they want to be known. Assuming they're the same people as those grave-robbers, of course. That graffiti's pretty ostentatious."

She had a point. The sight of one of their fearsome birds dismembered would definitely send warning bells ringing for the Venantium.

"Yeah, but... one of them *died* the other day. Aren't they distracted enough already?"

Mr Priestley. I'd only met him once, and he'd creeped me out slightly, but I couldn't process that he was *dead*. And it had happened right in front of me.

"That's why I don't think the two things are related," said Cyrus. "It's horrible what you saw, but I really think that ghoul—whatever it is—was acting alone. Melmoth was preoccupied with her when whoever killed the vampires came along. The same person hates the Venantium. It doesn't *seem* like there's a connection, but there has to be one somewhere."

There was. Me. The doppelganger looked like me. Mr Melmoth had been chasing her when he'd died. And that Skele-Ghoul had spoken to me, too…

Something big was happening right under our feet, I knew that much. But how it involved me, I didn't know.

"Well, whoever it is, they made one mistake," said Howard. "They tried to pick a fight with us."

"Howard, I told you, we're not fighting—"

"I'm sick of sitting around letting those *venators* have all the fun," snarled Howard. "Someone set those creatures loose on *our* campus! We have to show them they can't get away with it."

"We already burnt them to cinders, what more do you want?" said Claudia.

"That's probably majorly disrespecting the dead, too," said Cyrus.

"What, you think we should have reburied them?" said Claudia, with a snort.

"I wonder where they came from," said Cyrus. "Wait a minute. you don't think—?"

He began to rummage through his bag.

"What is it, Cy?" said Leo.

He pulled out a newspaper and unfolded it. I recognised it as the local paper.

"Picked this up today. Forgot to have a look. If there's anything in here about grave-robberies…"

"Ah, that's a point," said Claudia. "Those skeletons must have come from somewhere nearby."

"Well, they weren't from Blackstone," said Cyrus. "The

only cemetery's the old one in the churchyard, and that's right next to the Venantium's headquarters. The next nearest is in Hawthorn, the other village down the road."

"That doesn't explain why someone was able to summon a demon under the Venantium's radar."

"Maybe they didn't. I think they summoned the creatures outside. How they managed to walk past the barriers around Blackstone is a mystery—maybe because they're dead? But I don't think even a traitor *venator* could summon anything here. Too many defensive mechanisms."

"So someone let them into Blackstone?" said Berenice.

"Looks that way."

"Told you there was a traitor." And she looked at me.

I glared back. *She's determined to suspect me.*

"Nothing about local grave-robberies in here," said Cyrus, throwing down the paper. "Except in the readers' letters section. Hysterical letters from locals about seeing zombies on the streets. I wonder…"

"They probably walked out on the night of the Zombie Bar Crawl," said Leo, absently. He stared at one page of the journal, frowning.

"Well, it sounds a bit too much like those Skele-Ghouls. If they're walking the streets right under the Venantium's noses, we should be worried."

"Like I said," said Howard, sending Cyrus's character flying across the screen with a tremendous sucker-punch to the face, "We should deal with this ourselves."

Cyrus sighed. "First we need to figure out what's going on."

"Maybe the shape-shifter's the Skele-Ghouls' leader," said Howard.

"The Skele-Ghouls weren't here before, though," said Claudia. "Someone from the Venantium would have spotted them. I mean, I can understand how they could miss a shadow-creature if it was really a shape-shifter, but walking skeletons are pretty noticeable. And the harpies see everything."

"The one they killed won't," said Leo. "Come to think of it—it's weird that there was only one harpy, and it apparently took them on alone. They tend to have this swarm instinct. But there was just one corpse."

"Good point," said Cyrus. "Maybe it got too close. But if you kill a harpy with magic, it just disappears back to the Darkworld. That one was torn to pieces. Maybe there *was* a swarm, and they only *killed* one of them to leave a message for the Venantium."

"Which brings us back to where we started," said Claudia. "Well, I'm all for taking on a bunch of weak-ass skeletons, even if they have a creepy shape-shifting child leading them. But I dunno... something just doesn't add up. Someone let them past the Barrier."

"We need to leave it to the Venantium for now," said Cyrus. "They're more than capable of taking down ghouls. I'd say this is part of something bigger. And Leo," he said, with a stern glance at his brother, "Don't do anything rash. That goes for you too, Howard."

"Wasn't planning to," said Howard, pummelling Cyrus's character on-screen. The figure flew through the air and disappeared out of sight, over a cliff's edge. "I win," he added.

Cyrus sighed.

"Wait," said Leo. "I've an idea. Vampires and demons have the same ability; they can take energy from others. So vampires naturally have less magical energy than a normal sorcerer, even though they can use magic the same way. But of course, demons don't *need* to take energy from people—they just do it, it's instinct. They can draw on magic even from the dead. So... maybe the person responsible is trying to figure out a way to do what vampires and demons do naturally—take magical energy from others. Humans can't do it, after all. It's kind of a sketchy theory, I admit, but it's all I've got."

"You might have something there," said Cyrus, thoughtfully. "People don't think about this a lot, but summoning a demon—well, the energy has to come from somewhere. That's why you need a demon heart, a stone loaded with magical energy. Sorcerers started using them because otherwise the demons would make for the next available source of energy. In other words, the summoner. They still do, a lot of the time. That's why summoning one is such a stupid, risky thing to do."

I nodded. I remembered Terrence all-too-clearly. The demon had had a heart, an anchor, and had still killed Terrence. I resisted the urge to run my hand over my own demon heart, wondering for the first time where the energy inside had come from. I knew nothing about how one went about amassing magical energy, but it wasn't like I intended to summon a demon any time soon.

Would the fortune-teller know? *Why* had she disappeared now of all times?

Another, chilling thought struck me. *Can* I *take magical energy from others?* Was that what my reflection in the dream had meant when she'd said I was *one of them?*

You don't even have a heart. You can't love. You cannot be loved.

I shook my head fiercely. *No…*

"What's up, Ash?" said Leo, looking at me with concerned eyes. "You think of something else?"

"Nothing," I said. "I can't think of anything else."

Liar, said a voice in my head. How much longer could I keep this from them? Did I really belong amongst other magic-users? Did I belong to the demons instead?

I am you, *Ashlyn. You are a part of us now.*

THE WORDS REPEATED in my head as I left the Games Room, making the excuse that I needed to study. Leo asked again if I was okay. I said I was. What more could I say? That I was losing my mind? I couldn't mention the dreams without giving away my secret. I *needed* to talk to the fortune-teller.

I went downstairs into the common room. No one even noticed the Games Room, because during meetings Cyrus used some Influence on it to make it invisible to anyone but us. *I need to ask him how he does that,* I thought.

My mind kept jumping around from one thing to another. Seeing a girl about my height with brown hair at the union bar made my heart jump and my hand fly to the pendant around my neck, before she turned slightly and I realised it was someone from my seminar group. *Idiot.*

I hurried out of the common room and into torrential rain. Pulling up my hood, I jogged through the student village back to my flat, feet splashing in puddles. The grey sky made the forest look dark, uninviting.

I let myself into the building, shaking rainwater from my hair, and crossed the corridor to my flat. It was early evening, but it disarmed me how quiet it was. Probably people were hiding from the rain.

I unlocked the door, trying to suppress my sense of disquiet. A relaxing movie night with my flatmates—that was what I needed to take my mind off things.

Stepping into the corridor, I collided with a hooded figure. I jumped aside with a shriek, reaching out to the Darkworld. Ice sprang up along my hands, even as panic ripped through me. *Shit. How did it get in? My friends...*

Muffled giggles reached my ears. I frowned, glancing at

Sarah's door, then back at the hooded figure. A tall, cloaked, masked man, holding... a scythe?

Sarah's door burst open, and Alex and Sarah came out, roaring with laughter. Alex waved a camera in my face. "Oh my God," she spluttered. "That was amazing. You're a world-class actress, Ash. Thanks for standing right in front of the door!"

"Wha—?"

"Whoever put spy-holes in the doors is a genius."

"I am going to kill you," I said.

The hooded man unmasked, revealing a tall Indian boy. He grinned at me. "That's not much of a welcome, is it?"

This was too much. "What the hell is going on?" I demanded.

"Hey, now." Alex held up her hands. "While you were off shooting zombies or whatever you GameSoc people do, Mandeep here moved in. It just so happened we were formulating an evil plan at the time... and he offered to star in my horror-movie remake."

"What, you made him dress up as the Grim Reaper?" I said. "Couldn't you have asked Pete to do it?"

"Pete's passed out in the kitchen with lipstick all over his face."

"Ri-ight," I said, deciding I didn't want to know. "It's nice to meet you, by the way," I added to Mandeep. "Sorry about those two."

"Nice to meet you, too," he said, putting down the scythe. "They said you could take a joke. Your friends are too short to look intimidating in a Grim Reaper costume."

"Ha!" I said, as Alex made a noise of protest. "Give me that camera."

"No way. I'm putting this on Facebook."

"Like hell you are!" I attempted to wrestle the camera from her, whilst Mandeep and Sarah looked on, laughing.

I hoped my contacting the Darkworld hadn't been visible on camera. That would be a sure-fire way to get locked up by the Venantium.

Giving up, I sat down on the hall floor. "Glad you got a laugh out of scaring me half to death."

"Best. Scream. Ever," said Alex. "Oh God—seriously, Ash, you stole the show."

"I expect a cut of the profits," Mandeep said. "I stood here for half an hour!"

"Well, we didn't know *exactly* when Ash would come back…"

I shook my head. Really, with friends like mine, it wasn't surprising I was jumping at shadows. I'd never hear the end of this one.

Thankfully, the footage only showed the front half of me before I jumped out of the camera's sight. Not that I was thrilled at my humiliation being plastered all over social media, but at least I hadn't exposed my magic to the world. I couldn't do to my friends what I'd had to do to David, erasing and altering his memories to forget about seeing me use magic. And I couldn't forget how Terrence had messed with *my* memory, erasing our first encounter, when he'd stolen the pendant from me.

"Ash." The fortune-teller's voice spoke without warning, sharp and clear as though she was right in front of me. I froze where I stood. It *couldn't* be—I'd just been thinking about subliminal magic…

"Don't panic. I'm using mind-communication. I cannot speak to you right now, but it's important that you come and find me later. All of you. I need to talk to your friends, too."

Sure, I thought, not knowing if she would hear me or

not. I was sure we were somehow communicating through the Darkworld.

"Good. Make sure you come. It's important."

The connection to the Darkworld faded. My heart beat fast in my ears, and I steadied myself against the wall.

I had no idea what the fortune-teller wanted—but I was glad she was back.

15

SHIFTING DARKNESS

"So what are we all doing here?" said Howard.

We stood like a group thrown together by accident: me, Claudia, Leo, Cyrus, a surly-looking Howard, and an even surlier-looking Berenice. None of us had a clue why the fortune-teller wanted to talk to us here, of all places, in a deserted field midway between Blackstone and Crowley. Hills were on either side of us, and the only sign of human life was an abandoned farmer's cottage just visible behind a patch of trees. I couldn't help looking around anxiously, expecting the doppelganger to appear.

Leo, Claudia, and I had told her everything the moment we'd arrived at her stall in Blackstone. I could hardly believe so much had happened since the last time we'd seen her—though I didn't exactly make a habit of visiting, knowing how maddeningly cryptic she could be—but approaching her tent had felt oddly like coming home.

The usual sign was displayed outside: *Madame Persephone, fortune-teller*. That couldn't be her real name, I thought. It was another alias, like Aunt Eve. If you could change your appearance at will, you could pretend to be several people at once. For all I knew, she was, and anyone I saw might be her in disguise.

Good job it isn't a common gift. I'd never be able to trust anyone.

Berenice, Howard, and Cyrus had met us there, the former two looking displeased. Of course, since the fortune-teller hadn't said *why* it was so urgent that we meet, it had taken a lot of coaxing on Cyrus's part to get Howard and Berenice to come out. But the fortune-teller had only needed to look at them and say, in her quietest voice, "Come with me," and they obeyed. She must have used Influence, because I'd never known Berenice so compliant —she didn't even complain when we then had to trek across fields for nearly an hour, because she didn't want us using magic where anyone could see, or the Venantium could apprehend us.

Thinking about it, maybe she had us all under some kind of spell. No one asked any questions as we followed her, and it wasn't until we stopped, in the middle of a deserted field, that the spell seemed to break.

She faced us, looking from one to another. "I have something useful to teach you. Something that might save your lives."

She had our attention now, even Berenice's.

"What?" said Howard.

The fortune-teller gestured to the field around her. At once the Darkworld responded; the hairs on my arms rose. Tears in the universe opened all around us, like the world was merely made of fabric, the dark underside exposed.

"If a demon were to appear, right here, right now, any one of you could die. In fact, it's likely that the person it chooses as its host would perish instantly."

A chill swept through the group. I knew each of us was wondering the same thing: out of the group, who would the demon pick as its first victim? Would it be Claudia, or

Berenice, or Howard, who was always up for a fight? Or would the demon choose mild-mannered Cyrus—or Leo?

I recoiled from the thought, and from the accompanying cold feeling that I was the only one the demon couldn't choose, because I was immune to possession.

"It could be any of you." I could tell the fortune-teller chose her words with care. "I called you here because your lives are in danger from something far deadlier than the average shadow-beast. You need to be able to defend yourselves—and with more than just fire and light. If a true demon appears, there is a way to repel it from your mind. Don't use this lightly, because if misplaced, it can go horribly wrong. But I think you have all demonstrated that you possess the… maturity not to misuse this skill." I didn't miss her eyes flicker towards Howard for a moment.

"You sound like my old Chemistry teacher," said Howard. He still didn't look impressed.

The fortune-teller ignored him. "If a ghoul has managed to get past the Venantium's Barrier, then there is someone to be feared in this very area. You are the only people to my knowledge who do not have the Venantium's protection. Therefore, you will need to learn to defend yourselves."

"So get on with it already," said Berenice. "It's bloody freezing out here."

The fortune-teller looked at her sharply. She looked so imposing with her intense storm-grey eyes and her billowing black coat and wild fair hair that even Berenice seemed cowed. She lowered her gaze.

"To conjure a demon-proof shield—that is your goal. At first you'll only be able to keep shadow-beasts at bay, but with practise, you'll be able to repel all but the highest demons."

"Is that possible?" said Cyrus. "I know about the

Venantium's shields—our guardian used to tell us we'd learn if we joined up, but he never taught us anything about them."

"It is possible," said the fortune-teller, "but it isn't taught lightly."

She spread her arms wide, and the darkness between the gaps seemed to shift all around her. Then with one sweep of her right hand, a swathe of darkness moved to form a curtain in front of her. Somehow both black as night and semi-transparent, the shield surrounded her like a cloak.

Even Howard and Berenice looked impressed. "Can we try?" said Howard.

"You might not get it the first time," the fortune-teller warned. "But the basic gist is this. You need to imagine the Darkworld as like a long sheet of fabric, all around us."

Since this was what I'd been thinking anyway, I didn't have any trouble. But when it came to taking the shadows and using them to form a shield, this was where I fell down. It was like trying to keep a firm grip on a block of ice—and the Darkworld was just as cold. The darkness radiated iciness, and even I could feel it sapping away at my energy. Berenice started moaning that her hands were going blue, and it was more noticeable than ever that I was the only person who wasn't shivering.

Why do I need to learn this anyway? It wasn't as though I needed to conjure a shield to be safe from demons.

Maybe she wants me to keep the others safe, I thought. You could use the shield on as many people as you liked—and make it stronger by combining forces. That made sense.

Not that any of us had made much progress. Leo was the first to get the hang of grasping the darkness, but the shield never stayed in place for long; like a nebulous living creature, it slithered out of our grasp. Leo swore as the shield dropped.

"Nice one, bro," Cyrus called, attempting to drag the shadows towards himself. They moved in a whirlwind of black and grey, but again, as if swept aside by the wind buffeting the grass, the shield dissipated.

"What a waste of time," snarled Howard, blowing on his hands to warm them up.

We stayed there a good few hours. Neither Howard nor Berenice made much progress; perhaps the Darkworld could sense their impatience and refused to cooperate. Claudia managed to get a hold on the shadows on one occasion, but the biting coldness forced her to let go. Cyrus and Leo, however, were almost on a level of the fortune-teller by the end of the day. I watched in awe as the two brothers stood back to back and almost conducted the flow of shadowy smoke around them. Both had ice slivers in their hair by the time they dropped the shield.

As for me, I might not have felt the cold, but it didn't mean I was any good at manipulating the Darkworld. I was beginning to think of it as a personality all in itself. It certainly moved like a living thing. Though I supposed that it *was* mostly made up of spirits, which were living, if not in the conventional way.

I tried shutting my eyes to focus better, but all that happened was that Berenice walked into me, possibly on purpose.

"Hey!" she waved a hand in front of my face. "These aren't meditation classes, you know."

"I know that. I don't see you doing any better."

She snorted. "Come on, I thought you were the supreme magic-user."

"News flash? I'm not," I said. Whatever she thought was far off the mark.

"Stop arguing," the fortune-teller said, from where she stood watching, her hands buried in the pockets of her long black coat. "You'd do well to remember that you are on the same side—all of you. Fighting amongst ourselves is the worst thing we can do."

"Sure," said Berenice. "Whatever."

But when I looked at her, she didn't give me her usual glare. She returned to conjuring shields without another word. Sometimes I wondered what was going on in her head.

The fortune-teller stopped us when the sun began to sink over the hilltops, turning the yellow grass to gold.

"That's enough for now."

To my surprise, she escorted us all back to Blackstone. *She must be worried,* I thought, uneasy at the thought that something could unsettle even the fortune-teller. After the Skele-Ghoul had appeared on campus, though, nowhere felt safe.

We said goodbye to Howard, Berenice, and Cyrus in town, and the four of us began the walk back to campus along the country road.

"I have a question," Leo said to the fortune-teller. "How much do you know about what's going on? You're acting like you knew this would happen."

"I have always known that the Venantium's defences are not as faultless as they like to assume. There are cracks in the shield, if you know where to look—and no one knows that more than the members themselves."

"What, you think there's a traitor?" said Claudia.

"I believe the person responsible for the recent events is someone who knows the Venantium very well, whether they be a current member or a former one. But as to *who*… I cannot tell. There was a time when I knew every face that entered the gateway to the Venantium, but times change.

They need more help than ever, and as much as they might try to deny it, they are only strong together. The Barrier hangs upon a balance, and if it tips, ever so slightly, we might be lost to the Darkworld."

"So you're saying the demons might overpower the Barrier?"

The fortune-teller shook her head, deep sadness etched on her deceptively fair face. I had often been given reason to suspect that she was far older than she looked, and if ever her eyes looked old, it was now.

"The demons cannot take our world alone. As always, it is humans who we have reason to fear the most. This sorcerer is meddling with the very fabric of the Darkworld."

"Through making those Skele-Ghoul things?" said Leo.

"I fear that they are only the beginning. There is some information which is kept concealed for a reason, even from most *venators*. Mr Melmoth knew that as well as anyone, but…"

"Stop talking in circles," said Leo, his voice unexpectedly sharp. "I know you know more about Melmoth than you're letting on. Even his journal doesn't give much away. What was he looking for? What's this Death Child? It's no normal ghoul."

"That," said the fortune-teller, "is precisely what we should be afraid of. I *believe* the Death Child is a shape-shifting ghoul, but the fact that it is still present after I have spent the past two months searching with every method I have at my disposal proves that its summoner is no common sorcerer. Ghouls do not usually have a will of their own."

"And do you think this Death Child killed Melmoth and the vampires as well?" said Leo.

"I do not know. I haven't gathered enough information to be sure of a connection… but I do not believe in coincidence."

"Well, you *are* technically a fortune-teller," said Leo.

At that moment, we passed the ruins of the old Blackstone house. As usual, my eyes were drawn unwillingly to the stark black remains. Rooms had collapsed in on themselves, and the house leaned slightly to the left, its rotting frame barely supporting what was left of the upstairs floor.

The fortune-teller paused in front of the ruin. She wore that pensive, sad expression again, and shook her head. Then she carried on walking, giving no explanation.

We reached the foot of the hill and began the steady climb towards campus. The woods waited for us, and I found myself looking uneasily around as we stepped under cover of the sprawling trees. The image of the dismembered harpy was still fresh in my memory.

But we met no one. It seemed almost too quiet. On the path, I could usually hear singing and talking from campus, and there were always joggers and the occasional questing patrol of Role-Playing Society members on the path. It was like we were totally alone.

Then I heard laughter. Not the drunken laughter of students, but a quiet titter.

The Darkworld stirred around me and the pendant burned against my chest. I could sense a presence nearby that was tuned into the Darkworld—and that it wasn't human. I stiffened at almost exactly the same moment as the fortune-teller whispered, "It's here."

"Shit," said Claudia, as a girl stepped out from behind a tree.

She was my double; not merely someone who looked a bit like me, but my *exact double.* She even wore the same clothes as I did, like in the dream. Her tangled dark brown hair framed her pale face, and her violet eyes were shadowed, the result of sleepless nights.

That was the only difference. Her eyes were those of a demon.

"Holy shit," said Leo, looking at the girl in horror.

The fortune-teller faced the doppelganger, calmly. "What do you want?" she asked.

"I just want to play." I winced as the girl spoke in a mock-childlike way. It was creepy beyond belief to hear that voice coming out of my own mouth.

It's not me, I told myself.

"Oh, but I am," said the demon's voice in my head.

The girl threw back her head and laughed. It was a horrible sound, like hearing my own voice distorted almost out of recognition, but enough that I could still recognise it as mine. That made it even worse.

"I've heard about *you*," she said to the fortune-teller. "You think you know everything about us. You think you know our inmost secrets. But you don't have a clue what we can do."

She looked at me. "Your friend's a bit dim, isn't he? Fancy not noticing my eyes."

For a second I stared back, nonplussed. Then it hit me. *Conrad.*

"Why'd you do that?" I said.

"It was fun." She giggled again.

"Why are you pretending to be me?" I said. "You're the Death Child, aren't you?"

"Is that what they call me?" Another giggle.

"Why do you hate the Venantium?" Leo demanded.

The girl's face twisted. "They *stole my life*," she snarled.

"You're a demon. You don't *have* a life. Did you kill Mr Melmoth?"

"You know nothing about me!" shrieked the girl.

Holy crap, she's mad, I thought. "Okay," I said. "Why are you pretending to be me?"

"Because you're interesting to me," she said, her voice a petulant child's once again. "It's so *boring,* being stuck in this half-life. I can't even come and pay you a visit thanks to those pesky barriers. I had to send my Skele-Ghouls instead, and they're far less friendly."

"You killed that harpy? The Skele-Ghouls were yours?"

"They're disgusting, aren't they?" she said. "Horrible things. But they're trained to answer to any demon. Even me." She laughed. "He has no idea I took them. He won't be pleased. But it doesn't matter. He'll be next. I'll make him pay. I'll make them *all* pay."

"For what?" I said. "Who summoned you? Are they killing vampires?"

"Vampires?" She let out a brittle laugh. "You think I wanted to kill that sad loser who keeps following you? I admit it was tempting, but I won't waste my power on him."

The fortune-teller stepped forwards. "I have seen enough of your kind to know that original thinking isn't your forte," she said. "I don't suppose you want to reveal who your creator is?"

The girl laughed again. "That would spoil the game, wouldn't it?"

The fortune-teller raised a hand, and shadows gathered around her in a smoky cloud. Even I felt the temperature drop; the frost already coating the trees hardened, turning to ice. My breath fogged the air in front of me.

The girl's face stretched in a twisted smile. I wanted to hit her, do anything to break that awful parody of myself—but the fortune-teller gestured at me to fall back.

The shadows struck the doppelganger and she staggered backwards. She laughed, high and delighted, then her face twisted again. She let out a snarl and sprung at me like a wild animal. Caught off guard, I barely managed to fling out my arms to shield myself, ice forming.

A burning sensation ripped through the skin of my arms. It wasn't hot—it was deathly cold. But the ice was cracking; my skin felt like it was on fire. I screamed, yet at the same time I could hear my own laughter, underlain by the hissing laugh of a demon.

My vision went black. The doppelganger's laughter still echoed in my ears. The pendant burned against my chest.

"Don't fade away on us just yet, Ashlyn."

The pain was gone, but so was all other sensation. The world began to flicker back into being, tinted slightly purple.

Get out of my head, I told the demon.

"I am not in your head, human-demon."

You're lying. I blinked repeatedly, willing the world to go back to its normal spectrum of colour. It was like I was seeing through a purple glass lens. I knew I was lying on the ground, but I couldn't feel anything, only the pulsing energy of the Darkworld.

Is this how demons feel?

"Wouldn't you like to know?" said the demon.

Stop reading my mind! I thought, and tried to will feeling back into my body, like throwing off sleep paralysis.

And slowly, it came back. The purple faded, and the pain hit me again like a tidal wave. It was pain beyond tears. All other senses were dulled: I couldn't see, could barely hear the muffled voices of people around me.

I blacked out again, and this time the darkness stayed constant.

16

MIND GAMES

The first thing I saw when I awoke was the fortune-teller, bending over me.

"Ash? Can you speak?"

I started to say I didn't know, but the words came out as a slurred incoherent jumble. I tried again. "What happened?"

Claudia stepped into view. "You're damn lucky, girl, that's what happened."

I realised that we were in the fortune-teller's tent. The charms on the ceiling dazzled my eyes. I lay on my back on the bench, and I had a rush of déjà vu as I remembered being in this exact situation after the harpy had attacked me. I could smell something earthy, faintly herbal.

"The ghoul nearly killed you," said the fortune-teller. "I underestimated it. I had no idea that it had the sorcery skills of a human."

"What happened to it?" I said.

"The Death Child escaped. It's my fault—she attacked you so fast, and fled into the forest. I feared I might be too late to save you…"

"If it was so easy for her to kill me, why didn't she finish the job?" I said, sitting up. I felt dizzy, but I was no longer in pain.

"I don't think she meant to kill you," said the fortune-teller. "That would have... spoiled her game."

I wasn't sure I wanted to know what game that was. Whoever was in control of the demon, they knew how I used magic—the ghoul had hit me with the same ice-fire I used myself. Unless it *was* some kind of doppelganger, and we really were connected in some way.

You can't love. You can never be loved.

I shook my head. I'd thought demons knew nothing about me, but that ghoul had stolen every detail of my life, even to the extent that she could fool someone into thinking she was really me. How many people would tell the difference? Could you ever truly know anyone? Only demons could...

"What is it, Ashlyn?"

"Can demons read anyone's mind?" I said. "At any time?

"Yes. That is why it is pointless to lie to a demon."

Her words hung in the air like they were weighted. I shuddered, feeling more vulnerable than ever before. Every single time I'd been in the presence of a demon, all my thoughts had been laid bare. Every private thought, every whim, every contemplation...

"They wouldn't necessarily be concentrating on *your* mind all the time, Ash," said Claudia, as if *she'd* read my mind. Neither she nor Leo looked perturbed by the idea. But then again, neither of them had reason to expect contact from demons—certainly not as much as I did, at any rate.

"They read you through the Darkworld," said Leo. "They're tuned in to everyone in the immediate area, constantly. If you were totally alone with a demon, yeah, they'd be focused on you, but otherwise they wouldn't have any reason to be."

They would, I thought. *They speak to me.*

"Demons can use mind-communication," I said. "The one… last term, it spoke to me, in my head." No need to let on just how frequently this was occurring now.

"As spirits, it's how they communicate, yes," said the fortune-teller. "I learnt how to do it myself through deep study into the Darkworld, but few people are aware of the technique. It's a matter of contacting the surface thoughts, like using Influence, but on a more intimate scale. But meddling with the mind is something strongly condemned by the Venantium."

"Yeah, when they aren't using it themselves," I said, remembering the Angel Box. "Could the ghoul be reading my mind? Like, right now?"

"I doubt it. Mind-reading requires one to be strongly tuned into the Darkworld, and the ghoul cannot be so if she wishes to remain hidden from me. Strong she may be, but she is not stronger than I. She relies on her master—whoever that is."

I sighed and sank back onto the bench. No one said anything for a moment. I watched the tendrils of smoke from the burning incense sticks drift through the air like pale snakes.

"You need to stop nearly dying on us, Ash," said Leo.

"I'll try," I said. "Why is it always me?"

"Because you're a bad luck magnet?" said Claudia. "Honestly, no one can figure out demons. Wish we could read *their* minds."

"That would deprive you of your humanity," said the fortune-teller. "Only beings which are a part of the Darkworld entirely can use the connection to read others' thoughts. Even I don't have that power."

I had a feeling that that was an indirect way of saying that *I* wouldn't be able to read people's minds. Thinking about it, it was probably for the best. Anyone would be happier not knowing what people really thought of them.

"Well, anyway, demons tend to target the weak link," said Claudia. "They used to go for Berenice, mostly, before you came here. Till she learnt how to fight them off."

"It isn't like I can't fight them," I said, ashamed at how pathetic I must seem. I'd never seen any of the others suffer injury at the hands of a shadow-creature.

But then again, none of them are like me, I thought. Besides, that creature had taken a *venator* down. It could have killed any of us. So why hadn't it? I supposed it must have a particular grudge against them.

"I know," said Leo. "Hell, that ice-trick of yours is amazing. I've never seen anything like it. Talk about taking cold-shouldering literally."

"Do you know the limits of your power, Ash?" said Claudia.

"No, but I've never tried to freeze a lake or anything bigger. It only really happens when I'm angry, or protecting someone…"

"I can test you," said the fortune-teller. "Not now… you're still recovering. But another time."

"Right," I said. To my own surprise I felt hot anger rising in me. "I don't suppose you could have done that before I started accidentally freezing people? What if I'd done worse?"

The image of Terrence's face, sliced deeply by my own fingernails, crept to the forefront of my mind, like something wanted to nudge it into view.

The fortune-teller said nothing. Again, she looked deeply sad, almost pitying.

I couldn't have cared less. I didn't care how childish or irrational it was; right then I blamed her for everything that had happened recently. It was stupid, like I was a child expecting the adults to set the world to rights. But then, she was the all-powerful sorceress. I was just... an eighteen-year-old human-demon with no idea how much of a danger I posed to the world.

I held the anger in check, even as I felt ice start to form on my fingertips. I thought the fortune-teller was avoiding my eye, but then I followed her gaze and realised it was on the pendant around my neck. The amethyst glowed, faintly, and my skin tingled as the stone brushed against my collarbone.

"I would advise you against going into the forest again. Take the bus back to the university from the station. It is best if you do not travel alone—nothing will attack you when you are surrounded by other students."

Why? I thought. *Surely you know that I'm the one attracting all the trouble?*

The fortune-teller gave a tight nod of dismissal. "You had better leave. I managed to get past the harpies without being seen, but it was close. I dare not reveal myself tonight. You should know... the Venantium have me listed as a suspect for the ghoul summonings."

"They *what?*" said Claudia. "Are they completely dense? If it wasn't for you, they'd probably have overrun the town. I saw you," she added. "Don't pretend you haven't been adding your own defences to campus."

The fortune-teller nodded. "It's true that I don't have absolute faith in their protection. But they see me as a rogue sorceress out to make trouble. I have made enemies of too many sorcerers who have gone to them for protection."

"How'd you manage that?" asked Leo. "Did you stand in the cemetery handing out leaflets saying 'The Venantium Suck'?"

"It's just 'cos no one trusts a rogue sorceress," said Claudia. "Closed-minded idiots. We'd better be getting back, anyway. Do you have anything else to warn us against? Any more of those Skele-Ghouls walking around?"

"I have scanned the entire town. There's nothing. I would guess that the girl is still hiding in the woods."

"Well, there goes my morning walk," I muttered.

"Make sure you're careful."

I said nothing, ducking under the tent flap before I lost it completely. I couldn't control the anger; it followed me like a cloud of icy fog.

"Holy shit, it's freezing!" yelped Claudia. I realised I really *was* lowering the temperature. Thankfully I managed to stifle my instinct to apologise. *Moron,* I berated myself. *That's the kind of careless thinking that'll give you away.*

I felt hyperaware of the presence of the Darkworld even as we walked out into the streets of Blackstone. The town didn't look the same to me now, I thought as we waited for the bus, even though I knew that outwardly nothing had changed. The cobblestone streets and shadowy buildings, the Gothic cathedral and towering headstones in the graveyard had always looked vaguely sinister, but there was a new aura of menace to everything, now I knew that even here, in my once-safe haven, there were demons.

And that, really, was why I was so angry. Demons had invaded my private world, the only place where they'd never disturbed me before. Last term, all the crazy shit happened only when I was away from campus——at least, apart from Terrence and David messing with my head...

I wondered if David knew any more than I did about what was happening. Probably not. Judging from the Venantium's leaflets, they were clueless, and could only "urge any sorcerers to be wary when using magic, as we will be policing the Darkworld surrounding the area closely."

And a fine job they were doing of it. I might not have received the best impression of them, coloured as it had been by the others, yet I'd always implicitly trusted that *someone* was keeping the area safe from the demons. Now I knew that there was a creepy doppelganger running around, unchecked. Wanting to kill them.

"Ash, wait!" said Leo.

I'd unintentionally stormed ahead. I slowed down to let him catch up, breathing heavily half from exhaustion, half from anger.

"Look, I can't stand seeing you all worked up like this. That doppelganger's a menace. It makes me sick thinking of her walking around hurting people. The last thing I want is people blaming you for what *she* does."

"I'm surprised it hasn't happened already," I said. "I mean, she looks exactly like me."

"She doesn't look like you. Not at all."

A lump rose in my throat. "She's stronger than I am," I whispered.

"Like hell she is."

Tears pricked my eyes. How could he put that much faith in me?

"We can kill her," said Leo. "You can kill her."

I shook my head. "She's like a demon. She can make me see things that aren't there. That's one step away from mind-domination, right? She nearly killed me. It makes no sense that she didn't."

"You're not gonna get killed," said Leo, and he sounded so certain I wanted to believe it.

Wait. The doppelganger spoke to me in my dream. Had it *really* spoken to me? Had the dream been more than my own subconscious, but an actual encounter, on some other plane, with the demon? I vaguely remembered considering the possibility before—the idea that demons could manipulate the mind, even from the other side of the Barrier. Even here. Sleep paralysis and nightmares could well have been down to be more than my subconscious.

If demons could read my mind, could they control dreams, too? The thought made my flesh creep all over. Was I safe anywhere, even inside my own head?

17

HAUNTED

The first vision happened in an English lecture.

One second I was scribbling notes on Victorian poets, trying to keep up with the lecturer—the next, a girl appeared in front of me so suddenly I almost fell off my seat.

"Hi, Ash."

I recognised that whisper; it danced down my spine like an ice-cold finger, and suddenly I really, really didn't want to look up.

But I couldn't help myself. I raised my head to meet the doppelganger's gaze.

The Ash-double smiled, violet eyes locked on me. It was *standing in the desk.*

"You okay, Ash?" said Sarah.

I didn't answer. I couldn't take my eyes off the apparition. It wasn't there—at least, not quite. The doppelganger was semi-transparent, like a dark space, or a demon. But that wasn't possible. Not here.

I looked down out of habit, but the pendant was hidden beneath my shirt. It wasn't burning. I'd have felt it.

"You're not dreaming this time," said the demon, as if she'd read my thoughts. *"I can, Ashlyn. Your head is like a window to me."*

Stop doing that! I thought back, hand clenching around my pen.

"But it's in my nature, Ashlyn. If you could read minds, wouldn't you use it to your best advantage?"

No. I'd respect people's privacy. Strangely, the more I talked to the demon, the less she sounded like me. She might look like my exact double, but her mannerisms and way of speaking were different enough that even without the mind-speak, it should be obvious that we weren't the same person.

"You're such a fascinating character, Ashlyn. You still try to deny it?"

I'm not like you. You're a mind-meddling soulless bitch.

"Soulless? That I can't deny. But I thought you didn't even believe in souls, Ashlyn."

Stop reading my thoughts.

"I know everything about you, Ash. No one understands you better than me."

Something inside me snapped. *Fuck off.*

My hands were shaking. I'd almost forgotten I was in the middle of a lecture theatre; had she been solid, I might have hit her.

"You can't hide from me, Ash. I am you."

And she faded away.

I breathed out, unclenching my fists. I heard a faint crunching sound as I did so, and quickly hid my hands under the desk before anyone asked why they were covered in ice. And I'd snapped my pen clean in two.

Was I hallucinating, or had the girl found some way of manifesting in spirit form? Whatever it might say about my mental state, I hoped against hope that it was the former.

Like I'd be let off that easily.

She kept appearing. Silent as a demon, she came out of nowhere, always when I least expected it. I walked back from lectures with Alex and Sarah—avoiding Conrad—and there she was, hovering over the quadrangle, waving at passers-by. My blood ran cold. *Don't look up,* I told the universe in general, but as no one pointed at the sky, I concluded that she only intended to freak me out. It worked.

Back at my flat, I turned the key in the lock to see her materialise right out of the door. I couldn't hold myself back from jumping, which startled Alex and Sarah.

"You okay, Ash?"

"Yeah. Um, thought I saw something. No matter."

"Just your sanity breaking, Ashlyn," the doppelganger whispered.

Go away.

Alex and Sarah stared as I slammed the door on the illusion.

Great. Now I'm the freak that stares at nothing. Again.

I spent the evening in my room. As we had more deadlines, and everyone was busy—Sarah with her new job, Alex with her new boyfriend—no one really questioned it, but I'd forgotten about the Literature Society General Meeting. Alex knocked on my door when she got in to tell me that they'd voted Tombstone Hill as the location of the Halloween trip—*that night.* Like I needed anything else to worry about. I had no idea so many people were so keen on the idea of spending a cold winter night on the floor of an empty old house.

They can't go there. It's where Mr Priestley died. I can't let them go there.

My mind whirled. How could I deal with this? I thought about texting Leo, but he had enough to worry about already. Still, I couldn't leave this alone. My two lives were colliding and I hadn't a clue what to do.

My phone buzzed in my hands and I nearly dropped it.

"Crap," I whispered.

It was a text from Leo. "Mr Melmoth's body's been stolen. The Ghouls came to the catacombs today. I'm going."

No. He couldn't go there. Not alone.

I made my mind up. I'd run after Leo. We'd both go to the fortune-teller. She knew how to do Influence on a major scale. She could stop my friends going near that house, and help Leo find out who'd stolen his guardian's body.

There I was, putting all my trust in her again. But what else was there to do?

"I'm coming. Wait for me," I texted.

I got lucky. I ran out of my flat at the same time as Leo crossed in front of my block, and caught up with him, panting.

"Ash, you really don't have to come."

"I've got—to do something." I gasped. "My friends are idiots and have voted on spending tonight at Tombstone Hill."

"You're kidding me."

"It was meant to be the LitSoc Halloween trip, but it got postponed. For some reason they want to spend the night in a haunted house," I said.

"What, on Valentine's Day?"

"Is it?" The thought hadn't crossed my mind; I'd been so preoccupied with everything else. "Sorry. I know it's shit timing. But I've got to talk to the fortune-teller. She can stop them. I know she's got better things to do, but I can't let them go to that place. The doppelganger... she's been turning up everywhere. Like waking visions."

"Shit, really?"

"I've never heard of a ghoul being able to manipulate someone from the other side of the Barrier like that."

"That makes two of us," said Leo. "I've gotta go, anyway. Cy texted me, I think he's already there. The *venators* are being totally useless about it."

"Then we'll talk to the fortune-teller."

"Not sure she's been much help, but all right." Leo sighed.

"I'm sorry." I wished there was more I could say, but the words wouldn't come. To lose his guardian again... I couldn't even imagine what that must feel like.

"It's okay, Ash. I'm glad you're here."

We hurried through the forest, as neither of us had the patience to wait for a bus. A voice in the back of my head told me that this was a bad idea, that we were tempting fate, but I took no notice. We had bigger problems.

"Shit," said Leo, halting in the middle of the path. "Did you hear something?"

No. Not now!

Coldness stabbed me all over, like a thousand icy knives. The pendant around my neck burned.

"Do you feel that?"

Leo's eyes were wide. "Shit. It's them."

A clawed hand grabbed my ankle.

I jumped backwards, right into the grip of one of them. I spun around out of reach. Silent, walking skeletons had crept up all around us, some walking, some half-crawling as though they couldn't support their own weight. I looked down and saw that a skeletal hand gripped my foot. I could see every bone in the hand, some cracked, all covered in the mossy sheen of the long-dead, long-buried.

Violet eyes stared out of its skull, unnatural; and I saw

the dark space behind the skeleton, the swirling mass of shadows.

Fear had stopped my heart in my chest, but now it started pounding. I kicked out and the brittle bones shattered. Heat and light flared next to me and I looked towards the source. Leo grappled with one of them, fire streaming down his arms. The ghoul screamed, a high-pitched keening that raised every hair on my body. The blackness vanished, the violet eyes winked out, and the charred bones dropped to the ground.

I flared ice-fire as a warning, but they continued to come at me. They were clumsy, flimsy as scarecrows, yet the demonic forces kept them upright. Bones splintered, scattering, falling to the ground like leaves.

Then I saw her, standing amongst the dead, wearing a positively gloating expression.

"When will you learn that you can't escape me, Ash?"

Her skin glowed in the weak light, giving her—me—a ghostly appearance.

"Yes, it was *a stupid decision to come out tonight. I always know where you are."*

Stop reading my mind! I screamed, as ice fire flared from my hands.

"Don't you mean our *mind?"*

She stepped forwards to face me, holding out her own palms, which flared with blue, just like mine. *She's solid this time. No illusion.*

"You're going to regret this, Ash."

But anger had taken over me by now. Anger—and humiliation at having my face stolen by a monster. I stepped forwards to face the demon. Hands clawed at my feet, but I kicked them aside. I wasn't going to lose to her again. I couldn't.

The pendant around the doppelganger's neck glowed, and mine did likewise.

"Leave this world behind and become who you truly are, Ash."

"Like hell I will!" I shouted, and shot a dagger of ice directly at her demon's heart.

Laughing, the girl dodged. Then she fired back—but not at me. At Leo.

I reached out to the Darkworld and grabbed handfuls of shadows. Leo did likewise, wrapping them around us like a semi-transparent shield. The ice-fire simply glanced off it.

"Nice try, demon!" Leo shouted. The shadows had knocked the Skele-Ghouls out of the way, but they still stood around us, like limp, awkward puppets.

The doppelganger flew at me; before I could react, she passed right through the shield and grabbed me by the throat, lifting me off the ground. She was unnaturally strong, and I fought for breath, my hands clawing at hers, struggling to break free.

"If I push you to the brink of death, will you give in?"

No! I cried silently, kicking out both physically and mentally. The Darkworld responded and as my vision flashed purple. A jolt ran through me like an electric current and the other girl screamed.

Her hands were ablaze with a blue fire, but it wasn't her own. Somehow I'd broken through her shield. She cried out in pain; Tears ran down her face and a shudder of disbelief rolled through me. She was a demon. She couldn't feel pain in the same way humans did—could she?

As this thought crossed my mind, the flames faded. She'd dropped to her knees, but as she looked up at me, her face etched with lines of pain, pure hatred shone from her violet eyes.

She croaked, in a voice part demon, part me, "You'll

pay for that, Ash. You and your friend here. In fact, I'll kill him. In front of you." A smile twisted her features again. "Yes, that should do it. It should help you see that you really don't have a choice."

"Leo!" I shouted, but too late. She raised her hands and shot a stream of pure darkness at us. Leo conjured a shield in response whilst directing a jet of fire at her, but she dodged. Darkness streamed from her palms, weaving around us, trying to find a gap in the shield.

"Aren't you going to help your friend, Ashlyn?"

I didn't know what to do to defend us other than add my own strength to Leo's shield and hope it wouldn't break. The Darkworld shuddered as two parts of it were set against each other.

Without warning, a tremor ran through the shield like the first gust of a hurricane.

Leo looked at me. His forehead glistened with sweat.

"We can beat her, Ash," he said.

The girl laughed, an unearthly squeal of pure delight.

Then the ground split beneath my feet, and I fell down into deeper darkness.

18

TRAPPED

I screamed and soil filled my mouth. Choking, I tried to spit it out. I was still falling, the earth giving way as I did so. I tried helplessly to grab hold of something solid, but encountered only crumbling dirt that broke into pieces at my touch.

I didn't know how long I fell, but it seemed timeless. Wind rushed past me, roaring in my ears. It felt as though I was trapped in an earthy cocoon, dislodged soil and bone fragments hitting me all over. Every time I hoped there was a solid landing beneath my body, it gave way to nothing.

Hands grabbed me, skeletal hands; the Skele-Ghouls were falling, too. A grinning skull flashed past, and finger-nails scratched at my face. I hit out, knocking the mass of bones off me. I kept smacking into rocks and other falling debris. Once, a chunk of rock crashed into the back of my head and stars winked before my eyes.

Light flared from my forehead, but it lit up only earth and swirling darkness. There was no one else, only a tunnel leading down, down, down.

"*Leo!*" I cried; even my scream had died to a whisper.

But the fall was slowing; I could hear again, strange echoing shrieks punctuating stretches of eerie silence. Without warning, my back hit the ground and I rolled over on a slightly spongy surface. *Damp soil*, I thought dazedly, barely able to comprehend that I'd survived the fall.

I lay still, drawing deep, shuddering breaths. Every part of me felt numb.

When I could finally bring myself to move, I conjured another light. I was in a small cave, barely a couple of metres either way, and alone. No sign of any Skele-Ghouls —or Leo. What if he—?

No, I told myself. I wasn't going down that road. I had to find a way out.

There were tunnels on either side of me. I couldn't take too long to choose or I'd really start to panic. I was shaking already, and when I stood up, I nearly passed out. I dug my fingers into the wall, staying upright, trying to will away the fog at the edges of my vision.

Leo, I'll find you, I thought desperately. Someone would come to help... and even though I was God-knew-how many miles underground, the tunnels had to lead some-where. I hadn't even known they came this close to campus. Either some giant worm had dug them, or people had. I steered my thoughts away from giant worms, too. *Just walk. Don't think.*

I stopped as a chilling screech froze the blood in my veins. *Harpies.*

Before I could run or duck, they flew at me, scratching at my arms. I yelled, contacting the Darkworld almost before I was aware of it. Ice fire consumed the birds, and they burst into black ashes before my eyes. I stared at my own hands, hardly able to believe I'd destroyed them so easily.

Then another sound started up, a wail like a grief-stricken cry. It seemed to come from all around me. Although it wasn't as eerie as the sound of the harpies, it brought out the same flood of fear in me as a fire alarm accompanied by the smell of smoke would.

Had I triggered an alarm, or was there something even worse waiting for me ahead?

I couldn't stay where I was, so I decided to carry on, hoping I wasn't making a huge mistake.

The wailing continued to echo through the tunnel, like a siren, building to a crescendo. I threw my arms over my head to try and muffle the sound and ran flat out, panic taking over, my feet barely skimming the ground, even when I had to wade across a rushing underground river. I hoped it was just regular water.

Another harpy flew at me and I reacted without thinking, hitting out with a hand that was suddenly enclosed in solid ice—the harpy exploded into dust.

It frightened me how quick I'd reacted, but by now I was beyond terror. My feet stumbled over rocks and holes; at one point, I had to crawl under a sagging ceiling that threatened to collapse—and still the siren wailed, on and on.

Then rough hands grabbed me and pulled me out of the crevice. Human hands.

"So this is the little tunnel rat." Sharp eyes glared from beneath a hard helmet which looked out of place, considering he wore a sharp navy blue suit. My heart sank. He was with the Venantium.

"Come with me," he said. "You have some explaining to do, young miss."

He pulled me after him, never once loosening his vice-grip on my arm, but I was in too much shock to put up a fight. He kept up a continual mutter that told me the Venantium wanted to question me not only about killing harpies, but about the Skele-Ghouls. The ghouls were walking the streets in Blackstone.

"That wasn't me!" I protested. "There's a ghoul——"

But he didn't listen to a word. When the long, long walk was finally over, we came to a row of caves behind barred doors. *Cells*, I thought, as he threw me into one.

A second before I hit the stone floor, ice shot out of my palms, breaking my fall.

"Don't try anything!" shouted my captor, as the door slammed.

I sat and stared at the door in disbelief, wondering how in hell I'd ended up in this situation. How could they blame *me*? And Leo… where was he? Had he fallen too? Was he lost somewhere down here? I contacted the Dark-world and tried to will the locks to break at my touch, but whatever I did, nothing worked. Of course they were magic-proof.

"What did you do?" said a voice. It came from the cell opposite me. Someone was leaning against the bars of his own cage; with the poor lighting down here, I couldn't see any more than an outline. "They're really stirred up."

"I didn't do anything," I snapped. "A ghoul attacked me and there's Skele-Ghouls in the tunnels, and now they're blaming me for it."

"Tough break," said the guy.

I glared at him, even though I knew he wouldn't be able to see me.

"Say," he said. "Do you know anything about this Death Child? They say they're bringing her in soon. She's supposed to be a shape-shifting demon child."

I said nothing. A horrible thought had crossed my mind—I couldn't believe it hadn't occurred to me before.

"Do you? Wait a minute…" He paused. "Are you her?"

"No," I said.

I conjured a light, unable to stand not being able to see. The cell was only a few metres wide, and the ceiling barely cleared six feet. This couldn't be made for permanent accommodation; there was nothing in the cell, not even a bed.

With the light, I could also see my neighbour. He was a skinny guy who looked to be in his early twenties, with pale blond hair. He didn't look dangerous, but you could never be sure.

He saw me looking at him. "You better not delay them," he said. "I've been here for hours. I want out of here."

"What did you do?" I said, curious despite myself.

"Broke the law, same as you, right?"

"I guess," I said. "But I didn't do what they think I did."

"Doesn't mean a thing. Nothing changes their minds."

This wasn't helping. I needed to get out. I had to make sure Leo was okay—to say nothing of everyone in Blackstone, the thousand ordinary people who were probably running terrified from the Skele-Ghouls. And my friends were going to a haunted house.

I rested my head on the bars, momentarily overwhelmed. There had to be a way out of this.

"I can help you."

My blood turned to ice. I jumped back from the bars as though they were electrically charged and spun on the spot, my eyes roving all over the cell. No one was there. Human or otherwise.

"You can't see me, Ashlyn."

"What's up?" said the guy.

I shook my head. Either I was cracking up—or something really bad was going to happen.

Ice formed on my palms, and I had no control over it.

The pendant burned against my neck, and my hands moved by themselves, gripping the bars of the cell. Ice pinned them into place, and smoke began to seep out between the cracks.

I was *melting* the bars.

"What are you doing?"

"I don't kn—" I choked, the demon rising within me, cutting off my voice. My vision flashed purple, and a rush of searing anger overwhelmed me.

The guy yelled, "Demon!"

Everything happened very fast. Several shouts echoed down the corridor, and people came running. The ice disappeared and I let go of the bars—which had dissolved into shapelessness—just as the doors burst open. Several people ran in and seized me. A suffocating feeling descended on me, even worse than the sensation of falling through the earth. It was like intense air pressure, and pain, sharp pain grasping me all over like knives.

Then... nothing.

"Don't try using magic, demon. It's blocked." The speaker was a man with a face that looked like it was carved out of granite. He wore a badge which read, *Senior Supervisor.*

Blocked. *Is that what this is?* It felt like something fundamental was missing, like a vital piece of me was gone.

"I'm not a demon," I said.

"You were spotted using demonic magic on no fewer than *seven* occasions, as our various witnesses will confirm —and now you're being held responsible for the disappearances of several Venantium members in the tunnels. I think it's high time for you to be questioned."

And, a short, but tense walk later, I was back in the large, spacious chamber with the metal walls. The clinical smell in the air and the staring *venators* in sharp suits made me even more aware that I was covered in dirt. My jeans were soaked to the knees from the water I'd waded through.

This time, several people waited for me at the end of the room. I recognised only one of the faces: Jude. He wore a look of gloating triumph tempered by piousness.

"Doctor Philips will be your interrogator," he said, barely concealing a laugh, as the other man handed me over. My fists clenched, but there was no rush of cold from the Darkworld. They really had blocked my connection.

A hard-faced woman stepped forwards. She had a stern look that reminded me of the strictest teachers at school, the expression of one who rarely smiled.

"Come with me, Miss Temple."

Back through the metal door into the room where the Angel Box waited, glowing with that eerie, alien light. Fear rushed through me, and the only thing that made me follow her into the room and sit down was the desperate thought that they had to believe my story—I was innocent; I'd never hurt anyone.

She was direct and impersonal as though she questioned someone as robotic as herself. I answered her questions truthfully, admitting that Leo and I had been walking in the forest by campus when we'd run into the ghouls. I told her all about the doppelganger, as well as the connection to the grave robberies and that someone was summoning dark spirits to possess corpses. There were some things I kept quiet, such as my suspicions about the doppelganger being linked to my being human-demon, and anything that might give away what I was, but it was hard to think clearly, knowing that Leo was still out there somewhere, and that the world outside was in chaos. Her sceptical expression made the panic fluttering in my chest threaten to spill over, but I kept talking. Her expression never wavered.

"Please believe me," I finished. "I don't know who summoned it, but it's the ghoul you're after. She's the one you want."

"She?" said the woman. "You're talking about the demon as an individual? Were *you* the summoner?"

"It looks just like me!" I said. I didn't seem to have any control over my own mouth. It babbled all by itself. "I don't know who has something against me, but someone summoned it and made it look like me. Why would I want to create a double of myself?"

"I don't doubt that you young people have all kinds of schemes in mind. Magical ability in youngsters is a danger. I am in favour of it being eradicated. Even with our close monitoring, this can happen." Her cold stare was as penetrating as a demon's. "Would you like to tell me how you gained the knowledge to transgress our Barriers and bring the demon right here?"

"I didn't," I said. "I'd never been in the tunnels before the last time I came here. I didn't even know this place existed until a few months ago. It's the truth."

"This will test your truthfulness," she said, her mouth set in a grim line. "Get into the Angel Box."

"I thought my magic was blocked," I said, swallowing.

"So it is, but merely temporarily—for now. Even if the Box finds you to be truthful, you still used magic to attack our harpies, and for that, you must be disciplined as a caution. You are not a child; you are an adult and must take responsibility for your actions. We have therefore decreed that your connection to the Darkworld must be permanently blocked."

Her words rang in my ears as I stepped into the box, which again, muted all sound. White light flared around me, and I felt as though I floated in a dream. This couldn't be happening.

They'll find out what I really am, I thought. *If the Angel Box reveals the truth, I'm not safe. There's no way. They'll have me locked up for good, or worse.*

The box shuddered around me, bringing me out of my dark thoughts. I looked down; I'd been positive I felt a trembling beneath my feet.

I glanced back up at the woman, but she was no longer looking at me. Several people ran into the room, shouting, although I couldn't hear anything. I watched Dr Philips argue with the intruders, all of whom wore expressions ranging from desperation to stark terror. These must be lower-level *venators*—those fighting on the surface. The Skele-Ghouls had come to town.

I shifted position, and no one noticed when I pressed my hands against the glass, trying to find a way to open the door. But there didn't seem to be one. I ran my hands over the edges and found only smooth corners, no door hinges. Horror rose within me as I saw everyone leaving the room, seemingly forgetting I was even there.

"Let me out!" I screamed, as the ground shook again. I banged frantically on the glass, but it was in vain. I was alone.

The ground continued to shake, and the glass vibrated beneath my hands and feet. I searched over and over again, turning to each corner of the glass, trying to break past the block in my mind. I could sense it, the cold of the Darkworld, like it was on the other side of the glass wall, but as with the real thing, no matter how hard I knocked, it didn't budge an inch. My hands felt bruised, and I lost the fear that the glass would shatter and cut my hands. Instead, I had to face the real possibility that there was no way to break the glass at all. *Oh, God. No.*

"Need help, Ash?"

I looked up and saw my own reflection staring out of the glass. But it wasn't really my reflection, of course. We looked at each other, hazel eyes into violet, and I waited for her to smirk, come out with a snarky comment, taunt me.

"Come to laugh at me?" I said. My voice echoed strangely, caught within the glass.

The glass door fell open. *"Aren't you going to get out?"*

"Why are you helping me?" I asked.

Instead of answering, she faded away. I stepped gingerly out of the case, panting hard from the exertion of banging on the glass. *I have to get out of here.*

"Ashlyn?" Someone appeared in the doorway. Jude.

"What's going on?" I said, wary in case he came at me and shoved me into the case again.

"We're being attacked," he said. "You'd better come with me. I'll take you back to the surface."

Attacked? Who by, the Skele-Ghouls? Or... Leo and the others wouldn't do anything stupid to rescue me, would they? They didn't even know I was down here, I reminded myself, as Jude led me down another tunnel.

We walked for a long time, yet I was so preoccupied that it wasn't until I recognised several of the tunnels Leo had marked that I realised we'd long-missed the turning to the way to the surface.

"Where are we going?" I asked him, feeling the prickling of a suspicion. He didn't answer.

I stopped. "Hold it," I said.

He turned back to face me. "What?"

"This way doesn't lead to the surface."

"It's an alternative way. The main exit's blocked."

All the same, my feeling of foreboding didn't diminish. I was about to protest again, when without warning, something crashed into the back of my head and all went black.

19

BURIED ALIVE

I awoke in an open grave.

There was earth all around me, forming solid walls either side, the top open to the heavens—or at least, that was what I first thought. But then I realised that what I supposed was sunlight was the combined light of torches forming a ring around the wide chamber I was in, and the ceiling was lost in shadows black as the night sky.

I sat up, breathing fast. I had a sudden mental image of earth falling onto me and stood, looking for a way to climb out. It was shallow, and I could just about get a grip on the sides—

It was only when I saw a face staring down at me that I remembered what happened.

Jude said, "You're awake."

"Where am I?" I said.

"You're in the tomb of my ancestors," he said, gesturing around us. I couldn't see much above the high walls of the grave, but the murmurs of voices in the background suggested that there were several other people there.

"Huh?"

"The Melmoth family were once respectable," he muttered, half to himself. "Then my invalid uncle had to ruin everything. Well, you belong here with them, abomination that you are."

"Huh?" I said again. Maybe it was because the back of my head still throbbed, but this didn't make any sense to me. "You mean Mr Melmoth?"

"The very same."

"He was… your uncle?"

"He was no relation of mine," he spat out the words. "He rose to power despite being a monster. But I knew his secret. I knew he was a degenerate."

It took a moment for my thoughts to catch up. "Leo said… he said you led the campaign to get him sacked."

"He was right. My uncle was a demon sympathiser as well as a monster."

"You betrayed your own family?"

"Family!" he spat. "My parents died when I was a child, and everyone tried to shield the truth from me. But when I came here four years ago, I found out my uncle's little secret. I knew I alone could stop him from infecting the Venantium. He had to be removed. All of them have to die."

"You killed the vampires that had the cure."

"Cure!" He laughed. "That was a lie. What better way to draw them out? I was going to save Melmoth for last, but I couldn't resist it when he came so close to campus. Chasing you. You've been puzzling me for months, Ashlyn. I knew you were no regular spirit or ghoul. You act of your own volition, and can do things no other demon can. Mr Priestley was a good man. You shouldn't have killed him."

"I didn't kill him," I said. "That person wasn't me. It was the doppelganger. It looks just like me."

"A doppelganger. What a pity. It might have been convincing, were it not for the evidence before me."

"What evidence?" I said. My heart was pounding. "I'm human!"

"You're a demon," said Jude. "I have your demon heart right here."

He held out the pendant.

"I've tested it," he said. "I know."

And with a grim smile on his face, he extended his hand, flames engulfing it.

Pain. Such pain ripped through me that every cell on my body seemed to scream. Laughter echoed around the chamber, but I couldn't see, couldn't feel anything beside the pain. My vision flashed purple and then black, and the demon inside me cried out in a voice devoid of humanity. Two screams became one as human and demon alike were consumed.

Then it stopped. A small, hard object hit my face, but the pain was still too strong to open my eyes. My skin seared as though every inch of me had been burned like the pendant.

The pendant. I felt it burning at my side. He'd dropped it into the tomb, and somehow, I managed to move my hand to clasp it.

I floated, hearing voices, shouts, but in a disconnected way, as though I was hovering in another world entirely. Maybe the Darkworld.

Then I recognised a voice amongst the clamour.

"Ash!"

Someone took me in their arms. My eyes flicked open.

"Leo?" I said.

"Don't you die on me!" he said. "I've spent too damn long walking down these tunnels for you to die."

"Nice to know you care," I coughed, but before the

words were out of my mouth, he'd pulled me one-hand-edly out of the grave and was kissing me.

Someone made sick noises.

"Berenice, cut it out," said Cyrus's voice. "Seriously, though, bro, you really nailed the cliché romantic rescue scene."

"Except with it being in a crypt," said Claudia. "I'm not sure that counts as romantic."

"Fair point," said Leo. I was too dazed to do any more than stare at him, at his messy, dirt-specked dark hair and concerned grey-blue eyes.

Then I looked around me, thoroughly confused. Claudia, Cyrus, Berenice, and Howard were standing beside the rows of graves.

"What—what the hell...?" I said, standing. "What are you all doing here? Where's Jude? And who else was in here?"

"The fortune-teller," said Leo. "She clocked him one. It was amazing. She's been chasing the Skele-Ghouls," he added. "I've no idea how she knew, but she was on the scene as soon as you fell down the tunnel—I owe it to her that I didn't fall, too. I think she put a shield on you to cushion your landing, but by then the ghoul had run off, so we went after her. And then we found... never mind. What happened to you? Why did Jude have you in a *grave*?"

"I was with the Venantium," I said. "They blocked my magic. They were questioning me. But then something happened and they all left. I think it was the Skele-Ghouls. The doppelganger let me out of the Angel Box and I was going to leave. Jude said he was going to lead me outside, but he knocked me out and brought me here..."

The pendant was still clenched in my fist; I transferred it to my jeans pocket.

"He thought you were the doppelganger?" said Leo. I nodded.

"He killed Mr Melmoth," I said. "And the other vampires. He said he was ashamed…" My voice shook, and I realised I was trembling all over. A delayed shock effect.

"It's okay," said Leo. "We're all here now, and the fortune-teller, too. We'll make Jude pay. There's a special place in hell with his name on it."

"*Why* are you guys all here?" I said. "How's it possible?"

"I was talking to the *venators* about Melmoth," said Cyrus. "Then they got an emergency call to the surface. So I went to find these guys."

"We were at the pub," said Claudia. "And the fortune-teller showed up with Leo, saying you'd been taken. She used some kind of magic to scour the tunnels and took off after you. Dragged us miles underground. I've got blisters like you wouldn't believe."

"So is Jude working for the Ghouls?" said Leo. "The sly bastard legged it—we were on the other side of the chamber. We couldn't catch him."

"I don't know," I said. "He didn't mention the Ghouls —he was just talking about how much he hates vampires. Melmoth was his uncle."

"That's the connection!" said Leo. "His own dad was the leader of the Righteous. He'll have been raised to hate vampires. I guess he just decided to take matters into his own hands."

"He pretended there was a cure. I should have guessed —Conrad didn't know about it."

"None of us guessed. He played us all, even the venators." He looked pale and angry, but a determined glint shone in his eyes. "Want to get a hit in before I finish him off?" He turned to Cyrus.

"Damn right." Cyrus's jaw was set. "I never agreed with Melmoth on a lot of things, but the bastard who killed him won't get away with it." The brothers shared a nod of understanding.

I managed to calm my breathing enough to focus on my surroundings. "Where's the fortune-teller?"

Leo pointed to the other side of the chamber.

"She went after Jude—that way. Told us to stay behind and help you. She chased him away, threw some kind of shadow-magic at him. The door's blocked. I think they're fighting."

Fighting. The fortune-teller was a formidable fighter, I had no doubt of that—but all the same, the thought of Jude's maniacal expression filled me with unease. "Have any of you seen the doppelganger?"

Leo shook his head. "Did you say she *saved* you?"

"Don't ask me why. She disappeared right away, leaving me to get taken down here by Jude. If you ask me, she was involved with this, too…"

But that couldn't be right. She was a demon, and even Jude surely wouldn't resort to teaming up with the enemy. Still, it made even littler sense for her to help me after trying to kill me so many times.

"I'd put nothing past him," said Leo, who was clearly thinking along the same lines. "He sees murder as perfectly fine. But the fortune-teller says Jude used regular spirits to drain the vampires' life energy, not demons."

"How'd she know all that?"

"She caught him in the act, apparently," said Cyrus. "He ran off. That's when he must have gone back to headquarters, when the ghouls attacked. It would have looked suspicious for him not to be there."

"But he led me down here," I said. "Where are we, anyway?"

"In the catacombs under the cathedral in Crowley," said Leo. "I don't know why Jude would have brought you *here* to kill you—it gives me a bad feeling. Apart from all the Skele-Ghouls, that is."

A shrill wail echoed around us.

"Please don't tell me the dead are rising now," said Claudia. "That would be just bloody perfect—"

But a figure *was* crawling out of the ground. A person, a live, solid person. Conrad.

"Ash!" he wailed.

Is this really happening? He was covered in earth, having just climbed out of an open grave like the one I'd been in. The others looked at him like he was a ghost.

"What... the actual fuck," said Berenice.

"What are you doing down here?" I said.

"You led me here," he said, pointing at me. "What did I ever do to deserve this? You were going to leave me here, weren't you?" He looked as though he was about to cry.

"That wasn't me," I said, beginning to grasp what happened. "There's a ghoul, a shape-shifter who looks just like me. Did you follow her?"

"Don't leave me!" he wailed.

"You'll have to come with us," I said. "I'm sorry, honestly. I didn't know she'd do that."

"I believe you, Ash," said Conrad, coming towards me as if to hug me, but Leo took hold of my hand in a clear gesture. My heart kick-started in my chest. Funny how *this* had most surprised me today.

Another sound echoed, a crash, like a heavy object falling over. It came from behind the door the fortune-teller had gone through.

Cyrus and Leo exchanged a glance. "You don't think…?"

"That little twat's no match for her," said Claudia, striding over to the door. It had opened slightly, and unease skittered down my spine. No sound came from the other side.

"Stay close together," Cyrus said. "This gives me a bad feeling."

We left the chamber through the metal door, where another earth tunnel wound into darkness. I stayed close to Leo, who still held my hand, like he had the first time we'd been down here.

The tunnel widened out into another circular chamber. Pillars supported a ceiling so high it was just a mass of shadows. More graves stood around us; clearly, we were in another sepulchre. But this time there were people in here.

The fortune-teller stood in the centre of the room, not moving, like she was frozen in place. Around her, dead bodies lay beside their graves. I gagged on the smell of death.

But one was living. Jude. He was in the middle of it all, standing amongst the dead. A corpse sat upright on a grave beside him. Even from here, I recognised the face.

Mr Melmoth.

"*You're* the leader of the Ghouls?" said Howard, incredulous.

Jude looked up. "You again. Why don't you stay out of this?"

"Why don't you get the hell away from Mr Melmoth?" Leo countered. He let go of my hand and stepped forwards, body trembling in anger. "You're attacking my friends. You tried to kill Ash. And you have my dead guardian's body right there. Why don't you tell me what the hell you're doing?"

"I'm augmenting power," he said calmly. "I alone remain of the Righteous. I alone can fight the Darkworld. I need the power only a vampire can give me. I would have preferred to resurrect my father, but this way is better. I know my father wouldn't have wanted to be tainted by demons even after death."

"What the hell are you talking about?" said Leo. "You made the Skele-Ghouls, right? What part of that is not *tainted with demons?*"

Jude turned cold eyes onto him. "I wouldn't expect you to understand. The Ghouls were a distraction. I need my fellow *venators* to focus elsewhere. They do not understand my purpose. I had to know if I could bring someone back from the Darkworld using the energy of a dead sorcerer. Magic lingers after death, and it seems to be such a waste."

"You're cracked," said Leo.

Jude stood, brushing grave-dirt off one hand whilst the other remained clenched in a fist.

"Why can only demons access the true power of the Darkworld? Why must humans die at their hands? I experimented with giving demonic power to dead humans, but something is missing. I need to speak to the one sorcerer who gained the power of the Darkworld. I need to speak to Lucifer."

"Lucifer?" I said, blankly. "You mean, the Devil?"

"I mean the only human known to have survived the Darkworld," said Jude. "I will resurrect him in my uncle's body."

The fortune-teller made a barely perceptible movement.

"What have you done to her?" I said. I'd never seen her subdued like this before, utterly powerless. It frightened me more than the crazed madman before me.

"She's temporarily out of action." Jude looked at me

with those cold eyes, almost demon-like. "You should never have come in here. She wanted to save you, to distract me from killing you, but even the likes of her is no match for me." He took a step towards me. "Ashlyn, you are going to be my other sacrifice, and give your power to Lucifer."

"The hell I am," I said.

"Bring her to me," Jude said. "Rise, all of you. Kill the others."

And all around us, the dead began to rise.

20

DARKNESS FALLS

Skeletons pulled themselves out of the earth, bony hands grasping the sides of their graves. Heads rose above the ground, empty skulls filled only with staring demon eyes. Decaying flesh hung from their bones. The air filled with a ghastly stench: the smell of the recent dead.

"Shit," said Leo. "It's a mass demon-summoning. He's ripped a hole in the Darkworld."

Blackness descended all around us, but not because the torches were extinguished. I could still see them through the veil of semi-transparent darkness, but their light was dimmed, and I could see from the way the others were shivering that the temperature had dropped.

"We can take them," said Berenice, through chattering teeth. "They're only skeletons."

But she moved closer to Howard, all the same.

"You'll have to do better than that!" Howard yelled at Jude.

"You have no respect," snarled Jude. "None of you understand that our world will soon fall to the demons, unless I do something about it. Your deaths will feed the power in this demon heart."

Now I could see what he held in his hand. A piece of crystal, blue and glittering. A demon heart. "Now. *Kill them.*"

They came at us, lumbering awkwardly over the suddenly open graves. There was a hiss and crackle of flames springing to life in the others' hands; a swathe of darkness wrapped around us as someone conjured a shield. Cyrus and Leo. They moved to stand in front of the group, holding up the shield. Claudia, Howard and Berenice all held flames at the ready as the Skele-Ghouls clambered towards us.

The first of the army of walking corpses reached the shield. They stood awkwardly, like puppets propped up on the ground, but intelligence gleamed in their pit-like eyes— a hundred pairs of eyes, or more.

I could do nothing. I could feel my connection to the Darkworld, but it was like I was still trapped behind glass with the Darkworld on the outside. I'd never felt so powerless.

And Jude knew it. As the others faced off against the army of animated corpses, he beckoned to me. I didn't move. I was behind the shield; he could no more harm me than harm the others. But though it might keep out the ghouls, if he summoned a true demon, we were dead.

The fortune-teller's words echoed in my head as clearly as though she spoke now. *If a demon were to appear, right here, right now, any one of you could die. In fact, it's likely that the person it chooses as its host would perish instantly... It could be any of you...*

I had to stop him. But without my connection to the Darkworld, what could I do?

The silence broke as the first ghoul threw itself at the

shield. At once, several flames went flying at it, and the demonic creature screamed as demon and corpse alike burned. But a dozen more rose to take its place, throwing themselves at the shield and letting out ghastly screeching sounds. The shield wavered, splitting and coming together again, and in that moment, one of them broke through.

Chaos erupted. Claudia whipped out her fan and jumped ahead of the group, throwing fire at the Skele-Ghouls one after another. Cyrus swore and leapt to join her, while Howard tackled another ghoul which was in the process of sneaking up on us from behind. I hated feeling so powerless, standing behind the others with Conrad as they fought. But the sheer number of them was over-whelming. Jude had summoned enough ghouls to possess every corpse in the catacombs.

And still more rose at every moment. Fire danced around me; the ground itself seemed to be alive with flames. They seared my skin even from behind the shield.

"They aren't going down!" Cyrus panted, now standing back to back with Leo as they tried to pull the remainder of the shield together. Howard and Berenice had ditched the protection entirely—I couldn't see Berenice, but Howard ran along the tops of graves, shooting fireballs, looking as though he was having the time of his life. I couldn't see Claudia, at least until she emerged from a desecrated grave, scattering fragments of burned bone everywhere.

I looked desperately at the fortune-teller—and my blood turned to ice. Two Skele-Ghouls had targeted her, and as I watched, their corpse-bodies changed. Bony human arms became curved claws, poised for attack.

"Get away from her!" I yelled. I threw myself against the mental barrier blocking my access to the Darkworld, but nothing changed. *Stop. Please!*

Cyrus and Leo jumped into action. Still using the shield spell, they ran to the fortune-teller and placed themselves in front of her, blocking the ghouls' path. The two monsters let out guttural snarls at being denied their prey.

The shield now covered half the room, but parts of it were breaking down. I needed to get close to Leo and Cyrus again. And find a way to contact the Darkworld…

"I can help you, Ashlyn." The demon's voice cut through me like an icicle; I turned to see the doppelganger waiting for me… on *our* side of the shield.

"You—how—?"

Conrad, who'd been cowering behind a headstone, looked at her in horror. "Ash! I thought it was you!"

But there was no time to think, to react. She had me in a headlock before I could blink, impossibly strong arms gripping me, cutting off my oxygen supply. I fought to shake her off, to break through to the Darkworld, but my connection remained blocked. She threw me to the ground, and we rolled away across the floor.

"Get off her!"

I found myself flung to the ground as Leo and Cyrus both tackled the doppelganger at once. She still held onto me and the two of us rolled over on the ground.

The shield broke—and so did the block the Venantium had put on me.

Violet light flared across my vision; the pendant seared my skin. A paralysing chill pinned me to the ground. And *she* stood over me, grinning, her eyes as violet as my own.

Stop, I thought. *Please stop this…*

Then someone leapt into my line of vision and delivered a flaming sucker-punch to the ghoul's head, so powerful that the creature went flying. It took me a minute to recognise the person as Berenice. She glared at me. "Get up."

I tried to say I couldn't move, but my vision flared purple again.

Berenice backed away. "What... the... hell?" She looked from me to the fallen doppelganger and back again. "Which of you is the demon?"

I threw off the paralysis before her punch landed, and rolled out of the way. "I'm Ash!" I said. "It's me!"

"What the hell are you, freak? You possessed?"

I shook my head. *Shit,* this was bad. "No, it's her, she —" I pointed desperately at the doppelganger. "She's doing it."

"What's her problem?" said Berenice, kicking my double in the side, flames spreading from her foot. "Why won't she die?"

"No clue," I said, knocking another Skele-Ghoul away from me. Berenice finished it off, and it collapsed in a pile of bones, its demon eyes extinguished. They'd crept into the part of the room the shield once covered, blocking the exit—but that didn't worry me as much as the doppelganger.

"I am undying," snarled the doppelganger, curling up on the ground. "That is my curse. That is *our* curse, Ashlyn."

"What do you mean?"

Two Skele-Ghouls launched themselves at Berenice, and while she was preoccupied, the ghoul shuffled to her feet. She looked like she was genuinely in pain.

"You—will pay," she hissed.

"What *are* you?" I said. "You're no ghoul. Are you?"

Are you really me? I wanted to say.

"You forget I can read your mind, Ashlyn. No. But I was like you, once. A human-demon."

No. I stared at her in horror. *No...*

"I was, Ashlyn. But I was captured by necromancers and taken

to the house on Tombstone Hill. There, the venators mistook me for a true demon and killed me."

You're a ghost?

"No. I'm the demon I was. In the Darkworld, I cannot die. My anger brought me back, when someone broke into the Barrier. I have found a way to augment power. I can draw energy from demon hearts and become immortal."

She moved closer to me, and I recoiled as she laid a hand on my arm. "Join me, Ashlyn. We mustn't let him steal our power. If he contacts Lucifer, we all die."

I hesitated, torn. There was no reason for me to trust a word she said—and I didn't even know what to think about being cursed to spend eternity in the Darkworld. Just the thought opened a cold, dark place inside me. *It can't be true.*

"Come to me when you're ready, Ashlyn. I'll be waiting."

And she faded away, like smoke.

I looked around. Leo and Cyrus had conjured another shield to keep the ghouls away from the fortune-teller, while Claudia and Howard ran amongst them, striking the monsters down one at a time. Berenice ran to Howard, without as much as a glance back at me.

"Howard! You okay?"

"Course." He swung a fist at a Skele-Ghoul and hit it with such force he sent its head soaring across the chamber.

I ran back towards the fortune-teller, who still stood unmoving in the centre of the room, behind Cyrus and Leo and the shield. But outside the shield, tendrils of the Darkworld had begun to swirl around the place where Mr Melmoth's body sat, where Jude had been—

Where is he?

An icy presence stirred in the darkness, something apart from the ghouls and the doppelganger, something that brought a deeper chill. *A true demon?*

Had Jude managed to make contact?

"Ash, wait!" Conrad leapt in front of me, trying to kick away a Skele-Ghoul which had wrapped itself around his ankles. He didn't seem to have the hang of conjuring fire; every time he tried, it instantly extinguished itself. "I'm coming!" he shouted.

"No, you don't." Jude appeared from the shadows, tackling him to the ground. "I warned you, vampire," he spat. "This is your doing, all of it. Your evil kind brought the demons right to our doorstep!"

The fight slowed down as everyone looked at Jude.

"I live so that this *thing* may die." He held a long knife in his hand, and pressed it to Conrad's throat. Conrad whimpered.

"Don't kill him!" I shouted.

"Vampires all deserve to die," hissed Jude. "They killed us, so why shouldn't we repay them in kind?"

The knife slid out of his grasp entirely, but he hardly noticed. Flames danced along his outstretched arm, down to the fingertips still pressed against Conrad's throat.

Conrad screamed as the fire licked at his exposed skin, but at that moment, a jet of darkness hit Jude from behind, knocking him off his feet. He whirled around, staring incredulously at the fortune-teller. She pushed herself upright, using a dislodged slab of stone for support. Scars ran the length of her face, which was haggard and wrinkled, as though she'd aged fifty years. Her hair was white as bone.

"Ah, you're awake? Just in time."

"Don't think of using me as a vessel to speak to Lucifer. You'll destroy yourself." When she spoke, her voice was a hoarse croak.

"No, I suspect he might kill you if you contact him again. I've heard the rumours. *Demon lover.*"

The fortune-teller gasped.

"I thought so. Come," he said.

And he waved a hand. Mr Melmoth—I hadn't even seen him still there, amongst the chaos—stood. His skin was pale grey, his eyes sunken and sad. Not possessed—yet.

"Come, vessel. Serve me in death."

"Screw that, you fucking murderer." Leo launched himself at Jude, hands ablaze.

Jude cried out; Leo knocked him off-balance and the burns seared his arms. I rushed to help, but the ground was suddenly alive with livid shadows.

"No!" the fortune-teller screamed. "You fool—you've woken one of them. They're coming."

Jude turned away from a furious Leo, heedless of the flames licking at his skin. "He's come? Lucifer?"

The fortune-teller shook her head. Jude stood, raising a hand, and all the strands of the Darkworld in the room rushed towards him in a flood of shadows.

At the same time, the fortune-teller raised a hand.

21

WAKING THE DEMON

The torrent of darkness stopped, dispersing at the fortune-teller's touch. Jude snarled.

"You dare to interfere? You're nothing compared to me."

"You don't know what I am." The fortune-teller swayed, as though staying upright cost her a huge effort. "You don't know what I've done. Don't make me add to the burden. I don't want to kill you."

"You, kill me?" Jude narrowed his eyes. "You speak of burdens, but you have no idea what it is like to carry the weight of this task. I must poison myself with the Darkworld in order to rid the world of evil. I must consort with demons in order to destroy monsters like you."

"Monster?" said the fortune-teller, taking a long trail of darkness in hand, twisting it as though it was a rope. "I never claimed to be guiltless, but you are the only monster here."

She lashed at Jude without warning, speaking in a language I didn't recognise. It sounded like Latin. The Darkworld responded, wrapping around Jude like a cloak.

He yelled something back, and it loosened, becoming a shield instead.

"You still use the old language?" he said. "Living in the past, even now?"

The fortune-teller ignored his taunts, standing up fully for the first time. The haggardness faded from her face as the shadows whirled around her, and when they cleared, she was her imposing self once more, her silver-fair hair fanning out and her posture formidable and devastating.

"The past has power," she said quietly. "We may not forgive ourselves, but the memory gives us strength. And damn me a thousand times more if I allow you to try to take what you have no right to."

"No right?"

"You have no understanding," said the fortune-teller. "You are not superior, either to humans or to demons."

I had been so transfixed on the power-play between the two sorcerers that it I jumped when someone put their hand on my shoulder.

"Let's leave them to their games, Ashlyn." She smiled at me; it never failed to chill me that other than the eyes, she was my exact double, down to the muddy Converse on her feet.

"It should be an easy choice. The sorceress will die, as will your friends. You alone have the power we need to fight Lucifer. Your heart."

She held out her hand. I felt the crystal sear the skin of my leg through my pocket and winced. I instinctively reached for it.

"It can sense your will," she said, aloud. "It knows you want to be with us. In the Darkworld. It's your anchor. It will try to hold you back, like these mortals."

What was the Darkworld like as a place? Incorporeal, limitless. If we were all going to die... maybe it was my only option. I'd go there once I was dead, anyway...

Another voice shot through my head, louder. *Idiot. She's*

using subliminal magic on you.

Her smirk told me I was right. "It's for the best, Ash. You're a human-demon, the only child in a generation to have this privilege. Don't you want to know who fathered you? Which higher demon gave you their power?"

My hand clenched around the demon heart in my pocket. The sounds of the fortune-teller and Jude's battle were strangely muted. It was as though the doppelganger and I were trapped in a bubble, isolated.

You're falling under her spell again, whispered the voice in my head, and I shook it to clear it. I let go of the demon heart and instead tried to contact the Darkworld.

"I don't know," I whispered, trying to stall for time. "I don't think I want to give up on being human."

"But this way is so much more fun!" She gave her horrible, childlike laugh. "You were never truly human, were you? I told you, you can't love…"

Distract her…

But if she was reading my mind…

Shadows flickered at the edges of my vision again, and this time, the Darkworld answered, its cold embrace like an old friend. One blink and the world was tinted, violet, leached of all other colour.

I watched her through the demon's eyes and felt my mouth curl into a smile. "You're nothing," I said, ice flowing to my fingertips. "Stay away from me."

Another voice in the back of my head yelled at me to stop, but my hand was moving by itself. The doppelganger watched me, her violet eyes reflecting my own.

The attack was fast, sudden. Pain shot up both my arms, and I gasped. I would have fallen back, but my feet locked in place, and I couldn't control them.

The doppelganger smiled. "I can break you, Ashlyn."

"No!"

Fighting the pain, I summoned ice-fire. The coldness numbed me, and I let go, sending a blur of blue flame spiralling towards the doppelganger. She ducked, forced to throw herself flat on the ground to avoid it, and looked up at me, not smiling any longer.

The world was still violet. It hit me—she couldn't attack me mentally with the demon in control. But I could attack her. I summoned another icy flame. This time, I'd win.

She shrieked, as though stricken by a sudden pain. "Stop it!"

For a second I thought I was the one doing it, somehow, but then it registered that the fighting behind me had stopped. Jude stood triumphant, the fortune-teller at his feet again. And Conrad was there, too. Darkness flowed from the giant demon heart Jude held in his hands, wrapping around Conrad like ropes.

"What the hell are you doing?" Cyrus yelled. "You're going to rip the Darkworld apart!"

Is that what's happening? The Darkworld hissed, shadows moving along the walls and floor, whirling in the air as though they possessed a mind of their own.

"A vampire is a conduit of energy," said Jude, breathing heavily. "I can channel it into him—without a limit. A living vampire is even better than a dead one. Thank you for bringing him to me."

Guilt rushed through me, thick and unforgiving, pushing the demon's presence from my mind. My vision returned to normal, but the Darkworld remained, shadows writhing on the walls.

Conrad had followed me—or he'd thought he had. If he died...

"You—foolish boy." The fortune-teller managed to raise her head. "You can't handle that level of power.

There's no way of telling what will come through the hole you've made in the Barrier."

"Then I guess it's a good thing I'm not channelling the energy through a dead man."

Conrad let out a shrill scream as the ropes tightened. His face began to twist uncontrollably.

"Come on, vampire, access the power of the Dark-world. As a defender of humanity, I claim the power that should be mine. Lucifer, come!"

Darkness crackled through the room like black lightning, and the fortune-teller's body stiffened, cocooned in the shadows spilling from the demon heart.

Then she looked up. A scream rose in my throat. There was something wrong with her eyes. They glowed, but not with the violet light of a demon, but a somehow luminous blackness. Like the Darkworld itself was looking through her.

Jude saw, too. "What… what in seven hells are you?"

"You should know." It was a demon's voice, undoubtedly, but colder, more deadly, than any demon I had ever heard. At the mere sound of its voice I became aware of coldness as profound as Dante's ninth circle of Hell, a place where no life could survive. It was the voice of the Darkworld.

"Lucifer?" Jude's own voice sounded weak, uncertain, pitifully human by comparison. The presence that spoke through the fortune-teller laughed, and it was like a shower of icy rain.

"You should know that when you augment the power of the Darkworld, it attracts unwelcome attention. I am known as Belphegor, and I am a higher demon. And one of my progeny is where it doesn't belong."

The doppelganger screamed again.

"You have caused damage here, damage the others of the Seven may well take advantage of. You need not thank me for repairing it."

There was a shudder, all around us, and the shreds of Darkworld began to move. I could see them knotting together.

"And now, the price."

The air shuddered again. At the same time, the doppelganger froze on the spot, eyes wide open, and her body seemed to stiffen. A cry tore from her mouth, and she trembled. All around, the Skele-Ghouls dropped to the ground like stones. The presence lifted, and the Darkworld faded to nothing. Still screaming, the doppelganger fell to the ground. It didn't look remotely human any more—a formless mass, like a clot of blackness, which faded to nothing.

Someone took my hand. Leo. I wanted nothing more than to throw myself into his arms right then. I was bone-tired and my head whirled, overwhelmed with it all. My vision blurred. The doppelganger was dead, gone, and nothing remained around us but bones and ashes.

The fortune-teller shouted out a warning. I turned to see someone run past, and the door slammed behind them.

"Hey!" Howard shouted. "Murdering bastard—"

"He's gone, Howard," said the fortune-teller. I realised she meant Jude. *The higher demon let him live?* He'd killed the doppelganger, but left the real monster alive. A dull pain tore at my heart. She'd been angry and alone. Part of a human-demon. Like me. I didn't even know how to process that.

"Where's…" Leo ran over to Mr Melmoth. "God… he's still intact. We've got to re-bury him."

"Yeah." Cyrus looked pale. "I can't believe Jude did that. I can't believe he would… how anyone could…" He shook his head, and turned to the fortune-teller. "Are you okay? That demon didn't harm you?"

The fortune-teller gave him a weak smile. "No. The

higher demon merely used me to speak to him."

"Yeah, man, how are you still alive?" said Howard, as polite as ever.

"The higher demons rarely interfere with humans," said the fortune-teller. "This one intervened because of the damage Jude caused."

"But why did he kill the doppelganger and not Jude?" I said.

"Aren't you grateful?" Berenice gave me a shrewd look. "Unless you and the demon child were buddies?"

No. But she'd been drawn into this by accident. *That's demonic justice for you.*

I shook my head, too weary to argue. "Jude got away, is all."

"He won't come back," said the fortune-teller. "We're going to tell the Venantium exactly what he did."

"And they'll believe us?" I said, unable to keep the scepticism out of my voice. "They locked me up just because they thought I was the doppelganger."

"I'll deal with them, Ashlyn."

And, absurdly, I trusted her. Despite everything I knew she hadn't told us, I trusted her to get us out of this mess.

First, she had to re-bury Mr Melmoth. We were more or less directly beneath Crowley, so it was just a matter of finding the right room. I felt bad for the others who'd been dug up and used for Jude's games, but we didn't have the time to deal with that now.

"I'm sorry," I said to Leo, as he stared at the headstone. *William Melmoth.*

Leo's arm wrapped around my shoulders. "Don't be. I'm glad you're here." I turned to face him. He gave me a smile, and despite my still-shaking limbs, despite the still-present cold pit of terror inside me, I smiled back.

"I second that," I said.

22

WHO WE ARE

Blackstone looked so pristine, I had a hard time believing that the dead had walked the streets not an hour beforehand. That much could be said for the venators' skill in cleaning up after themselves. Only the occasional blackened bone kicked into a gutter gave away the unnatural nature of the attack. As for the people— well, judging by the sound of singing echoing from the Coach and Horses, things were well and truly back to normal.

For them, at least. I couldn't say as much for us.

If the fortune-teller hadn't been there, we'd have been in a world of trouble—especially me. But somehow she managed to convince them that I had been falsely accused. She subjected herself to testing so they could see if she was truthful, and it was impossible to deny the evidence. One of their own had betrayed them, and after that, it hardly mattered whether I was guilty of misusing magic or not. Once they had several witnesses' testimony that there had indeed been a doppelganger wearing my face, that seemed good enough evidence to drop the accusations. It was obvious from the magic tests that I'd not done any of the things the doppelganger had been seen doing, and Mr Melmoth's journal accounting his hunt of the Death Child was considered undeniable proof that there was indeed someone else.

So they let me go.

At least the Inner Circle didn't get involved; they were too busy reinforcing the barriers and flushing every rogue spirit out of Blackstone. In the end, it was the fortune-teller who convinced them—through what means, I didn't know —that I'd killed the doppelganger and helped defeat the necromancer. She was a miracle, that woman. I couldn't thank her enough for saving us, even if she did scare me a little. More than a little.

But I wasn't off the hook yet. Berenice took me aside whilst the others were still being questioned. Her own questioning had been over the quickest since she had the least history with the Venantium, and she hung about in the corridor when I came out of the interrogation room. She beckoned me into an alcove and I followed warily. After everything that happened, I doubted I'd ever feel comfortable in those tunnels again.

"I know," she said.

"Huh?" I said, rubbing my eyes—the Angel Box's glare was still imprinted on them.

"I'm not thick, *Ashlyn*. You're part demon, like her, aren't you?"

She would have seen the answer on my face even if I'd lied. "Yeah. I am."

"I thought so."

I waited for her to say she'd tell the others, even tell the Venantium—it hadn't registered on the tests they'd done on me, in the end. The demon in me hid herself well. But the thought of the others—especially Leo—knowing still made me recoil.

However, to my surprise, she said, "I won't tell them. The Venantium are suspicious enough without having something else to hold against us."

I should have figured she'd have a selfish motive. But at this point, I was so relieved she didn't intend to tell the others that I didn't care.

"Is that why she went after you?"

I nodded. I felt slightly misguided; I don't think we'd ever had a conversation before where she hadn't made some uncalled-for sharp comment. She'd never given me the chance to be friendly.

"Honestly, it was all her doing," I told her. "I never hurt anyone."

"I know. You're too much of a wimp. But if you turn on us, don't expect any mercy from me."

Figures.

I just nodded again. I wasn't in the mood to argue the point. I felt battered all over, mentally and physically exhausted.

"So," she said, giving me a piercing look.

"So what?" I said.

"You and Leo," she said. "Like I never saw *that* coming."

I didn't say anything. This wasn't exactly something I wanted to discuss with Berenice, of all people.

"Well, I hope you know what you're doing. If he gets hurt, Howard will never forgive you."

So that was it. Howard.

"Why aren't you two going out?" I said. "You obviously like him. He likes you—"

"None of your business," she said haughtily. That figured, too. *Some people never change.*

We paused for a minute, listening to the bustle of people moving around the tunnels. I saw Dr Philips walk past and was glad that she hadn't been involved in my interrogations this time around. Berenice fiddled with her hair; even her salon-perfect curls had acquired a light coating of dust from the time we'd spent down here.

"If you ask me, this is only the beginning," she said. "The message to the Venantium was pretty clear. The demons want revenge. They want to break the Barrier."

I'd never considered that before. "I thought the demons were acting on orders from Jude. And he only summoned them to use their power."

"Yeah, but they *wanted* access to our world. I don't think so many have got through since the Demon Wars. And now they know they can feed on the magic of *dead* sorcerers…"

"I don't get that," I said. "I thought magic was a part of the Darkworld."

"Once you're a magic-user, the connection never really fades away. It's part of us, living or not. And the demons know it. This is who we are."

She seemed to echo the sentiment of the fortune-teller.

Once we'd all been questioned and were finally on the surface again, I managed to corner the sorceress before she disappeared. I finally told her the full story of the doppel-ganger—how she'd been just like me once. I hadn't even told Leo that. It seemed too personal, and it still numbed me to the core that the higher demon had taken the spirit's life without a thought.

"Why?" I said. "Why did he do that? Is it because she's dangerous? Doesn't that make me the same? I don't know what I can do. I could… hurt people…" Like the doppelganger. What would have happened if the higher demon hadn't interrupted the fight at that exact moment? Would the demon inside me—who, I was starting to think, was a being apart from me—have killed her?

To my shock, the fortune-teller embraced me. Although she seemed to have let down her barriers considerably, she'd never used such an intimate gesture—even as Aunt Eve, as far as I remembered. I didn't know how to react.

"It's your own will that governs your actions. Remember that. The doppelganger was a creature of hatred; that is what sustained her, kept her demon side alive when she should have been dead. You aren't like her. You will never be like her."

"But... I kept dreaming," I said. "I dreamt that I hurt people, that I was turning into a monster. And whenever the doppelganger, was around, my vision would turn into a demon's. I had no control over it."

"Didn't you?"

I shook my head.

"It was her," she said. "She had a hold over you. Even here, your mind was open to the Darkworld, and once she crept past the Barrier, she was able to beguile and confuse you."

"Bad dreams," I said. "Even the sleep paralysis... was that her, too?"

I felt like an idiot for not telling her from the start. Every dream last term, even the one that finally revealed what I really was... had she been the cause?

"They used to say nightmares were caused by evil spirits. *Nightmare*, or the German *alpdrucken*, originally referred to a creature which would sit on your chest when you slept, preventing you from moving."

I shuddered. "Is it the demons?"

"I would say it is. Demons can read the deepest fears in

our hearts, and your... position makes you especially vulnerable."

"She told me that I couldn't love, that I'd never be loved."

"Ridiculous. You are far more human than that Jude, for one. Much more so than your flatmate, Terrence, even though he was biologically human through and through. Some people fail to grasp the essence of humanity. It means nothing that you have demonic lineage. In you, the human won out."

"Did you know?" I said. "Before? That she was like me?"

She shook her head. "No human-demons have been around for twenty years at least. I didn't know about the girl. If I had, I could have saved her." She sighed, that pensive expression crossing her face again. "So many I could have saved..."

"What was there...? I mean, he said you... and Lucifer..." I couldn't seem to string a coherent sentence together to ask what I wanted to. It sounded too personal, and judging by the fortune-teller's reaction, too painful. As I expected, she shook her head.

"Lucifer and I... I am not the first, nor shall I be the last, to fall for the promises of a demon. When I learned what he was... it formed an irrecoverable bond between us. That's how I managed to channel the Darkworld and speak to Belphegor. My gifts are quite exceptional, however much they might cost me." Her eyes were dark.

I'd never seen her so vulnerable until recently. Her weakness before the necromancer had scared me more than he had, more even than the appearance of the higher demon. But of course, I should have expected her to have a limit. She was only human.

"Ash, that is how I came to possess your demon heart."

"Huh?"

"Lucifer, chief of the higher demons, entrusted it to me. It was he who told me to watch over you."

"But why would he do that?" I said. "Unless…"

"Yes." She nodded, as if she'd read my thoughts. "I expect it must be so."

Lucifer was my ancestor. The thought had little impact; I was too worn out with fear already.

"The others? Do they know?"

"You mean the Six? I do not know. They rarely interest themselves in the affairs of humans. Except Asmodeus. They call him the demon of lust, and his reputation is not without reason."

I grimaced. I got that higher demons could take on human form, but the idea of doing *that* with one baffled me.

The fortune-teller's next words turned my thoughts away from demon fornicating. "This isn't over."

"What isn't?" Jude was gone, and the barriers around Blackstone restored, more securely than ever. It was once again a demon-free haven.

"The battle. Jude almost succeeded in contacting Lucifer—the false Lucifer. He styled himself as the greatest human sorcerer, and he alone managed to infiltrate the Darkworld. They say he haunts it like a ghost would haunt our world, never quite there, never quite here. The higher demons have long since done as they pleased, but if this sorcerer appears to tip the balance… I dread to think of the consequences."

"I don't understand," I said. "This Lucifer—he's human? I thought that was one of the higher demons."

"The sorcerer took the name of Lucifer when he cast his own aside, but he was human once. In a manner of speaking, he still is. There are dangers involved with abandoning oneself to the Darkworld. In the Darkworld, time has no meaning; one can spend a hundred years there and not die. But there's a price, the loss of your human body. If you return you must possess another—very much like a demon would. Lucifer alone knows how to navigate the Darkworld, and I fear he may be coming back."

"Don't the Venantium know?"

"It is what they've been preparing for. And it isn't something we're ready to face." She sighed. "In any case, we should not trouble ourselves with that tonight. We have stopped a great evil and prevented many deaths."

"There's one thing I don't understand," I said. "The Vampire's Curse. Is there really no cure? Because Mr Melmoth seemed to be working on something."

The fortune-teller sighed. "He worked on the cure for years, but had no results. He fought against it, but succumbed again and again... until it was too late."

That seemed enough of an explanation for Cyrus, at least, but Leo told me outright that he didn't entirely buy into the fortune-teller's explanation of events.

"That woman's not telling us something," he said, as we watched the fortune-teller leave, after thanking her, once again, for her help.

"That's nothing new," I said. "I think she likes being an enigma."

"Well, yeah... still, I don't completely trust her."

I hadn't trusted her since she'd admitted she'd disguised herself as my aunt for years, but the slight insight I'd had into what happened to make her the way she was made me feel a little sorry for her. She seemed to know of dark things the rest of us could only see the surface of, and I would have been more troubled by her words if I hadn't long since worn out my worry quota for that day.

At that moment, a *venator* appeared to call Leo back

down into the tunnels. I made to follow him, but someone grabbed my arm. Conrad.

"Hey, Ash," he said.

"Conrad," I said, tensing.

"Look, I'm sorry about everything," he said. "You know the doppelganger actually told me to stay away? But I followed her anyway, and look what happened." He hung his head.

"Sorry," I said, awkwardly. "Sorry she toyed with you like that." *She was lonely,* I thought. She might have killed Mr Priestley—and possibly other *venators* too, I hadn't asked—but she was just a young girl, lost.

"Anyway, I hoped we could be friends, but you guys run into too much trouble. I think it's probably best if I stay away."

"Good call," said Cyrus, before Berenice or one of the others could say something more cutting.

I sighed when he walked away. *Thank God that's over with.* Running to catch up with Leo, I found myself face-to-face with Dr Philips.

"Ashlyn," she said, face poker-straight as usual.

I said nothing. Surely she couldn't find another excuse to lock me away?

"I wanted to apologise, Ashlyn, for the way you were treated earlier. Please understand that we do what we do for the good of everyone, sorcerer or otherwise. We must protect everyone from demons, or else our world will fall to darkness."

Well, that's intense.

She waited for me to speak. I swallowed. "Um, I understand," I said.

She gave me a brief nod, then left.

Shaking all over, I hurried to the interrogation room to find Leo already leaving.

"They want to search the house again," he explained. "I'm going with them."

He'd stuck by me throughout the entire interrogation, even when it put him under even more suspicion, so I made up my mind. "I'll come, too," I said.

Even though it meant walking through the tunnels to Crowley once more, it was worth it to hold his hand and feel tingles up and down my arms. I marvelled at how swiftly fear could be replaced by hope, shadows by comfort.

The *venators* clearly wanted to go home as much as we did; they spent barely five minutes combing the house. After the search, we found ourselves faced with walking back from Crowley above or underground.

"I'm not going down there again," I said, firmly.

Leo checked his watch. "It's four a.m. First train's in an hour. D'you want to—" He paused. "Aren't your friends still in that haunted house?"

I met his eyes, which glittered with amusement.

"So they are."

"I happen to know a way in."

The Venantium had cleared the damage in the tunnels, leaving them more or less exactly as they were. I guessed they did sometimes use magic for a useful cause after all. All the same, we hurried through them as fast as we could, and it was a relief to find the stone steps leading into the cellar of the old house.

I couldn't hear voices as we climbed the stairs. I wondered if the Literature Society had had a restful night.

"C'mon." Leo pushed the trapdoor upwards and peered out into the hall. He swiftly dropped it again. "They're camped out in the hallway, would you believe it?" he said in a whisper.

"This is perfect," I said.

I ran my fingers over the underside of the trapdoor, enough to make a distinct scratching sound. It took a couple of minutes, but I heard someone whisper, "What's that?"

"What's what?" That was definitely Alex.

"That sound."

"Probably a bat," said Alex.

"It sounded like scratching," said a guy's voice. Rex.

Leo did a pretty convincing ghoul interpretation, accompanied by more scratching. I felt the hairs rise on my arms even though I knew it was only Leo.

Someone upstairs shrieked.

"There's someone else in here!"

I shook all over with silent laughter as I whispered, in my best death-rattle voice, "Alex."

Alex let out an ear-splitting scream. "Holy shit! It said my name!"

More scratching from Leo, who raked his fingernails over the trapdoor. I could hear people moving around above us.

"Where's it coming from?"

"I think it's in the walls," Alex whimpered. "Shit."

There were more noises, people running about. I held my breath, lifted the trapdoor, then slammed it, hard.

"It's upstairs!" someone yelled, and there was a thunder of footsteps, the sound of several people falling over each other.

I looked at Leo, scarcely able to believe it. We had the perfect opening.

Once we were sure there was no one in the hall, we crept out of the cellar and made for the door. A tangle of sleeping bags lay sprawled in the hallway. Leo stepped over them and pushed open the front door.

"Leo, what are you doing?" I said, as he shut the door behind us. There was a click. "You locked them in?"

There was another crescendo of screams. Leo pulled me into the shadow of a tombstone.

"When're you going to let them out?" I said. "This is taking it a bit far, isn't it?"

"Idiots shouldn't have come to a haunted house," he said, and laughed.

"Seriously, though, let them out." I gave him a stern look, even though I was still laughing.

"I will in a minute. Wouldn't want you to turn your icy powers on *me* next."

"You make me sound like the witch-queen from *The Lion, the Witch and the Wardrobe*."

"Is that your secret identity?"

"Nah. I'm actually the Grim Reaper."

"That explains the scythe. So, what d'you want to do for our first date?"

I flushed, a pleased shiver running through me.

"Something normal," I said.

We stood hand in hand, watching the sun rise over Crowley, leaving a golden trail across the horizon. Black-stone was safe again now, and the dark tunnels beneath were as harmless as the memory of a nightmare.

It was only then that I realised: my hand, the one that held Leo's, was *warm*. Not ice-cold, as it had been for over a year. When had that happened? Was it when the doppel-ganger died?

I'd worry about that later. For now, I smiled as I snuggled against Leo, taking comfort from warmth I could finally feel again.

ABOUT THE AUTHOR

Emma is the New York Times and USA Today Bestselling author of the Changeling Chronicles urban fantasy series.

Emma spent her childhood creating imaginary worlds to compensate for a disappointingly average reality, so it was probably inevitable that she ended up writing fantasy novels. When she's not immersed in her own fictional universes, Emma can be found with her head in a book or wandering around the world in search of adventure.

Find out more about Emma's books at
www.emmaladams.com.

www.ingramcontent.com/pod-product-compliance
Lightning Source LLC
Chambersburg PA
CBHW031426200626
46814CB00016B/2339